Cicero Lamont dealt drugs in massiv and lots of enemies until one night he was introduced to a steel bumper in a hit-and-run and now he's dead. His daughter, Jade, has also just learned that her mom has committed suicide and now her brother, Richie, is missing. Jade hires Nick Crane to find Richie and to track down whoever murdered their father, but as the old saying goes, 'be careful what you wish for', because 300 million dollars cuts an awful lot of family ties.

Arnold Clipper, vile, cunning and deadly, accompanied by Richie, has been to see Ron Cera, Jade's former boyfriend. It didn't go well and shortly after Nick speaks to Ron, his decapitated corpse turns up on Skid Row. James Halladay, the Lamont family lawyer, pays Nick a lot of money to keep his name out of the investigation, only now the cops are pissed and jamming Nick for Ron's murder.

When it seems like it couldn't get any worse, several members of Los Muertos, an outlaw motorcycle club, pay Nick a visit at his home. Unfortunately for them, Nick's close friend, ex Vietnam vet, Bobby Moore, who has been helping him with the investigation, gets the drop on them with bloody consequences.

Reggie Mount lives in a lovely house in the Hollywood Hills. Interestingly, the original owner had an underground labyrinth built, full of ornate rooms and mysterious passageways. Either Reggie or Arnold Clipper has filled the labyrinth with strange art and weird books and a chapel with an altar. Only no one is expecting to find the madness that's decomposing on that altar.

As the pressure builds and pigs feed on flesh and bones, Nick, Bobby and Jade discover as much about themselves as they do about each other and the horrors that humanity can, and often does, heap upon each other for the most powerful motivator of all -- money.

Who will live and who will die and who will be forever changed by this journey into the dark horror that can hide behind the nicest smile? Read on and find out.

CICERO'S DEAD

PATRICK H. MOORE

U.S. iNDiE BOOKS

Cicero's Dead
© 2014, Patrick H. Moore

Library Of Congress Control Number: 2014945141

ABOUT PATRICK H. MOORE

Patrick H. Moore is a Los Angeles based Private Investigator, Sentencing Mitigation Specialist, and crime writer. He has been working in this field since 2003 and has worked in virtually all areas including drug trafficking, sex crimes, crimes of violence, and white-collar fraud.

"There's no feeling quite like walking into a prison to consult with a client knowing that he or she is facing many long years behind bars, unless you can thread the needle and convince a skeptical Federal judge to give your guy or gal a second chance. Criminals are not known for putting a high priority on telling the truth; neither are cops and prosecutors."

This is no easy task but mastering this job, which combines art, science and intuition, has given Patrick the tools to write realistic crime fiction that depicts the unpredictable and violent world of cops, convicts, prosecutors and defense attorneys.

Since February of 2013, Patrick has been running All Things Crime Blog, a true crime and crime fiction website, which is one of the most popular (if not the most popular) true crime blogs in the United States. What sets All Things Crime Blog apart from the competition is the high quality of the writing from its many excellent contributors, and Patrick's idiosyncratic, personalized approach to writing about crime. This is not merely reporting the alleged facts; this is interpreting the facts and tying them in to our everyday experience as we attempt to survive in an increasingly hostile and terrifying world.

Patrick holds a Master's degree in English Literature from San Francisco State University where he graduated summa cum laude in 1990. Prior to moving to Los Angeles, he was lead vocalist and played rhythm guitar for Crash Carnival, a San Francisco rock 'n roll band, and experienced the "naked lunch" of life on the streets for the better part of two decades.

Cicero's Dead, Patrick's debut crime novel, will be followed in 2015 by *The Mental Health Club*, the second in the Nick Crane series.

ACKNOWLEDGEMENTS

For Warren Larry Foster, Vietnam veteran, American hero and friend unto death. May he find the peace that every Vietnam veteran longs for.

To Patricia Wong, smooth, true, brown.

And to Max Myers, publisher, friend and inspiration.

Table of Contents

PART ONE

CHAPTER I
Jade, Los Angeles, October 24, 2003

JADE LAMONT MET ME IN the lobby of her Wilshire Boulevard high-rise. She was striking, on the petite side, with enough cleavage showing to make things interesting. She had purple and gold butterflies tattooed above each breast, and wore her hair blunt cut in back and long on the sides. Her navy blue designer shorts gripped her thighs like eager friends. Her legs were long and brown and seemed to glisten as she led me to the elevator and we rode up together to her 23rd floor condo. I assumed she did her shopping on Rodeo Drive.

We sat across from one another at a glass-topped breakfast table, sipping tea, which she served with heavy cream and sugar. She had clear green eyes, a café con leche complexion and lovely sculpted lips. I had the impression we were alone, or maybe that was wishful thinking. Not wanting to stare, I cut right to the chase.

"I'm sure I'm not here just to keep you company."

"I wish you were." A brief smile washed across her features. "You come highly recommended. They say you're persistent and are the soul of discretion."

I smiled. "They are correct. Whoever they are."

She took a sip of tea and shook her head sadly. "It's my brother, Richard. He's disappeared." She paused and I waited. "His cell phone is disconnected and I haven't heard from him. That's not like him. He usually calls me every few days. We're very close."

"How long's it been?"

"Three weeks."

"Did you see it coming?"

She shook her head, her eyes turning inward as if the answer lay somewhere behind her retinas. Her chest heaved slightly and the smooth tops of her breasts seemed almost plaintive. She stood up, crossed to a black lacquered sideboard and took out a photo album. She sat down, and pushed it toward me across the table.

Richard Lamont had brown eyes under his dark curly hair, and looked comfortable in front of a camera. There were pictures of him and Jade, his arms wrapped around her while she gazed up at him. In one photo he stood on a diving board, hair tousled by the breeze. His youthful physique was powerful, with broad shoulders and a deep chest. In another picture, he wore a top hat and held a knife in either hand like some demented circus impresario.

"Handsome kid."

"He was," said Jade. "He's much thinner now."

I turned the page and came to a family photo. Father wore a dark pinstriped suit. Well-barbered with swarthy features, he appeared pleased with his family. Mother was maybe five four and wore designer clothes, voluptuous with good features and the same green eyes as her daughter. Jade stood next to her father. Oddly, in this picture, Richard looked worried, lacking the camera-ready confidence that was so pronounced in the other shots.

"Everybody's gone," said Jade. "One right after the other."

"What do you mean, 'everybody'?"

Her composure cracked slightly, and she looked down at her hands, fingers long and slim like a pianist's. When she spoke, her voice was barely audible.

"Daddy, Cicero, was killed in a hit-and-run in the Valley, on August 16th. Two months before that he and Mother separated. She moved to San Francisco to be close to her boyfriend. She died twelve days after Daddy."

"Died? How?"

"It was ruled a suicide."

"What d'you think?"

"Mother wasn't the type to kill herself. She was always steady even when things were rough. And she adored Richard. It doesn't make any sense."

"How old are you and Richard?"

"I'm 22, he's 20."

"How old was your mother?"

"She would have been 39 in two months, on December 12th. Daddy was 10 years older. Her maiden name was Dominique Dominguez, from the Virgin Islands."

"You've been through a lot."

Sadness reshaped her mouth, and she nodded matter-of-factly. "It hasn't been easy. Losing Richard would be the final blow. I love my brother."

"I'm sure you do."

Although there was a hint of liquid in her eyes, she kept her poise. "He's a good kid but he's messed up. He was never that close to Daddy, which makes it even worse."

I thought it over. "Why do you think he's disconnected his cell?"

"I dunno. Why do people do that?"

"Lots of reasons. They wanna shake someone, or don't wanna be found. Drug traffickers change burners, phones, all the time. Sometimes people just want a new number to shake off people they don't want calling 'em anymore. That's probably not the case here. Richard would have let you know." I thought for a moment. "Anything in particular I should know about your brother?"

"I know he was messing around with drugs but I don't know the details. It's hard to know for sure with him. He could be pretty secretive."

We paused for a moment and looked at one another. "And?" I asked.

She shrugged. "I don't think he's an addict or anything. More tea?"

"Sure."

She rose and glided over to her stainless steel stove. Her body moving made me uneasy. She poured us each another cup and sat back down.

I hoped she hadn't noticed me staring, but women like her don't usually miss a trick. I cleared my throat. "What kind of work do you do?"

"I work for one of the downtown law firms."

"Are you an attorney?"

"Hardly. I do paralegal stuff. Daddy got me in. He knew a lot of attorneys."

"Which firm?"

"Waldrop & Hemsley."

"What do they think about what happened to your father?"

She shrugged, a smooth up and down motion of her shoulders. "We don't talk about it. But what is there to think? Unsolved hit-and-run."

"Unsolved?"

"Aren't they usually?"

"Actually a lot of them are solved. Were there any witnesses?"

"Sure. They got a description of the vehicle, a silver late model Honda Accord. Someone even got a license plate, but they never found the car. I've heard that more Accords are stolen than any other vehicle."

"That's true. Is there any reason anybody would want to hurt your father?"

She looked at me quizzically. "Of course. Cicero Lamont was a baller. He called the shots and too bad for anyone who didn't go along with the program."

"What was his business?"

"Daddy was in refrigeration. Produce. But he did other things too."

"Dope?"

She shrugged. "I dunno. Maybe."

"You said he was a baller. That implies that he was involved in some type of criminal enterprise."

"Cicero had a way about him. Exactly what he was into, I dunno."

She was avoiding the issue, so I let it go. "What about his friends? What were they like?"

"Just like you'd imagine. Some were young guys in Hugo Boss suits, Gucci shoes, expensive sunglasses and Beamers. Others were older guys who looked like they ate metal for breakfast."

"They sound like a fun crew."

"As far as I know, Cicero sold most of his warehouses in 2005."

I nodded. "What about Richard? Did he associate with your father's friends?"

She shook her head. "Not really. My brother usually went his own way. My father was frustrated with him."

"Why?"

"It's not that he wanted Richard to learn the business necessarily; my father just wanted to be acknowledged, while Richard just wanted to be acknowledged for being Richard. You know how fathers and sons can be. Competitive. Not unlike mothers and daughters except--" She fell silent and her eyes searched the room.

"Except what?"

"Oh, it's just something Cicero used to say, 'the big difference between men and women, is that women don't have hair on their chests.' He had a way of summing up the world in a single phrase."

I laughed and was damn sure this girl didn't have hair on her chest. "Were you close to your father?"

She nodded. "Daddy doted on me. I was his little could-do-no-wrong princess. When I started to date, he watched me like a hawk."

"What about your mom? Why did she move out?"

"Mother was very strong-willed. That's why it's hard to believe she killed herself. She was just a kid when they met, but over the years she wised up and grew tired of being invisible to Cicero. Money can only go so far when you've got no one to share it with."

"Did your father mess around?"

Jade frowned. "I'm sure he did, although I don't believe that was his thing. He was a man's man and women weren't that important to him."

"But you were."

"It's different with daughters. Fathers and daughters go together like wine and roses."

I sat back for a moment and chewed this over. "It sounds to me like we've got three mysteries; your brother's disappearance and the deaths under questionable circumstances of your parents." I met her eyes and she nodded slowly. "Why would anyone wanna kill your mother?"

"Why not? Mother was no dummy. She knew far more than Daddy ever wanted her to."

"But he was already dead when she died."

"I know. It doesn't make a lot of sense, does it?"

I shook my head. "These things usually don't until you've had time to put the pieces together."

Jade took a sip of her tea. "Find my brother and if you discover anything about my parents' deaths, so much the better. I just wanna know he's okay."

"I understand."

She extracted a manila envelope from the back of the photo album and pushed it across the table. "I'm counting on you. This should help you get started."

It's always a heady feeling to start a new case and I felt a peculiar exhilaration. We shook hands at the door; her grip was warm and firm and I felt the electricity roll right up my arm.

"You might start by talking with one of Richard's friends, the actor Ron Cera," she said softly. "His address is in the packet."

"Thanks."

On the way down in the elevator I opened the envelope. It was a cashier's check for $10,000 made out to Nick Crane.

Outside, the wind was blowing in off the desert. Already the weathermen had warned of fire danger. In 24 hours, the Santa Anas would be shrieking in the canyons.

Before going home, I stopped in at Philippe's to have a beer with Tony Bott. He works narcotics for LAPD. We've been pals for 20 years, maybe because we're both originally from the Midwest and both like guns and basketball. Tony has a magnificent weapon collection: swords from medieval France, scimitars from the days of the sultans, blow guns from South America, and, of course, the obligatory Kalashnikov AK-47. In the dark world of law enforcement, he may be a little crazier than most.

"Hey, bro," grinned Tony, hugging me as he gripped my hand.

"What's new? Still beating up on the homeless?"

"Only if they force my hand."

We laughed and grabbed beer and coleslaw, planting ourselves in a booth on the lower level. Philippe's is a L.A. landmark, just down the street from the Federal Detention Center and a few blocks from the downtown courthouses. D.A.'s, lawyers and cops come here for French Dip sandwiches and beer.

Tony grinned. "Dude, I'm getting ready to arrest 10,000 meth dealers."

"Better be careful. You don't want to work your way right out of a job."

We have this running gag. The basic notion is drug dealers are interchangeable; you take out three or four and five or six new ones spring up like weeds.

"Nick, I'm confident that there will always be plenty of dealers. The lure of easy money never goes away."

"I wish some of that easy money would come my way."

"That's what my new girlfriend says."

"Where did you meet her?"

"At this sushi bar. She's Japanese."

"I love sushi."

He grinned. "Yeah, me too."

"Where's she work?"

"At this aerospace firm. She's some kind of manager. Gets her very stressed, so we fuck like bunnies to relieve it."

"Sounds like a match made in heaven."

"She wants kids, though. Not sure that's for me."

"Why not? You'd be a great dad."

"I know, but I've made it this far without any serious entanglements. Why ruin a perfect record?"

"The time comes for all men."

"Not all."

We ordered a second brew and I asked, "Ever heard of a guy named Cicero Lamont?"

He took a long pull on his beer. "Let me just take a second to flash through the memory bank." He placed both hands on his temples, his usual mannerism when thinking. Then he swallowed more beer. "That's a name you don't forget. You don't run into many Cicero Lamont's. Why would I have heard of him?"

"He might've been dealing weight, and he got clipped in a hit-and-run last August."

"Dealing what?"

"Dunno. Skag, probably. I don't think it was meth."

"I'll check on it."

The next morning the Santa Anas were blowing at near gale force and the fire danger was off the charts. When I got to the office, I jotted down a few notes concerning my meeting with Jade. Cicero Lamont getting popped was a hazard of the drug trade. I knew Tony would jump on it and might be able to steer me in the right direction as to whom, and why. What was much harder to figure was the death of Mrs. Lamont. Why off her with Cicero already worm food? Jade had given me the check for ten large as casually as if she was loaning me a Jackson. Was there a fortune in the picture? And with Cicero and her mom out of the way, Richard and Jade could be next in line. I decided to send one of my investigators, Audrey, to talk to Jade to get a handle on the cash situation. She mostly takes care of our adultery cases, and she was glad to get into something new.

"Nick, sounds like this chick may not be leveling with us."

"Maybe you two can bond and get her into therapy while you're at it."

"Just because I think *you* need therapy, doesn't mean everybody does."

"Wouldn't you, if your parents died in the space of two weeks?"

"I'd need it even if they didn't."

"You'll like Jade," I said finally. "She's a righteous babe, among other things."

"Yeah? Maybe we can get it on."

"Maybe, though I don't recommend it. Anyway, find out everything you can. She's pretty friendly, so ask her about credit cards. See if we can trace Richard that way."

"I'm on it, Boss."

I put the phone down and stared out the window. I tried to envision a web of interlocking relationships, marked by greed and violence with Richard and Jade at the center. For all I knew, they could both be living on borrowed time.

Richard's friend, Ron Cera, lived in the Valley just north of Studio City. I slid into my silver Camry XLE, and drove north on Alameda. Just after Union Station, I pulled onto the 101. Traffic was heavy as I drove north through Echo Park and Silver Lake, then up into Hollywood. The freeway threads through the Hollywood Hills and just past Universal City, I turned off onto Laurel Canyon. Valley Village consists of mostly two story apartment buildings and duplexes, sandstone colored dwellings that have a clipped and manicured Midwestern feel.

I parked down on the end of Ron Cera's block and walked slowly toward his building. I had my set of lock picks and my Colt Commander .45 holstered in the small of my back. As I walked up the driveway, I noticed an elderly lady with gardening shears watching me closely. I waved and she snapped her head away. Chuckling, I climbed the stairs to Ron's second story apartment.

I knocked hard three times and waited. I was about to pound again, when I heard grunting, some movement and the door swung open. Ron was about 6'2" and a dead ringer for a young Nick Nolte. Same strong jaw, same singular intensity.

"What the hell, Buddy?"

I smiled. "Sorry. I know it's kind'a early."

"Fuckin' A. I'm on Hollywood time." He wore sweats and an Ozzy Osborne tee-shirt with a bat hanging upside down below his name. "Who the hell are you?"

"I'm a private investigator." I flipped open my wallet and showed him my license.

"You working for Arnold Clipper?"

"Never heard of him."

"You're lucky." He stepped back from the door and motioned me inside.

The living room was small with hardwood floors, off-white walls that could stand a coat of paint, and brown trim. The famous poster of Humphrey Bogart holding the shot glass was framed above his couch. Some boxes were stacked in the corner and I wondered if he was in the process of moving.

Ron noted my interest in the Bogart poster. "Bogie was the man."

"You got that right."

I sat on the couch, and the faint but unmistakable odor of marijuana drifted down the hall.

"Hang on," said Ron, "I'll be right back."

He disappeared, probably to slam down another lungful from his bong. As I waited, I glanced at the magazines on the solid oak coffee table that filled most of the space between the door and me. The room lacked windows and the stuffy, weed-tainted air was probably giving me a contact high. Ron returned carrying a bong filled with dirty water, a zippo lighter, and an ashtray. He set everything down on the coffee table, went into the kitchen and came back out with a straight-backed chair.

"I was just about to get high when you knocked on the door. I assume you don't mind?"

"You could be smoking seaweed with a turpentine chaser, and I wouldn't care."

He grunted, sat down, lit up and sucked a huge hit of designer weed into his lungs. Exhaling, he repeated the performance and looked at me with satisfaction. "Wanna hit?"

"Thanks but spliff gets me way wrecked."

"More for me," he grinned. "Sorry I acted like a jerk just now. I get like that in the morning. I work late and need my beauty rest."

"Me too."

He chuckled. "You sure you're an investigator, or is this some kind'a screen test?"

"Do you know Jade Lamont?"

"Yeah, I know Jade Lamont," he confirmed bitterly. "Butterfly girl. That little cooze used to jump my bones like it was Christmas and she was Mrs. Claus."

I laughed. This guy was pretty funny.

"I was just about to fall in love with her, or at least fall in love with her money when she dumped me like a fresh laid turd. I still haven't gotten over it. Makes you realize how women feel when they get used." A flash of sadness darkened his eyes. He shrugged it away and took another hit.

"She's a beauty."

The THC was having its desired effect, as he exhaled smoke propelled words. "You know those butterflies above her breasts?"

I nodded, recalling the tattoos emblazoned into her caramel skin.

"Dude, that's nothing. She's got a red cobra tattooed on one of her hot little ass cheeks and a green mongoose on the other. Never seen anything like it."

"Wow. I've missed out. She was very sedate when I met her."

"That's 'cause she wanted something other than your dick. That girl's gonna be a star one day, if she lives long enough. She may be the best actor I've ever met."

"She retained me to find her brother."

He raised his eyebrows and suddenly looked concerned. "Yeah? Huh. If I know Jade, she's freaking out. They were very close."

"Were?"

"Things change. You're aware, of course, that he has certain proclivities?"

"I thought there was a possibility."

"She didn't tell you, did she? Ms. Lamont is very selective when it comes to releasing classified information. She could be a spook if she didn't come from a crime family."

"I did get the impression that her father may have been running a little weight on the side."

"A little?" he smirked. "I believe it's called Persian brown. You mix it up with lemon juice before you slam it. The high's supposed to be amazing, but I stay away from that shit." He shivered, took another hit off his bong and shook his head as he held in the smoke. 20 seconds crawled by. "I almost feel guilty having told you that. Almost. Anyway, I like Richie. He's a good kid. I was flattered when he hit on me, except I don't swing that way, but he was cool. When I asked him why, he couldn't answer. Made me think that what he really wanted was a father who gave a damn. I felt bad for him. Then a few weeks later, Cicero gets splattered into road pizza. Small wonder the boy's a mess."

"That's good character analysis."

"Thanks."

"So how's the career going?"

Ron sighed. "Terrible. You see, these days it gets down to Nick Nolte and Johnny Depp. Do they want the moody sensitive yet swashbuckling type, or do they want the masculine, hard-bitten Nolte type? I'm more Nolte than Depp and it's just not happening for me right now."

"You're in the wrong era. Go back 50 years. Who did you have then? Glenn Ford, Spencer Tracy. Kirk Douglas. Hell, John Wayne, Robert Mitchum. Even William Holden before he got fat. And of course Bogie. Those guys were men. They weren't pretty boys. They didn't need to be."

"You're a genius. I think I'll kill myself."

"Don't be in any rush. Not until you help me find Richard."

"He can be very elusive. My guess, he's in trouble."

"I get the impression Jade agrees with you."

"She doesn't know the half of it."

"Is that right?"

"Yeah, and I'll tell you why and then I've got to get ready for work."

"I'm all ears."

"I met Richie and Jade about a year ago, in a club on Melrose. Later that night, we drove out to Malibu and partied on somebody's private beach. I had some bud with me, Jade was drinking wine and he was wired on meth. He'd just discovered it and was completely amped. I mean, dude, he couldn't shut up. I learned a lot about the Lamont family that night. Probably too much. After she got hammered, Jade started talking too. This was almost a year before their parents died. I saw her off and on for about 11 months, or rather, she saw me when she felt like it. The last time was about a month after Dominique walked out on Cicero, which was maybe three weeks before he met up with an unforgiving bumper. Or at least that's the way the story goes."

"And you don't believe it?"

"I don't know what to believe. Jade did give me the impression that the separation was only temporary. Just a little vacation to sort things out. Anyway, Cicero had no time for his wife. He had his business enterprises and, according to Richie, his Vietnamese massage girls in Westminster. He didn't care if mamma had a fling or two. Boy, Jade hated those call girls. She could be very high-handed considering her own *laissez-faire* morals."

He paused for breath and absently poked at the weed in its container. I waited patiently for him to continue as I considered this new info.

"In case you haven't figured it out, Jade has expensive taste. And she can afford it. That's what I learned that night in Malibu, and I'm not sure either of them remembers telling me. I learned something else, though. Something peculiar. It was about four in the morning. I don't know if you know what happens when you're up on crystal meth and it starts wearing off, but you get quiet and depressed. Your body's all fucked up and you wanna kill yourself. Anyway, we're all huddled together 'cause it's cold. Jade has her arm around me and I'm kissing her neck, when Richie gives me a funny look, comes around on the other side of her and puts his head on her chest. Next

14

thing I know, the damned guy is licking her butterflies. I'm weirded out but hell, you know, it's Hollyweird. Jade and I barely know each other and her brother is licking her butterflies. I mean, shit, man."

"Yeah, that's kind'a freaky."

He looked at his cell phone. "Sorry, gotta hit the shower and split for work."

"No worries."

"Wish I was rich, but I don't wish I was Richie."

"When did you last see him?"

"Little less than a month ago and man was that weird. It got me freaked."

"Why?"

"Tell you what, meet me at Milford's on Vine in the parking lot at 2:00 a.m. That's where I work and I'll fill you in on the rest of the story. After that, no offense, but I don't ever wanna see you again. Jade and Richie are bad news. I need to disconnect."

"Where do you think I can find him?"

"Oh, he's around. Try the gay bars, or the clubs on Sunset. He swings both ways. The women love him. How could they not? He's a dead ringer for John Garfield."

Ron opened the front door and we shook hands. "Thanks, Ron."

"You seem like a cool guy. I just don't want to end up dead when I'm not even 25."

CHAPTER II
Arnold Clipper

I LIVE IN WHITTIER, 18 miles due east of downtown Los Angeles, with my wife Cassady and Maleah, our 11 year old, adopted Chinese daughter. When I got home, they were dancing to Gwen Stefani in the living room. Gwen was yodeling and Maleah, who sings like a bird, was yodeling right along with her. Cassady's a couple years younger than I am, but looks about 30. She was a punk rocker when I met her, and still really is at heart. She's a helluva good mother, and she and Maleah are joined at the hip. I sank into a recliner and as I watched them, I thought about Ron Cera. *'Why was he so scared?'*

Five minutes later the doorbell rang. It was my old college friend, Brad Tanner, with a suitcase in either hand. Tall and skeletal, his hair, now bone white. Behind him, I could see his mud-and-insect splattered, burgundy Volkswagen Passat parked on the street. The last time I saw him was three years ago in the Bay Area where he was living with his wife and daughter. It had been obvious then that his marriage was deteriorating.

"Hi," he said. His brown eyes were dead serious.

"Hey, Brad, come on--"

"--Sorry to drop in like this, but I seem to remember you telling me to stop in any time."

"You okay?" I stood to one side and he stepped into the hallway.

"Uh, you know, life."

"Put your bags down and let's go see Cassady. She's in the kitchen."

"I hope she doesn't shoot me."

She was in the kitchen finishing off a stir-fry, a light film of moisture across her forehead. She looked at Brad and knew immediately something was wrong with him. "You're just in time for dinner."

I wanted to kiss her.

Before we ate, we took his luggage to our downstairs guest room. "Can I smoke?"

"Sure, but on the patio."

I grabbed a couple of Perriers and we sat outside in the cool jasmine scented night air. Around us, crickets chirped and buzzed away into the night. He lit up a Marlboro and inhaled deeply.

"You want one?"

"No, I'm good, thanks."

"I really appreciate you guys letting me crash."

"No worries."

"You have a beautiful place. Quiet. Peaceful."

It was obvious that he was hurting. "How're you doing, Buddy?"

"I'm good, you know. Six months now, since the divorce."

Brad was handsome in his gaunt aquiline way. Although sadness floated in his brown eyes, they were not entirely devoid of their old familiar sparkle. He looked at me, cigarette in one hand, the other folded atop our ceramic patio table.

"You ever hear from her?"

"No, except to talk about our daughter. And then she's strictly business." He crushed out the butt in the ashtray and lit up another. "It's been a little rugged, but I'm through the worst. Time to put the shoulder to the wheel, I guess."

We've been friends for two decades and have hardly ever touched except to shake hands. I wanted to hug the guy, but knew that a friendly touch would most likely cause him to break down, and men don't cry easily in front of other men.

"It's good that you're here because I've been wanting to introduce you to a pal of mine, Bobby Moore."

"Who's that?"

"Nam vet who's been to hell and back. He helps me when I need muscle."

A tic appeared above Brad's left eye and he swatted at it impatiently. "I hear you, man. Don't worry. I'm not gonna fuck up."

Cassady served the delicious stir-fry with a Greek salad and fragrant Basmati rice. While we ate, Brad filled us in on his recent tribulations. After his ex-wife Keri had given him the heave-ho, he'd spent six months in rehab with the muscle-tee and mullet crowd in Eureka, up near the Oregon border. After that, he moved in with his parents in Redding.

"My folks are great. I love them dearly. Still, it can be a little rough when Fox News plays 24-7. The real point, though, is I'm a little too old to still be living with mom and dad." He paused. "This adobo is something else. You're one heckuva chef."

Cassady still wears her thick red hair punked up, has never completely shed her youthful rebelliousness and loves being complimented on her cooking. "Thank you. I'm teaching Maleah and she's getting pretty good too."

"We're foodies," said Maleah. "There's a new Asian supermarket at the top of the hill. We go there every Friday when I get out of school."

After we'd finished the main course, Cassady brought out a delicious carrot cake with walnut frosting, and we retired to the living room, where she and Maleah entertained us. My daughter sang the Fergie song, "Big Girls Don't Cry", with Cassady accompanying her on piano. Then she sang her three octave special from Pocahontas.

"Young lady," said Brad, "you've got a fine voice."

"Thank you," said Maleah. "Does your daughter sing?"

"Tressa sings. But not like you. She's really good at gymnastics."

"Is she going to visit us?"

"I hope so. If I can talk her mother into it."

After I'd put Maleah to bed, I came back into the living room. Brad and Cassady were huddled in earnest conversation.

"You should see her," he said. "She's gotten way weird and has purple hair. Thinks she's still 25. I mean, it's ridiculous. She has a lesbian therapist and a masseur who gives her butt massages."

Cassady offered gently, "I guess Keri's trying to put her life back together. Nothing wrong with that."

"Yeah, but everyone's telling her I was the problem."

"You were drinking like a fish."

Brad looked unconvinced. As smart as he is, he hasn't handled his divorce well.

"Anyway, you should be celebrating. You've got a whole new life ahead."

"You're right, Cassady. I'll have a Heineken."

"Don't make me shoot you."

We laughed. It was good to have Brad around. It had been a long time and I realized how much I'd missed him.

The alarm went off at 1:00 a.m. Two hours sleep is hardly optimum, but in my profession you get used to it. I snapped on the bedside lamp and looked at Cassady. The blankets were pulled down, revealing her arched torso. She's 41 and still smoking hot. Her head was half off the pillow, her long throat pale and vulnerable. I leaned over and kissed her, from the hollow at the base of her throat, to the curve of her chin. She sighed softly in her sleep. Reluctantly, I dragged myself out of bed and pulled on some jeans.

After splashing water on my face, I went downstairs to the guest room. Brad was sitting bolt upright, still fully dressed. He cracked open his eyes and I said, "C'mon, we've got work to do."

We each grabbed a mug of coffee and went out to my car. The night was luminous and traffic on the 60 was light. Escalades and Navigators rolled on by, the preferred mode of transportation of nefarious Nighthawks and those that pursue them.

"Man, I had some god awful dream," said Brad. "Don't remember what it was. Something about a woman, but it scared the crap outta me."

His long face was skeletal and for a moment, I wondered if he was going to make it back to the realm of the living. I pushed the question out of my mind. We turned off the 60 onto the 101 and drove up to Hollywood. At Melrose, we exited and headed west through Thai Town, past the shops and restaurants. Just for the hell of it, I turned off on a side street and drove through a residential section. A great deal of L.A. is rundown, but even the ghettos are beautiful. The old craftsman bungalows, built after the first war, just knock me out. The palms float upwards like sentinels greeting the weary traveler. The small yards and detached garages shimmer in the mist, while the bungalow porches with their rocking chairs and flower boxes beckon.

"It's nice," said Brad. "I like it here."

"It'd be real cool to own one of these. They cost a fortune. Maybe someday when Maleah's grown up and off to college."

"What's a fortune?"

"Oh, maybe 1.3 million for a three bedroom, one-and-a-half bath. 1500 square feet with a small formal dining room, with coved ceilings and wainscoting. Cassady would love to have one of these."

"Me too. Maybe I can just sell my body."

Brad's a raw-boned, 6'3" veteran of many skirmishes. "Good luck."

He grinned.

Milford's on Vine, between Melrose and Santa Monica Boulevard. It's a seafood and sushi joint that does a good weeknight business, and hits the jackpot on the weekends. We pulled into the parking lot at exactly 1:55. It was emptying out, and we watched the late night customers stroll to their vehicles.

A few minutes later I walked to the back of the restaurant. I had a miniature tape recorder in the inside pocket of my jacket and although I don't usually record conversations, I figured Brad could be brought up to speed by listening to it. I didn't want to spook Ron.

After about five minutes, Ron walked out carrying a black gym bag. He was wearing a white tuxedo shirt with the sleeves rolled up, black slacks and shoes. His dark blond hair was plastered against his forehead. When I stepped out of the darkness, he showed no surprise.

"Busy night?"

"Very, but lucrative. That's the good thing about being a waiter, instant cash." His Honda Civic was parked three slots down from my Camry, and if he saw Brad, he didn't react. "I know a place where we can talk."

He and I got into his car and drove north on Vine. After a few blocks, we slid through residential streets until we came to one that curved uphill away from the bungalows. At the top, it circled a small grassy area with benches and a fountain. Ron parked, reached into his gym bag and took out his pipe. It was already loaded and I watched as he sparked a flame, inhaling deeply.

"That's quite a habit you've got there."

"This designer shit is way addictive. But it's still just marijuana."

"Maybe," I thought. It was so hi-tech, it smelled like perfume. He put his pipe away and we quietly climbed out of his car, and sat on one of the benches.

"Occasionally I bring girls here. It never fails to charm them and no one ever bothers you. I've even sat here till dawn and sometimes, it's as if the flowers talk to you while the sun comes up."

I watched him closely as the weed took effect. He took a moment to compose himself and looking down the dimply street, he began. "I don't even know why I'm telling you this. It's the sort of thing no one should ever hear. Maybe it's because I want to help Jade. Maybe it's because she gave me the best pussy any man's ever had. But after I tell you this, I'm going back to the restaurant and like I said earlier, I don't ever wanna see you again. Deal?"

"Deal."

"Okay. She and I had this sex thing going, and I was falling in love with her. Richie was hanging around the fringes and for some reason, Jade started to get bored. She disappears and I always kind'a knew that a chick like her, you know, she was probably gonna do that, so I let her go without a whimper. Still, Richie kept coming round, so I kind'a still had a tie to her, and then one night, he got a little too friendly and I told him I didn't swing that way. It was obvious I'd hurt his feelings. I felt bad and told him we were still buddies. He and Jade had their bizarre thing going on, and he had way more money than a spoiled kid could handle. So anyway, one night he shows up completely deranged, crying, and tells me that his parents are dead. I gave him a hug to, you know, comfort him. Not exactly my idea of a good time, but the dude was in need. He calms down a little, so I let him sleep on my couch."

"Still no sign of Jade?"

"No and after that I didn't see much of him either, apart from the couple'a times he stopped in to say 'hello.' Anyway, last night, I'd just got home from work and was watching "Crash," which as you know is one dynamite film, when there's a knock on the door. It was Richie and someone else and dude, the kid was wired like a goddamned power station. So I turned off the movie and gave 'em a beer."

"Who was the friend?"

"His name is Arnold Clipper. I guess he's about 30. Seemed cool, composed. You know, the type who looks good in a headshot. He was wearing expensive workout clothes and oddly, worn-out white Reeboks. Richard was meth babbling and to make it worse, he had a switchblade, which he kept opening and closing. A couple of times he jumped up and charged my Bogie poster like he was going to run it through. I was pretty toasted and since I didn't wanna obsess on him and his knife, I kept fixating on why this fashion plate was wearing these old mud-spattered running shoes. After a while, Arnold got sick of listening to Richie's babble and sez, '*Hush up, Richard. Sometimes you talk too much,*' or something like that."

"What did he do?"

"Before the come down insanity sets in, meth heads like to communicate, and he's one that wears his heart on his sleeve. You could see the emotions fire across his face in rapid succession. Hurt, surprise, a flash of anger, the realization that Arnold was right. Trippy and kind'a sad. Arnold put his arm around him, and began gently stroking his cheek."

"That calmed him down?"

"Yeah, you could see the tension wring out of him. The hurt morphed into gratitude and he squirmed up against Arnold, who's a half head taller. I felt embarrassed and was about to head into my kitchen when he pushed him away and said, '*Easy baby. Time and place. And put that knife away.*'"

"And did he?"

"Yep. I shot Arnold a grateful look. He shrugged and smiled, but his eyes were very cold, like a snake, you know, and that scared the shit outta me. I wondered what in the hell Arnold was doing to Richard to be able to check him like that, but I didn't wanna find out."

"Fear can be a powerful control mechanism."

"Yeah. I knew there was more to this visit and suddenly Arnold grabs his face and squeezes his mouth together. You know, puckered it up?"

"Richie's?"

He nodded. "It looked like it hurt, but he didn't move. It was scary, dude. Then Arnold locks eyes with me and says, *'As you can see, I like handsome young men with sensitive features,'* and squeezes the last remaining drops of blood out of Richard's mouth, and still he doesn't pull away, even though his eyes were watering. I knew I was way out of my depth. I got mad. The son of a bitch had no right to hurt him like that, but at the same time, I felt this peculiar terror. You ever felt that, anger and terror, all rolled into one?"

"All the time. Not a good feeling." To my surprise I realized I was sweating even though the night was breezy and mild. My tape recorder was whirring away in my pocket and I wondered what Brad would think when I played it back to him.

"No, it's not," said Ron, embarrassed. "I wanted to get them outta my place, but I was too scared to do anything in case this Arnold dude had a gun, or maybe was good with Richie's knife."

"Yeah, I would've been too."

Ron looked grateful for the lie.

"*'Mr. Cera,'* sez Arnold. *'What do you think of Jade Lamont?'*

"*'She's very pretty. Cool.'*

"*'Do you like fucking her?'*

"I said, 'Hold on, Man. I haven't even seen her in weeks.'

"*'It's come to my attention that Ms. Lamont is trying to hurt Richard.'*

"I was lost and told Arnold he was going to have to explain himself.

"He goes, *'Certainly. Ms. Lamont has told Richard that she is going to press rape charges against him, based on that time in Malibu when you forced Richard's face down between her--'* He stopped and cleared his throat. *'-- Womanly parts and then watched while he fucked her.'*"

I shivered. Something about this reminded me of what I'd always heard about Hitler. The Big Lie approach to power mongering. Always tell the big lie and it keeps everyone guessing."

"This is pretty weird. Who is this guy?"

"He's the very incarnation of evil. You should've seen him. All the while he's telling me this, he's talking like he's Christopher Walken in 'True Romance.' It was freaky."

"Great movie."

"Yeah, anyway, I knew I was being blackmailed to help them get to Jade."

"But that doesn't make any sense."

"That asshole, Arnold, then tells me that if I don't help them find her, Richard's prepared to swear under oath that I raped him one night. Right here, in my place."

"What?"

"I know, crazy."

"Why do that when Jade hired me to find Richie?"

"You're not too smart, are you?"

"I have my moments."

"Arnold doesn't give a crap about her or him. He wants the whole ball'a wax, man. The empire."

"But Richard's got plenty of money. All Arnold has to do is get him to fork some over, or give him power of attorney."

"Not exactly. See, Jade's already got that over Richard's end of the trust fund. He gets a certain amount each month, but that's it until such time as Jade, and the family lawyer, decide he's mature enough to handle it on his own. Considering his current condition, it could be a cold day in hell before that happens."

"How much money're we talking about?"

"Enough to offset the national debt of a small country."

"That's a lotta motivation."

"Yep."

"How did it end?"

"Arnold let's Richie go, and kisses him gently. So weird, dude."

"And Richie didn't say or do anything?"

"No. Arnold heads for the door, holding his hand. He stops and looks at me, giving me that psycho death stare."

"That's it?"

"And sez, '48 hours,' and leaves."

A cat hurtled past us, startling us out of the intensity of the moment. "Shit," is all I could croak out, somewhat embarrassed.

Ron dragged a nervous hand across his mouth and took several deep breaths. We sat there for a while in silence, and when we'd sufficiently calmed, got in his Civic and headed back to Milford's. By now the streets had emptied out as we drove through the mist, neon and soft air that seemed to promise things it could never deliver.

Ron pulled into the empty slot a few cars from mine, and kept the motor running.

"You've burned 24 of the 48. What're you gonna do?"

"Move. Tonight."

We shook hands and I got out. He gave me one last look, and pulled away into the night.

As we drove east on Melrose, I played back the tape for Brad. I dropped down to 3rd and hung a left, and we listened as we passed through downtown and Skid Row. Tent City was flourishing with its army of lost souls. Some pushed shopping carts full of woe, while others dragged themselves across the stained and littered asphalt. We passed my office and the warehouses that stretch east toward the river. There's a restaurant on Traction Street, Abel's Market Diner, tucked in between a couple of abandoned warehouses. No one would know it was there unless they knew the area. It opens at three a.m. and caters to the early crowd: cops, working men and insomniacs drinking coffee, eating eggs, hash browns and Abel's legendary blueberry pancakes. The booths were half-full, mostly tradesmen and a few homeless types nursing cups of coffee.

Brad asked, "What if Jade turns out to be the bad guy?"

"We're all bad guys. It's only a question of degree."

It was 5:00 a.m. when we got back to my office. It's pretty basic but it does have a few good features. Some soul with foresight had installed a hot plate, a small refrigerator and a shower. I asked Brad to answer the phone and check my email.

I took a long, hot shower, trying to rinse off the mounting layers of weariness. About 15 minutes later, I dressed and went into the office.

"You've got three emails. One is from a woman named Audrey, who says you need therapy. She also says to call her immediately. The second is from Tony, who says something stinks."

"And the third?"

"It's from Bobby Moore, the guy you want to introduce me to. He wants to know when you're coming over."

I called Audrey. She sounded sleepy but as soon as she recognized my voice, she perked up.

"Sorry to call so early. I had a long night prowling around Hollywood, got back to the office and saw your email."

"That's all right. Ramona is still asleep and Tim's in the shower."

"How did your meeting go?"

"I didn't connect with Miss Jade until 10 last night. She claimed that they'd put her on a rush case at Waldrop & Hemsley, and kept her working 'til nine."

"Do you believe her?"

"Not exactly, but I don't understand why she works at all though if she's so wealthy."

"Maybe she's industrious."

"Maybe. Anyway, I met her at her condo on Wilshire. During the course of our conversation, I made several specific observations. One, Jade is beautiful. So beautiful she brings out the lez in me. I've got some lez you know."

"We all do."

"Two, she dresses very well. And not just the usual designer stuff. The girl has taste."

"I'm aware of that."

"I'm not so sure you are. I don't believe you can tell Ann Taylor from Dolce and Gabana. Three, she probably spends more money in a week than I make in a year. How much was the retainer?"

"$10 K. But I guarantee you there's more where that came from."

"Nice. Can I have a raise?"

I grinned.

"Right. Number four; I feel she's all right. She really does love her brother, and she may have even loved her parents. She has that stricken, helpless look and five, they're very, very rich and no, Richard doesn't use credit cards. He did have one of Jade's, but she took it back once he'd maxed it out. So now he's allowed to draw up to $30K a month."

I whistled softly. "That's as much as some people make in a year."

"Exactly. So about my raise--"

"--Who makes these decisions?"

"The administrator, James Halladay. He's their lawyer, but Jade is the trustee. Do you know him?"

"I know of him. He used to represent 'made guys' way back in the day, and now probably represents their replacements. Did she say anything about having a boyfriend?"

"There's no one currently, but I haven't got to the best part. There's something weird about her father's death. Maybe her mother's death too, but that's harder to figure. When Cicero Lamont was run down, Jade was on vacation with her friends in the Austrian Alps and here's the odd part, she wasn't informed until three days after his death. She flew back immediately, just in time for the memorial service, which was at Forest Grove. Apparently Jade's mother had Halladay's office make all the arrangements. It was a small service, family and close friends only."

"Who contacted her?"

"Halladay."

"Why not Richard or her mom?"

"You tell me. And, they had the body cremated because it was mangled beyond recognition."

"That's strange. It's usually easy to identify hit-and-run victims."

"Jade was contacted by two uniformed officers from the Mission Hills Division the evening she returned. They informed her that sometimes this type of accident is never solved."

"Did she get their names and badge numbers?"

"Uh-huh. Jim Fishburne and Stanley Koncak. They stayed in touch with her, daily reports at first, but it's dwindled as there's nothing new to report."

"Should be easy to trace, if they exist."

"Nick, are you saying that Cicero was not killed in a hit-and-run?"

"I have no reason to believe he wasn't, but I just had an interesting conversation with a witness who shed some new light on the situation."

"So what do you think happened?"

"I don't think. I just collect evidence. Once I have enough evidence, then I start thinking."

"Okay, asshole. I just don't believe it's at all surprising that Cicero would get whacked. He was a major narcotics dealer and undoubtedly had enemies. Could be he got popped first, and then they made it look like a hit-and-run."

"Was there a coroner's report?"

"I didn't ask for it, but there has to be."

"I'll check on it."

"What is suspect is that everyone waited to inform her that her father was dead."

"Correct."

"When do you sleep?" Brad yawned.

I shrugged. "Gets pretty hectic sometimes, especially at the beginning of a case, but it sure beats a real job."

"Such as?"

"I dunno. Never had one."

"In any event, you don't happen to have a bed around here, do you?"

We pulled an air mattress and a couple of blankets out of the closet behind my desk, and Brad sacked out on the floor.

I called Tony, leaving a message that I was in the office and available to meet, and then extracted a 24" by 36" inch piece of white poster board from the closet. Clearing some desk space, I went to work creating a red ink time line.

Late summer 2006: Ron Cera meets Richard and Jade Lamont.

Summer 2006 to July 2007: Ron and Jade engage in sexual relationship.

July 2007: Jade disengages from Ron. Ron remains friends with Richard.

August 2007: Ron spurns Richard's advances.

August 16, 2007: Cicero Lamont killed in hit-and-run on Sepulveda Boulevard in Mission Hills.

August 28, 2007: Dominique Dominguez Lamont commits suicide in San Francisco.

Late September/October 2007: Richard vanishes out of Jade's life.

October 24, 2007: Richard and Arnold Clipper confront Ron. Jade contacts N.C.

I had just finished the dates when the phone rang. It was Tony. "Nick, meet me at Philippe's."

"When?"

"In 30."

"Okay."

Brad was stretched out on the air mattress with the blankets pulled over him but was apparently awake. "Where are we going?"

"I thought you were sleeping?"

"I was until the phone rang."

For the next 25 minutes I wrote notes below each date and connected them with arrows.

August 16, 2007: Cicero Lamont…

Obvious Perps:

1) Unconnected bad driver who panicked or didn't want to be caught.

2) Rival narcotics crew.

3) Traitorous member(s) of Cicero's crew.

4) Enemy unconnected to drug trade.

Question: Why was Jade not notified until three days after Cicero's death? Why was Jade contacted by Halladay, rather than by her mother or Richard?

There were lots of possible explanations but I didn't like any of them. A strong woman like Dominique would certainly have contacted her daughter. Furthermore, someone had located Richard or he couldn't have been at Cicero's memorial. I made a mental note to talk to James Halladay. If it pointed at a cover-up, the question would be why? Arnold Clipper could easily be involved with Richard, for any number of bad reasons, but might have had nothing to do with Cicero's death. The extreme mangling of the body, though, was weird and could be the work of a psychotic.

I moved on to Dominique's death.

August 28, 2007: Dominique: Suicide or murder? If suicide, why? Jade is skeptical of suicide theory.

If murder, why? Obvious motivation is "the money." With Cicero out of the way, the list of heirs grows shorter. Perp could be the same as in the death of Cicero. Could Arnold be responsible for both deaths? Seems unlikely. Psychotic killers, on the other hand, can be fiendishly clever. No reason to believe Arnold is a psychotic killer, other than Ron Cera's observations. Where is Richie?

Brad had brewed coffee in the kitchenette, and was staring at the whiteboard. "Any conclusions?"

"No, it's foggy and I'm worried because if Jade and Richard are not involved in the deaths of their parents, and I certainly don't believe they are, it doesn't take a rocket scientist to figure out that they could be next."

"What do we do?"

"Find Richie, and figure out who killed his dad."

"How?"

"We shake the trees."

He nodded.

"Let's go."

We sat in our usual booth on the lower level of Philippe's.

"Tony, this is Brad."

Tony grinned as he looked Brad over. "Doesn't surprise me. Another one of Nick's weird-ass friends. I don't know why I hang out with you."

Brad took it in stride and as they shook hands, I replied, "'Cause you love me and you love my friends."

"That must be it."

"Tony collects weapons. He's got the best collection of obscure instruments of destruction in all of Southern California."

"Yeah, but I'm getting worried about Mary; I couldn't get her off me this morning."

"That worries you? Give it time. You won't be able to get her on you."

"I'm not kinky, like you fools." He made spanking motions and looked pained. "I don't want that kind of responsibility. I don't even want a serious relationship." He turned to Brad as if for sympathy. "What do you think? You look like a lady's man."

Brad took a swallow of coffee, shrugged and thought about it.

"Brad's depressed," I said. "His ol' lady gave him the boot."

"She did, yeah? Why?" asked Tony, all ears.

"I developed a little drinking problem."

"No wonder you look like shit."

"Thanks."

"Just kidding, but you do look a little ragged out."

"So," I interjected, "in your email, you said something stank."

"Beyond rancid."

"You gonna tell me or do I have to bribe you?"

Tony grinned. "I checked out Cicero Lamont and you were right, he was into weight. Heroin. He did a four year bid in Soledad, back in the early 90s. Didn't seem to phase him. He came out the same swinging dick as he went in, but with one big difference; he was a whole lot smarter. He got involved in legitimate business. Warehousing for the produce industry, refrigeration and had warehouse facilities all over the South Bay. Word is that while he was cooling his nuts in stir, he studied refrigeration. You know, big industrial refrigeration units?"

"Yeah and?"

"Imagine you walk in and there's a mountain of cabbage crates. It's a good place to stash drugs or bodies. Problem is, we could never get probable cause. His lieutenants would do 20 and not even think about rolling. What made it even harder was that Cicero had connections with the spooks. They'd help him fly shit in from Afghanistan and take a hefty slice. If I could do one single thing, it would be to bust those fuckers. How can we make real inroads into the narcotics trade, when the goddamned CIA is bringing it in? Pisses me off."

"Yeah, but proving it's another matter."

"And people that poke their noses into government shit, usually get 'em cut off," added Brad.

Tony nodded as anger flashed across his eyes. "To make it worse, Cicero had a real smart lawyer, James Halladay. I'd like to garrote the son of a bitch. Anyway, in the summer of 2002, Cicero sold Lamont Refrigeration to an investment group out of Atlanta."

"What did he do with the money?" asked Brad.

"You tell me."

I said, "You would have got Cicero, if you hadn't been stuck busting meth dealers."

Tony shook his head. "Nice thought but truth is he was ironclad. I'm sure we'll pop some of his lieutenants, although it's almost a waste of time, as most of 'em have moved on. It wouldn't be the same as if we'd put the blade to Cicero at the height of his operation."

Brad chewed absently at a hangnail.

I sipped my coffee. "I don't see how anything can be rancid when it's refrigerated."

"You're a real wit," said Tony. "Anybody ever tell you that?"

"Never."

"Why are you interested in him?"

"I've been hired by his daughter to find her missing brother, who just might be using daddy's product."

"Sounds like a genius," said Tony. "Anyway, there was an unsolved hit-and-run on Sepulveda, on August 16th. Only problem is the victim wasn't Lamont."

The earth shifted and a cold flush ran through my body.

"The victim was a gangbanger out of Sun Valley, Mario Cantrell. The blood trail was over 200 feet, making him, as you can imagine, very hard to ID. However, they matched him because most of his teeth were still in what was left of his mouth."

"Were there any other hit-and-runs on Sepulveda that night?"

Tony shook his head. "No."

"Damn."

"Mysterious, 'eh?" He stood up and looked at Brad. "Nice meeting you."

"Yeah, you too."

"Don't let this guy talk you into anything I wouldn't do."

Brad and I stepped outside, and braced ourselves against the wind that was blowing even harder. We drove toward City Terrace, in East Los Angeles, which is where Bobby Moore had chosen to make his last stand, in a ramshackle house built into the side of a hill. He keeps goats and has secured his property with an electrified, eight foot high, cyclone fence. Woe to the foolish man who wanders onto his land without an invitation.

I met Bobby in 1986 in a Criminology class at S.F. State. 225 pounds of rock-hard Vietnam vet, with an in-your-face attitude, who wears shorts 300 days a year showing off thick hairy thighs, and a titanium prosthesis, courtesy of a Vietcong Dole pineapple mine. When he really wants to scare people, he wears a lime green muscle tee with the word FEAR emblazoned across the front, and a baseball cap bearing with the words, LONG RIFLES. He keeps his bullet head shaved clean, and speaks in a soft southern drawl.

A few days before his 1970 tour of duty was up, he'd subbed in for another paratrooper who had the flu. That was the day the mine blew up at his feet, and his life became a nightmare. Before that, he might have made the Big Leagues. Now PTSD fueled rage become the monkey on his back. Years melted into one another, and Bobby roamed the country in a black Dodge Daytona which he'd bought with his military disability money. He also smoked crack and meth, which only increased his paranoid anger. Between 1968 and the present, he'd had any number of psychotic breakdowns. I try not to count the number of times I had to go out and rescue him during those lost years. Like a lot of PTSD vets, he's a news junkie, has a satellite dish and can even pick up Al-Jazeera. He's on a batch of psychiatric drugs now which keep him halfway stable, but the pain is never completely gone from his sad brown eyes. To this day, he sometimes asks me if I think the CIA was really after him. I tell him, *'you never know for sure.'*

Bobby met us out front and I introduced Brad. He gave him his meaty grip, and we climbed his hillside, parting his goats who nuzzled our sides. We sat in his living room on thrift store furniture, amongst stacks of newspapers. CNN was on the huge flat screen T.V. that Bobby kept staring at.

He wrenched himself away and scrutinized Brad. "Where'd you meet homeboy?"

"Same place I met you," I replied.

"How come I never met him?"

"I was too busy drinking," said Brad dryly.

"Brad's staying with Cassady and me, for the time being."

"Same as me when I first moved here. Cassady's a saint and I love that woman. Don't know how she put up with me, 'cause man, I was delusional. I've been getting so bored I've been thinking about eating my goats, and that's not me. Not really."

Brad had this mesmerized half-smile.

"So what," asked Bobby, "is our plan? I assume you're here for a reason."

I ran down the basics while Bobby listened carefully.

He asked, "How we gonna find this kid who apparently has been bewitched by this Arnold psycho?"

"We've gotta hit the bars in West Hollywood and the clubs on Sunset."

"In the event I find them, do I have your permission to impale Arnold?" asked Bobby earnestly.

"We need to keep him alive, at least until we find Richie."

Bobby looked crestfallen. "Okay, tell you what, I won't hurt the asshole unless you give me the green light. What I do get, however, is to have sex with Boytoy's sister."

"In your dreams. She's the one paying us."

Bobby sighed. "What do I get then?"

"Money."

"I'm in. Just one rule. You," pointing at Brad, "kick my ass if I show any signs of getting a hankering for any nose candy, and I kick your ass if you start reaching for the bottle."

"How," said Brad, "am I going to kick your ass?"

"Easy. You just sneak up behind me with a sledgehammer."

CHAPTER III
James Halladay

LIKE A LOT OF PEOPLE, Audrey is scared of Bobby. The fact that he's been in therapy off and on for three decades, and has shown no signs of improvement, disillusions her. He's indifferent to her, but not her boobs, which he stares at like they were CNN. With Audrey and Brad, however, it was a different story. When we walked in, they both perked up immediately at the sight of one another.

We kicked around various possibilities and came up with a plan. Bobby and Brad would work together. They would comb West Hollywood and Sunset, hit the bars and clubs and ask questions. Audrey would concentrate solely on the West Hollywood clubs, places like I Candy and Mickey's. These joints have become more preference-mixed in recent years.

I gave them cash for expenses and they hit the street. I phoned Jade and set up a meeting at 1:00 p.m. at Rubio's, next to the downtown library. Then I got on the internet and brought up Vital Chek, which contracts with the California Department of Public Health Office of Vital Records. In California, like most states, you cannot be buried or cremated without a death certificate. In cases of foul play or traffic accidents, the coroner's office does its investigation and signs the death certificate, but, if death is by natural causes, all that is required is that a physician, or in some cases a peace officer, sign the death certificate. Everybody who's died since 1905 is theoretically on record.

I ordered an informational death certificate for Cicero Lamont. Vital Chek will usually spit one out in four or five days. Then I phoned the coroner's office just to make sure. They put me through the usual interminable robot menu but eventually directed me to the right person who assured me that they had no record of Cicero Lamont.

I studied the time line. Nearly everything about this case bothered me. I'd been hired to find Richard Lamont, but was obsessed with the death of Cicero Lamont. Killers may appear to be smart because they have endless time to plan and execute their crimes, but still they often leave clues. The tough part for the guy trying to put the pieces together is working against the clock, because he has only days, and sometimes only hours to recreate what happened.

At a crime scene, the homicide squad secures the area and goes over everything with a fine-toothed comb. The coroner does the same with the body. A victim can have a big hole in their forehead, but the coroner checks everything, and often performs internal tests. And things are not always what they seem. I still had very little to go on, though the death certificate could change that dramatically and in the interim, I kept coming back to the same question: '*Why had James Halladay contacted Jade with the news of Cicero's death, and why had he waited three days?*' In this era of modern communication, Jade could surely have been found more quickly, and it shouldn't have taken more than 24 hours to locate her. It would not be so suspicious if the cause of death had really been hit-and-run. But if Cicero had been killed by other means, it could signal that the killers had been buying time to get their ducks in order.

I slapped myself gently. James Halladay was a giant, and a legend in the legal field. He would never risk his career and freedom to cover up a murder, so I was barking up the wrong tree. Still, I couldn't get it out of my mind.

I called Tony who was in no mood to talk. "Make it quick. I'm tailing a banger in Sun Valley. A six pound deal is about to go down."

"Good work. I need you to run a check on two LAPD officers out of Mission Hills. I think they might be dirty."

"What if I were to tell you I don't give a fuck?"

"I happen to know you *do* give a fuck."

"Damn. The perp just walked out of a liquor store carrying a monster energy drink. This guy's gonna be caffeinated from here to Venice Beach."

"Wonderful. Listen, their names are Jim Fishburne and Stanley Koncak."

"You're an idiot. I know both those guys. They happen to play in our Saturday afternoon football league. I've even ridden dirt bikes with them a few times. They're good people."

"Lots of guys seem like good people. Doesn't mean a thing."

"I'm getting pissed, the Perp is heading toward Pocoima. Fucker's leading me in circles. I've been made."

"What do Jim and Stanley look like?"

"Jim's a tall black guy who has never gotten over the fact the Raiders moved back to Oakland. He thinks Tim Brown was the most underrated receiver of all time. Stanley is stocky, has one of those lame spiky haircuts white guys have these days. I always tell him to put his hat on."

"Do me a favor, ask Jim and Stanley if they were the officers who informed Jade Lamont that her father had been creamed in that hit-and-run."

"I guarantee you they weren't for the simple fact he wasn't killed in a hit-and-run."

"That's why I want you to verify it for me."

"Buddy, you got way too much time on your hands. Get a real job."

"Like yours?"

"Yo' momma."

I still had an hour before my meeting with Jade, so I ran a Merlin check on Arnold Clipper. Bingo! Two Arnold Clippers came up in southern California, both in the Los Angeles area. One was 60 and lived in Orange County, but the other was 35 and lived in the Hollywood Hills. I copied down both addresses and phone numbers on separate sheets of paper and attached them to the whiteboard.

I left the office, drove downtown and parked under the library. Five minutes later I met Jade in front of Rubio's. She was wearing some kind of dress-for-success business suit with a lavender blouse and some sexy high heels. She was still stunning, even with no visible butterflies.

"Let's talk outside in the library garden. I think it's a bit more discreet."

She gave just the slightest shrug. The downtown branch of the Los Angeles Public Library is surrounded on three sides by idyllic gardens where stately oaks and wrought iron benches afford a resting place to both the homeless and the literary. We found a secluded area and as we sat down, I tried to ignore her knees and the three inches of fishnet encased thigh displayed above them. Problem is, she kept crossing and uncrossing her legs, which only made it worse.

I decided against the oblique approach, as I was increasingly convinced that both she and Richie were in danger. I described my meetings with Ron Cera, naturally omitting any description of her sexual escapades. Her eyes were alternately amused and concerned, tough and tender, and I had a sense of being dragged deeper into those liquid pools.

When I got to Ron's encounter with Richard and Arnold, she reached out and took my arm. "I know what you're thinking, Mr. Crane, and it's not true. I usually try to avoid purely sexual encounters, no matter how hot the guy is. I don't like to hurt people.

This time, though, I went too far. Ron had that devil-may-care, I don't care if you fuck me or not quality, that really turns me on."

'He's not too turned on now,' I thought, but instead asked, "What I don't understand, is why didn't you contact Ron after Richie disappeared? You knew they were friends."

"I did call him a couple of times, and left messages, but he never got back to me. I was reluctant to go over there because I knew he was mad at me. When he didn't call, I figured he hadn't seen him. I didn't really start to get worried until ten days ago, when I hadn't heard from Richard for two weeks."

"Who recommended me to you?"

"James Halladay. He said you were good, and so far you haven't proven him wrong."

"He doesn't know me from Adam."

Jade shrugged and thought it over. "He and my father were very close. Mr. Halladay, as the administrator, is very protective of our interests."

"Interests being money, I assume."

Jade frowned. "It always gets back to that, doesn't it? The money. The whole world wants it but then when you've got it, it just makes things more complicated." She released my arm. "Look, it's actually pretty simple; Richard and I have trust funds and most of the money is invested. Last I looked, the combined trusts were worth in excess of 300 million dollars. When my father died, most of the money went to Mother. When she died, it turned out she had no will, so now the money's in probate. It's expected to be released soon. My brother and I will inherit the entire amount, and split it 50/50."

I tried to conceive of that much money, not as a number, which was easy, but as a force that changed lives and influenced decisions. "Where would the money go if you and Richard weren't around to receive it?"

For the first time, Jade looked rattled. Confusion creased her face in ripples. Then it was smooth again. "I don't know. How does that work? Doesn't it go to the grandparents and siblings of the deceased parents?"

"Only if there are no direct heirs."

Jade was silent for a long time. Her long manicured fingers played uneasily at the hem of her skirt. I wanted to take her hands and give her some form of comfort, but I restrained myself. Finally, she spoke. "Do you think we're in danger, Richie and me?"

"Perhaps."

She blanched. For a moment she looked twenty years older. Then she regained control, but the frantic look in her eyes remained. "It doesn't end, does it? My father's gone. My mother's gone, and now Richard's gone. I'm all that's left."

"Let's not bury him yet and keep in mind, there are happy endings."

"I'm not sure I believe in them anymore."

I recounted Ron's description of the night Richard and Arnold Clipper came to call. Jade listened, her expression resigned. I had the sense that I was telling her something she had already known for some time. Not in so many words, perhaps, but in essence.

"My brother," said Jade, "is very troubled. Sometimes bad things happen to people and they're never the same." She reached into her purse for some Kleenex and dabbed at her eyes. A tall, red-haired homeless guy, wearing dirty chinos and a striped pullover shirt, wandered past us and sat down at a nearby bench. He leaned back, his mouth half-open and stared at the sky.

"When we were young, Richard and I were very close. Maybe it was because Cicero was never home, and Mother liked art openings and nice restaurants. Anyway, Richard and I were raised by our maid, Sofia. There was the four-year stretch when Cicero was in Soledad. I was six and Richard was four when that happened and, of course, we didn't know why. He never let us visit him. After that, Mother tried harder. She enrolled me in soccer, and Richard in tee-ball and even came to our games. She fit right in with the other mothers in her ultra-chic jogging outfits, but her heart wasn't really in it and pretty soon she let Sofia take over completely."

"Sadly, that's not an unusual rich kid story."

She nodded and looked around thoughtfully. "This is a nice place. I need to come here more often, as it's not far from my job." She turned her gaze on me. "I don't want you to take this wrong. Mother loved us in her own way, and when she was in the mood, she would tuck us in bed and sing lullabies. Richard spent a lot of time sitting on her lap, but she was just too young and L.A. was too big and exciting."

"What about when your dad got outta the joint?"

"He looked ten years older and to his credit, I guess, he went right back to work like he hadn't missed a day. By then, Richard was eight, just the age when a boy needs to bond with his father, but Cicero had bigger fish to fry. He'd discovered that there was a fortune to be made in refrigeration, and worked day and night to build his empire. Once or twice a year we would take a Sunday afternoon drive, the four of us, to Wilmington and Long Beach and Carson. Drab places that were nothing like our beautiful Westside neighborhoods. We would drive by his warehouses, and Cicero would tell us that they all belonged to the family and that one day, they would belong to Richard and me. Mother was always a bit distracted on those drives, and I had the feeling she would much rather be shopping or lunching with her girlfriends."

"Who were they?"

"You know, mostly the wives of successful Beverly Hills Jewish guys. Ladies with plenty of money and old world manners." For a moment Jade seemed far away like she was remembering things better left forgotten.

"I've worked for a few of 'em," I smiled.

"Richard and I really only had each other, so we spent a lot of time together. Then for a while I had a girlfriend and felt guilty for abandoning my brother. Then her family moved back east and once again it was just Richard and me." She stopped and looked at me, her pretty lips trembling. "We'd watch movies, just the two of us, trying to make the world go away. He was the age where he should have been playing basketball with his friends, and instead he was watching Pretty in Pink and The Breakfast Club with his big sister."

She smiled ruefully and I wanted to comfort her.

"It's a lot to take in, I know, Mr. Crane."

"Nick."

"Nick," she repeated, rolling my name around her tongue.

I glanced over at the red-haired homeless guy. He was still staring into space, his breath ragged as if he had a respiratory problem.

"Nick," she said reaching out and taking my arm, "when I hired you I just knew that you were a good investigator because James Halladay recommended you, but now, based on what you've told me, I'm in your hands. If you can't help me, who can?" She leaned over; her scent, like tropical fruit, intoxicated me as she brushed her lips across my cheek.

The moment passed and I felt as needy as any junkie.

She sat back and tugged at her skirt again, knees pressed together. "For a long time I did everything I could to help my brother, at least I thought I did, but the world was just too powerful. When Richard was 15, we moved from Brentwood to the Hollywood Hills. He started hanging out with a group of rich delinquents, and one night they broke into the house of an elderly lady and tied her up, just for kicks. They drank her liquor and got wasted. Two of them passed out, but Richard woke up, snuck out and came back home. He woke me up at three in the morning, terrified. He knew he'd really messed up." Jade shook her head. "Somehow the old woman managed to untie herself and called the police, who got there just in time to arrest Richard's friends. Naturally, they rolled over on him and daddy just about had a heart attack. I'd never seen him that mad. I don't think it was so much what Richard had done; they didn't hurt the lady, just scared her half to death, but rather the fact he was so damned stupid.

The prosecutors took this very seriously and he was lucky to only get two years in Youth Camp. There was talk of trying him as an adult, which would have been disastrous. Nonetheless, when he got out, he was different. He never talked about it, but I could see it in his eyes. He went back to school and even did pretty well for a while; he's far from dumb. As we got older we started going out together on the weekends. I went to USC and took pre-law but after graduating from high school, Richard didn't do much, just waited for life to come to him."

"I suppose that's when he got interested in knives."

Jade thought for a moment. "Actually, that was earlier. Cicero used to always say that a knife was a great equalizer. Richard apparently took that to heart."

"Apparently." She looked at me quizzically, but I didn't comment further.

"Part of the reason I prolonged my relationship with Ron was because I thought he might be good for Richard. They seemed to like each other and I thought Ron was a pretty stable, normal guy. The truth is I was grasping at straws. I've been doing that for a long time with Richard."

"Jade, unfortunately Ron is a little too normal. He said no when Richard wanted him to say yes."

"That's Ron," she replied ruefully, "just an average guy." She brightened momentarily. "You know, he's really a very good actor. I don't know about the movies, but he's excellent on the stage. I saw him last fall in a local production of Cat on a Hot Tin Roof, put on by a Culver City theater workshop. He played the alcoholic husband, the character Paul Newman played in the movie version. He got a standing ovation."

Her cell phone rang and she looked at the screen. "I have to take this."

I smiled, *'sure.'*

"Hello, James...yes, he's right here."

She handed me the phone. I could smell her perfume on it and wondered if, just for a moment, if this was as close as I was ever going to get to her lips. The thought evaporated when I heard his voice. "Nick," barked Halladay in what is best described as hard, authoritative. "I need to talk to you right away at my office. Something's come up that you should know about."

"I can be there in 30."

"Sooner if you can. You know where we are and don't say anything to Jade."

I stood up and walked away out of earshot, passing in front of the homeless guy. Perhaps disturbed by my presence, he pulled his head down out of the clouds, watching me vaguely as if there were an invisible film between us.

"About what?"

"Her father. I assume you've figured it out by this point."

"Correct."

"We'll tell her, of course, but before we do, we need to be sure what the fuck we're talking about."

I couldn't argue with that. "Agreed."

"Tell her to lay low and be careful. She's kind of like a daughter to me and it would kill me if anything happened to her."

"On my way." I handed her the phone. "Jade, you have to stay alert. I'll see you after work in the lobby at Waldrop & Hemsley, and we'll decide what to do."

"What do you mean?"

"There's a very good chance we're being followed right now."

Her eyes widened and I saw the fear in them.

I flicked my eyes toward the homeless guy who had been contemplating his naval. She looked at him and frowned. He stood up, gave us a quizzical look, and wandered off across the garden.

Jade's hand flew to her mouth. "Oh shit, that's Officer Koncak."

We took a cab to her office, which was a few blocks away in California Plaza, on Grand Avenue, and I escorted her clear to the 32nd floor. We paused for a moment in front of the glass doors.

"I trust you. Please don't let me down." The doors opened inward and it was tough to watch her go. I headed back down the elevator and hit the street.

Halladay, Reynolds, Tosh & Mukaskey takes up several floors of the old Southern California Edison Building at One Bunker Hill. The status of a pricey white collar law firm is measured by how much empty space they can afford to waste. The receptionist's desk stood alone in the middle of a huge expanse of gleaming hardwood floor. I squinted at the meaningless art that was so distant, I would've needed binoculars to make it out. These are the trappings of power, a sense of entitlement so profound that wasted space becomes a virtue and mediocre art simply the shrug of indifference.

The pretty blonde receptionist smiled. "How can I help you?"

"Nick Crane to see Mr. Halladay."

She nodded, dialed and purred quietly down the line. A few moments later, another young, pretty secretary came out.

"This way please, Mr. Crane."

She led me across the endless hardwood, through glass doors, up escalators, around a good-sized gymnasium, down a hallway and up a private elevator that opened into a high-ceilinged anteroom, with busts of noted legal figures of yesteryear mounted on the walls. Finally, we passed through an open door into James Halladay's expensively furnished office suite. A smile played across his mouth as she smiled at him. He nodded at her, fixed his gaze on me and came forward, hand outstretched.

"Good to finally meet you, Nick."

His handshake was crisply efficient. Thick chested, his iron-grey hair rumpled just enough to indicate that this was a man with the confidence not to care. I was in the presence of a powerhouse. He knew it and knew that I knew it.

"What can I get you to drink? Perrier, Evian, iced coffee?" He crossed to a refrigerator set against the wall under a photograph of Chief Justice Cardoza.

"Iced coffee."

Halladay handed me a Starbucks Frappuccino. He had gripped an Evian, and motioned me to a brace of white leather armchairs, facing a mahogany grandfather clock, which struck 3:00 as we sat down. The leather was cold and I stifled an impulse to shiver. I took a long swallow of my Frappuccino.

Sipping his drink, Halladay looked at me thoughtfully. "When I brought you into this case, I had no idea it was going to turn out to be so complicated. I'm sure you have questions. I know mistakes have been made, but I don't believe they're fatal. At least I hope not."

He paused as if expecting a reassuring reply. I took another sip and waited.

The moment was not lost on him. He half-smirked and continued, "I was friends with Cicero for a long time, and have represented him since the beginning. Because of my long-standing career, I was able to keep his sentence down when he went to Soledad and after his release, I represented him through all his business ventures. Of course, he wouldn't always take my advice."

"You knew about his narcotics dealing?"

"I've heard you're the soul of discretion. That must not change." He locked eyes with me. His were like cannons staring out through portholes, ready to fire at the slightest provocation.

"I understand."

"Good. The world operates in peculiar ways. Did you know that George W. Bush's grandfather was Adolf Hitler's American banker?"

"Uh--"

"--Or that Joe Kennedy was a rum-runner? Our 19th century shipping magnates ran opium. Citibank is sitting on 80 billion dollars worth of bad paper. Why does this happen? Why is it allowed? It happens because powerful people are greedy and really don't care who gets hurt."

"Are you justifying Lamont's dealing?"

"All nations operate in a nexus of power that has little, if anything, to do with common notions of ethics and morality. What is nonetheless important is loyalty and that loyalty must be absolute. Do I make myself clear?"

I nodded slowly. "Absolutely."

"Good. Then we can go forward. I'm sure you have questions."

"Just two, or rather one with two parts. How and when did you become aware that Cicero Lamont was not actually killed in a hit-and-run?"

"That's the rub. I should have been on to it earlier. I found out two hours ago when the death certificate arrived in the mail. Here, let me show you." He rose, crossed to his desk, picked up a piece of paper and handed it to me, shaking his head.

It was signed by a Dr. Joseph Tarkanian. Cicero had died at home on August 16, 2007. Myocardial infarction. The document seemed entirely unremarkable.

"It was the birthday of a Spanish diplomat, whom I represent in his American business interests and I was in Ibiza, staying with mutual friends. I was pursuing a 28 year old woman who didn't care that I'm old enough to be her grandfather. One thing led to another, and when it became clear that she was mine for the taking, I turned off my phone and bedded her."

"Expensive?"

He ignored me. "My staff have instructions not to contact me when I'm on vacation, unless it's an emergency. When it became obvious that my young beauty was not going to wake up, I got out of bed and checked my voicemail. Lindsay had apparently thought that the death of one of my oldest clients was sufficient cause to leave a message."

"Efficient."

"You're the master of understatement."

I smiled. He didn't.

"Anyway, it was Saturday morning, which meant it was around midnight, Friday, in California. I had to wait 'til evening to contact anyone. Cicero was dead, so as it really made no difference, my young lady and I spent the day swimming and sunbathing."

I tried hard not to envision Halladay in a speedo, tan and leathery, an old satyr cavorting on crystalline beaches with his youthful trophy, but the horror of it was already etching its way into my memory.

"I called Lindsay at home at 9:00 a.m. California time. She informed me that an Officer Fishburne had phoned Friday afternoon with the news that Cicero had been killed, and the Department had been unable to contact his next of kin. Although his body had been badly mangled, his face was largely intact."

"Allowing for the dental record ID."

"Yes and Nick, at that moment, I felt the cold fingers of death creep down my spine. I had been very fond of Cicero. He wasn't necessarily a good man, but he was a real man and he was my friend."

"Who ID'd the body?"

He gave an almost imperceptible shrug. "I called Dominique and even though we've never been friends, we've always respected one another. She didn't take it well. Estranged or not, you don't disconnect overnight from someone you've spent over twenty years with. Dominique requested that I make arrangements to have Cicero cremated and buried at Forest Grove."

He drained his water and grabbed another, spun the cap and took a long drink.

"In retrospect, I should have flown back to L.A. immediately, and not waited as long as I did to contact Jade. I just couldn't bear to make the phone call." Halladay paused and his grey eyes misted.

"Yeah, those calls are tough to make."

He nodded. "Instead, I stayed there for another three days. Cicero's death reminded me of my own mortality, which I denied by pretending I was still young and in love. On Tuesday morning, my new girlfriend told me she was married and lived in Minneapolis with an insurance executive. Somehow I wasn't surprised. We flew back to the States together and separated at LaGuardia. It was not a heartfelt good-bye."

I felt no sympathy and wondered how many times Halladay had had his way with pretty young things, based on his position and innate power. In the silence, we both knew it was time for me to make the next move.

"When I met Jade just before you phoned, we were followed by Officer Koncak, disguised as a homeless person. He's the same officer who contacted her, along with an Officer Fishburne, when she got back to L.A."

Alarm played across Halladay's leathery face, settling in his eyes. "Why would he follow you?"

"Why does anyone tail someone?"

"Information."

"Yeah, and based on my source, he's not the real Koncak, who works out of Mission Hills PD, and is clean, as is the real Fishburne."

"Is your source reliable?"

"Very."

Halladay shook his head. "Shit. This is bad."

"You're the expert, but I believe we have solid ground here for a criminal investigation. As we both know, covering up a man's death and impersonating a police officer is no small matter. Neither is murder which, I imagine, is what we're looking at here."

Halladay said nothing, clenching and unclenching his fists. He stopped and locked eyes with me. "I see one very serious flaw in your thinking; Cicero was not popular either with local law enforcement, or the Feds. When a bad guy gets whacked, no one, particularly cops, give a damn."

"You're right, and that's why I'm convinced Jade and Richard are in danger."

Halladay shook his head stubbornly. "Let's assume they are, although I'm not convinced; either way, the police won't do anything unless they have proof."

"But they all know you and could give Jade pro--"

Halladay exploded. "--Shit, Crane, don't be ridiculous! If I'd wanted to deal with idiots, I wouldn't have hired you."

"Wait a second!"

"How are they going to protect her? This isn't RICO, so what's in it for them?"

I've learned that it is not a good idea in this business to react emotionally to someone else's outburst, unless it's absolutely necessary. It was obvious that Halladay didn't want this matter made public and I couldn't blame him. The esteemed firm of Halladay, Reynolds, Tosh & Mukaskey would look downright foolish if it was revealed that it been suckered by bogus cops, in the murder of one of their more notorious clients. As a practical matter he was right; the cops do suck when it comes to protecting people, unless, of course, they have a deeply vested interest in keeping them safe.

On the other hand, we were sitting on a stack of felonies that could land us all in stir. I comforted myself with the thought that if this ever came out, in all likelihood, the charges would be federal. There are far worse places to spend time than in minimum or low security federal prisons. Halladay and I could amuse ourselves playing basketball and tennis.

He stood up, drained his Evian, and studied me. "You will protect Jade Lamont and you will do a damned good job of it. You will also find Richard, if it's humanly possible, not that the kid is worth it, but, his sister loves him, and I promised Cicero that I would always look after them if anything ever happened to him. If you fail me, you will never work in Los Angeles again."

He crossed to his desk, mumbled something into the telephone, then made me a copy of Cicero's death certificate, which he placed in a manila folder. Lindsay came in, handed him an envelope and left. He placed it in the manila folder and handed it to me.

I took it and stood up. He eyes drilled into me again. "We're clear, Crane?"

"Yep."

Lindsay was waiting for me at the door to Halladay's office. She gave me a curt smile and led me back through the maze to the huge empty lobby. I thought she was looking at me strangely, but it could have been my imagination. When I reached the lobby of One Bunker Hill, I wished fervently for an emergency exit. None appeared and I had no choice but to exit through the revolving door onto 5th Street.

CHAPTER IV
Safe House

THE SANTA ANA WINDS WERE stronger now, and fingers of ominous gray-brown haze filled the sky to the northwest. I stood in the lee of the building scanning for taxis and unwelcome faces. It was five long blocks back to City Plaza.

People experience anxiety in different ways. Some develop headaches and turn into tyrants. Others experience heart palpitations, flushing and a sure knowledge of imminent disaster. My particular symptom is a swirling pressure somewhere in my head that scrambles my thoughts and makes it hard to think straight. I was reassured by the familiar feeling of my Colt Commander tucked into the small of my back. I've shot two men in the course of my career, both times in self-defense, and both guys survived. One walks with a limp and is doing 10 to 25 at Folsom. The other is in a wheelchair at Soledad.

I hailed the first taxi heading west on 5th. The turbaned, bearded driver spun a left on Figueroa and headed east on 6th.

I dialed Cassady. "Hi, Baby," she said. "How's your day going?"

That's a joke we have. In today's world, people are prone to using that greeting so Cassady beats them to the punch."

"It's been interesting."

"How's Brad?"

"He's good. He and Bobby are working together. What have you heard about the fires?"

"They're bad but nowhere close to us."

"What about the Whittier hills?"

"Not much wind here. So far so good. Maleah had a good day and she's off with Salina and her grandmother. They're having bobas."

"Okay. Gotta get back to work."

"What time're you gonna be home?"

"Around eight."

"Don't be late."

The taxi spat me out on Grand. I tipped the driver and he shot back into traffic. It was a little early to meet Jade, so I considered wandering around the City Plaza shops, but decided against it and took the elevator up to Waldrop & Hemsley. I had no sense of being followed. When I got to the lobby, I went inside and spoke to the receptionist.

"I'm here to meet Ms. Lamont."

"Is she expecting you?"

"Yes. Please let her know I'm here."

"Sure."

The lobby is, if anything, even larger than the lobby at Halladay's firm. The artwork is different, though. Instead of paintings, Waldrop & Hemsley favor polyurethane wall hangings, plastic sheets of random shimmering color that appear to signify nothing, other than an attempt to please the eye. I sat in an expensive, black leather armchair and waited. Five minutes later the receptionist walked over.

"Ms. Lamont is running behind, but asked that you wait."

I glanced at my phone. 4:15. "Okay."

She went back to her desk and I went back to my deliberations: what kept tripping me up were several simple but complex questions. How did Cicero's killers manage to get his body cremated and interred at Forest Grove when it was never at the coroner's office in the first place? If Halladay's office had really given the coroner's office instructions to release Cicero's body, wouldn't they have checked to make sure everything proceeded according to plan? And why was Halladay so unconcerned with finding Cicero's murderer? If he'd really been so close to him, that should have been as much a priority as protecting Jade and finding Richie. Yet he seemed more concerned that I keep my mouth shut. I opened the envelope, slid out the check and blinked several times, but the zeroes didn't go away. I replaced it and took a long, deep breath to steady myself.

Her touch was gentle and brought me back to Earth. Jade stood there, a single worry line cleft horizontally across her forehead. She removed her hand from my arm and I stood up. "Sorry I kept you waiting," she offered. "I had a deadline."

"Not a problem," I smiled.

"You look tired."

"Occupational hazard."

"You wanna get some coffee?"

"I'm going to move my car to your parking garage. When I'm ready, I'll call and come up to get you."

She frowned. "We're going somewhere?"

"I'll explain everything as soon as we're on the road."

"I'm in danger, aren't I?"

"We're all in danger," I replied cryptically.

I left her standing there, her fingers clenching the strap of her Dolce and Gabana handbag. I hit the street and hailed a cab. Same beard, different driver. I had him drop me off in front of the library, and took the outside elevator down to the parking garage, getting off and on several times to shake anyone who might be following me before retrieving my car. When I reached City Plaza, I pulled into the garage and parked three floors down. I buzzed Jade, took the elevator back up to the 32nd floor, and found her sitting in the same armchair I'd recently occupied.

"Time to move."

"What about my car?"

We reached the street and cut through the downtown maze, swung down 2nd toward Alameda and as nearly as I could tell, no one was on our tail. I called Bobby. No answer. Ditto with Brad, but I connected with Audrey.

"Where are you?"

"Mickey's."

"Any news?"

"Negative."

"Anybody seen Richie or Arnold?"

"Possibly. Nothing definite. I did put the word out."

"Okay. I need you to go to a Goodwill and buy Jade a disguise."

"What?"

"And bring it to Bobby's place."

"Let me get this straight. You want me to go to a second hand store, buy a disguise for Jade and bring everything to Bobby's house?"

"Precisely."

"Cool. I'm going to turn her into a hag."

"That's the spirit."

"I hate leaving Mickey's though. Richard or Arnold could walk in the door at any minute, and half of L.A. is offering to buy me drinks."

"You're still there?"

She hung up.

We crossed Alameda and took the back route to Highway 10. It took us twenty minutes to travel the three miles to City Terrace, during which time Jade just stared out of the window, occasionally shooting me a wary glance. I turned off the highway and pulled into the gravel parking lot at Leo's Brake and Paint Shop. He's been running this place for 30 years, and it's a slice out of old Mexico. Nobody but Leo speaks English, and the corridos play constantly. I pulled right into the paint shop and parked. Some of the help looked up curiously from behind their spray guns but kept on working.

"I'll be right back."

Leo is from Sinaloa, and grew up among cocaine traffickers, but has never sold a gram. Instead, he saves his money and invests in real estate.

"Orale, Nick."

"Hey, Leo."

As we shook hands, he looked at me intently. "I been hearing shit about you, Holmes."

"Yeah?"

"The street's got ears."

"What's it saying?"

"Watch your back, compadre."

"I am, believe me."

"So what you need?"

"Paint my car Forest Green."

"For real?"

"Yeah, but I don't need it to be showroom."

"A cover up, 'eh?" he grinned knowingly.

"How much?"

"$250."

"Can I pick it up in the morning?"

"Oh, come on, Holmes. The paint ain't even gonna be dry."

I looked at him but didn't respond.

He sucked on his teeth, made a disapproving face and grinned. "Okay."

"Can you give us a ride to Bobby's?"

"That crazy vato?"

"It's the safest place I know."

"Orale. Let's go."

Leo dropped us off and rumbled away.

Jade gave Bobby's place the once over and frowned. "What are we doing here?"

"This clapboard mansion belongs to my very good friend, Bobby Moore. You're going to stay here for a while until we sort things out. He'll take good care of you, and you'll be very, very safe."

Jade watched curiously as I tested the fence with the back of my hand. "What're you doing?"

"Had the juice been on, if I'd had my fingers the other way, the muscles would've involuntarily contracted and locked around the fence."

"Wait. It's electrified?"

"I told you, you'd be safe."

"You weren't joking."

I negotiated the combination padlock and we climbed the hill to his door. Our unexpected visit aroused his goats and they sniffed us eagerly. Bobby keeps a spare key under a rock in a weed patch that might once have been a garden. I retrieved it, unlocked the door, and we stepped inside. Jade's eyes swept from the big flat screen, to the unadorned walls, to the stacks of magazines.

"Bobby stays abreast of the news. A lot of Nam vets are that way. Anyway, sit down and make yourself at home."

Jade hesitated, then sat on a tattered southwestern blanket that was stretched across Bobby's sofa. Sitting back, she tugged at her skirt and crossed her legs.

"I know this all comes as a shock, but your life has taken a turn that no one could have predicted."

She sighed and sucked in her bottom lip that was beginning to tremble. "Thanks for looking out for me."

"No worries, Jade." She nodded. I shifted to face her more directly. "This is what we know, and I don't mean to sound harsh or blunt."

"It's okay," she said quietly.

"What's become clear is that your dad wasn't killed in a hit-and-run. A Dr. Tarkanian, out of Glendale, signed his death certificate -- heart attack, supposedly in his own bed. Those fake cops might be in with Arnold Clipper, but that's speculation. They could be working for somebody else, or they could be working alone."

"Christ, what a mess."

"Even though Arnold's put pressure on Ron to set you up, it still doesn't mean they're connected to him."

"Maybe they've hurt Richard." Tears were beginning to fill her eyes.

"I dunno, but I doubt it, not with Arnold protecting him."

Right there in Bobby Moore's weird-ass living room, the dam broke and tears streamed down her face. I don't like watching people cry; it kills me when Maleah occasionally wails, but it's even worse when adults are doing the weeping. Maybe she'd been holding it all in for too long, or maybe the time had just come for release but she wept, at first quietly, and then with an intensity that scared me. Audrey thinks I'm cold-hearted but actually I'm not. I put my arms around her and trying to comfort her, stroked her smooth, thick hair. How absurd it all is; wealth and power delude the world and, worse, deceive those that possess them.

Jade began to regain control. Reluctantly, I pulled myself away, went into the kitchen and again stared in disbelief at the $100,000 check Halladay had given me. I shook myself loose and placed it in my wallet. I took two Bud Lites out of the refrigerator, grabbed a glass for Jade, unscrewed the cap and took a long, welcome swallow. She was visibly embarrassed over her breakdown, and barely glanced at me as she filled her glass, and drank it like a veteran in four or five long swallows.

Bobby and Brad arrived at 7:30 carrying Chinese take-out. Five minutes later, Audrey who loves to shop and had made the most of this opportunity, arrived. I helped her carry several bags into the house.

I watched them eat fried rice and chicken l'orange. "We'll go over everything first thing in the morning, and as of right now, everybody's on payroll."

"I don't want your money," said Bobby. "I want your wife."

"I'll take either," added Brad.

I turned to Audrey. "Could you drive Brad and me back to Whittier?"

"Why not? I'm already about seven hours late."

At 8:15, we trotted in as Cassady was putting the finishing touches on some salmon steaks. Maleah was playing on the computer and talking on the phone. I was damned glad to be home.

Immediately after dinner, Brad, who was exhausted, went down to the guest room. After Cassady and I put Maleah to bed, we went into our room. Cassady usually sleeps nude, but tonight she put on a lacy negligee with a scooped neckline. As soon as I got into bed, she grabbed me and pinned me down.

"How come you smell like perfume?"

"Don't ask."

She slapped me hard across the face and then made love to me. When I met Cassady, 22 years ago, I thought she was the hottest woman in the western world. She combined artistry and passion and we would make love 'til we were exhausted. As the years passed, we discovered that we actually liked each other. Having met so young, we've each had flings over the years, but never anything serious enough to threaten our marriage. Since adopting Maleah nine years ago, I've been monogamous and I believe Cassady has too. We've never actually talked about it; it just seemed that once you're a parent, you forego extracurricular pleasures for the sake of the family. When we were finished, Cassady lay her head on my chest and we talked. I described the case and Jade's breakdown and the 100K retainer.

I felt Cassady tense up. "That's too much money."

"Yeah, does seem a little excessive."

"Halladay's dirty. He's buying your cooperation, just in case."

"Or maybe it's just really important to him not to be exposed. His incompetence in this instance is pretty shocking."

"I hate to say it, but maybe you should give the money back."

"I thought about it, but it's not that easy."

"Why the hell not?"

"Jade and Richie. They're in real danger."

"Can that danger reach us here?"

"Maybe."

She raked her eyes across me and got out of bed. Naked, she crossed to the closet and pulled something off the upper shelf. I felt myself grow aroused again at the sight of her rippling dancer's thighs and her trim curved ass, which tightened as she stood on tiptoe. She came back carrying two boxes. One held her 9 millimeter Beretta, double action, semi-automatic handgun and the other, her cleaning kit. She sat down cross-legged, pulled the sheet over her thighs and went to work, methodically disassembling the pistol. She ran the bore brush carefully through the breech end of the barrel, pulling it back with great care to avoid damaging the muzzle. After several passes, she dripped solvent onto a clean patch, wrapped it around a jag, and ran that through the barrel three times before extracting it. The gun hadn't been cleaned in a long time and the patch came out fouled and black. She repeated the process with a clean patch. Better. Then a dry patch, which came out nearly spotless. Her lips, usually full and pliant, were set in a hard line. She cleaned the slide with a toothbrush and ran it along the frame grooves. Then she lubricated each piece separately and reassembled it. Her model takes a fourteen round clip, which she loaded with standard 9 millimeter, NATO shells. She flicked the safety to the '*on*' position, and placed the gun back in its box. She returned the boxes to the closet and before getting into bed, very deliberately ran her oily fingers across her breasts 'til they glistened. We made love, silently, with a ferocity that was frightening.

After we were finished, she licked my throat and whispered in my ear, "There's one thing you can never forget."

"What's that, Baby?"

"My aim is true." She chuckled, a throaty purr that reminded me of a sleek jungle feline, eyes on her young, ready to kill at the slightest sign of danger.

CHAPTER V
First Blood

IN THE MORNING, THE NORTHWEST sky was almost black in contrast to the grey and brown to the south and east. The fires had precedence over all other news, and we sat glued to the TV. Maleah demanded to be driven to school so that she and her friends could have breakfast in the cafeteria. When I dropped her off, I gave her an especially big hug, which she accepted reluctantly. Friendly almost to a fault, she is not a touchy-feely person and has no use for constant physical contact. Our most intimate moments generally occur when watching horror flicks and children's comedies together. She curls up next to me in the den, and we dwell there together in an almost perfect world.

Today, as she was about to get out of Cassady's gold Altima, she stopped. "Dad, are we in danger from the fires?"

"Not here. Our town's very protected."

"That's what I thought. Okay. Bye, Dad."

She slung her shoulder bag over one shoulder and marched toward the cafeteria, not a tomboy, not a girly-girl either, in her jean jacket and straight-legged jeans. I felt a rush of love and intense protection, against the Arnold Clippers of the world.

On the way to East L.A., as Brad steered us through the morning traffic, I was struck by a sudden thought. "I forgot to tell you guys, but Arnold Clipper wears the most fucked-up, dirty and disgusting old Reeboks you can imagine."

"Maybe he's got a new pair."

"Sure, maybe so, but people might recognize him based on the old pair. It was an obvious affectation. Didn't match his smashing workout outfit."

Brad nodded thoughtfully. "Bobby and I talked to a lot of people yesterday. Although nobody told us much, I had the feeling that a couple of people knew exactly who Arnold was, and maybe Richie too, for that matter."

"How did Bobby do?"

"Fine. He looks like the ultimate rough trade masher."

"Don't tell him that. Might hurt his feelings."

"He's a good guy. Reminds me of some of the guys I met in rehab, except he seems more sincere. When I was in recovery, a lot of guys were still scamming; heavy *persona*, very little substance. I don't think that's the case with him."

"Correct."

"He told me something very interesting."

"Yeah?"

"He said that what puts a guy with PTSD over the edge, is not getting shot at or living in constant fear, or sleeping in the jungle in a foxhole with centipedes crawling all over you. It's not even necessarily seeing your friends killed."

"What is it then?"

Brad glanced over at me. "Killing people. We're not set up for that. God knows, we're capable of a lot of raunchy shit, but killing people and being human don't go together very well."

He changed lanes, smoothly pulling in front of a Kenmore 18-wheeler. I thought about the two guys I'd shot. I was glad they'd both lived, even though they'd had it coming and the world was better off with them out of commission.

The first guy was a white meth head in Fontana. It was back in my early days before I had Audrey to tail the adulterers. I was sitting in my car. It was about 120 degrees, and I had the windows down. The husband was in Room 211 at the Easy Rest Motel, on the edge of town, getting nasty with a peroxide blonde. Suddenly this freak appears at my window, brandishing a stainless steel hunting knife. Tells me to give him my wallet, get out of my car and leave the keys in the ignition. I complied with all three requests and a fourth he hadn't asked for. As he was getting in, his amped-out jaw twitching like a jackhammer mashing rivets, I shot him in the back of the leg with my .38. It was ruled self-defense on my part and the freak, who had a record, got 10 to 25 for attempted armed robbery, brandishing and carjacking. I remember my lawyer telling me that I was very lucky this happened in Fontana and not in a more liberal community. This was during the late '80s when victims still had more rights than perps in some parts of California.

I felt sick for weeks, haunted by the thought that I didn't have to shoot him; I could have just clubbed him with the gun. The people I talked to, though, including Tony, told me I'd done the right thing. Clubbing a guy is too risky. He might not go down and turn around and stab you.

The second time was one of those occasions you try to bury so deep you hope it never comes up. I'd been retained by a desperate mother to find her six-year old son, who had been kidnapped by her psycho ex-husband. Perp was running on empty, armed and dangerous. The police were in on this one, too, but I just happened to get there first, tracking him down in an apricot orchard, north of Corona. When I got there, he had his son tied to a tree with a gag in his mouth. He was digging a grave for his boy with a short-handled spade, with the intention of burying him alive, or so he claimed later. Maybe it was the sixth sense of the insane, but he realized I was coming up on him from the leeward side, my .45 leading the way. He went for his gun, which turned out to be a useless .25 piece of junk. I fired first, hit him in the shoulder and kept on squeezing. They don't call 'em semi-automatics for nothing; by the time I stopped, he was down and nearly out. One of the bullets had grazed his spine, and he's now in a wheelchair doing life in Soledad. This time I was a hero, but the damage was done. For the next several years I avoided the violent cases, yet here I was seven years later, once again feeding at the trough of never ending violence.

Brad dropped me off at Leo's Brake and Paint Shop. My Camry oozed forest green, and this was not the first time Leo had swapped colors to help me throw goons off my trail. When I got to Bobby's, everybody was in the kitchen. Jade in baggy jeans and an oversized work shirt still looked utterly desirable. She was spooning pancake batter into an old cast iron frying pan while Bobby, who looked ten years younger, was pouring coffee. Brad, who is a good cook, was stirring scrambled eggs. For a split second I thought that maybe Jade had graced Bobby with the gift of her body. I dismissed the thought. What Bobby loves more than anything is the chance to be part of a family unit, real or imagined, and here he was, happy as a clam.

I was eager to get moving, but let them take their time and enjoy a leisurely breakfast. I sipped coffee and agonized over whether to send Bobby out in the field. If he stayed here with Jade, she would be protected but his talents would be otherwise wasted. I also wasn't too keen on having Brad work alone. Careful by nature, he was nevertheless green. Bobby's forbidding presence tends to protect everyone in his orbit.

Sometimes a coin flip is every bit as valuable as thinking things through. In the end, it was decided for me.

Bobby cocked a thumb toward Jade. "If I hang here with Beauty, I'm useless for anything else. I say we go out and Jade stays here, and keeps her eyes open. Anything looks fishy, she phones us pronto. We'll trade phones. I take hers, she keeps mine. No reason to think mine is being monitored." It sounded reasonable. For all his eccentricities, Bobby is one crafty dude. "And, we'll turn on my electric fence."

"It's running?"

"Sure, I just don't use it that often. I don't like to shock people without probable cause."

"What about the goats?" asked Jade.

"They know the rules. Venture too close to the perimeter, they get zapped."

I gave Bobby and Brad each $1,000 and sent another $1,000 along for Audrey. "Spend it freely. You want to buy people drinks and get them talking."

After they left, Bobby in his PT Cruiser and Brad in his Passat, I huddled with Jade. We spoke about how the alleged Fishburne was not tall and African-American like the real one; rather, he was short, pale and thin-faced, with slicked-back, straight black hair. The Forest Grove representative presiding at Cicero's memorial service, William Jameson, was spare, elderly and smarmy. He had shaken hands with each guest, and Jade recalled his solemn diction and clammy palm.

Before leaving, Bobby had shown Jade how to turn on the electricity which was activated at the breaker box on the back porch.

I showed her my spare gun, a Glock 17. "You know how to use it?"

She took it from me, expertly ejected the clip, popped it back in, pulled back the slide ejecting the bullet and caught it with a smile.

"I'll take that as 'yes.'"

"You do that."

I opened the front door. "Soon as I'm gone, turn on the juice."

"It's nice having some men around to take care of me."

"No fear."

As I drove toward Glendale, the smoke from the northwest seemed blacker and more ominous. A thin sun bled through the darkness and traffic was snarled. Finally, I turned off I-5 and took the back route past the warehouses on San Fernando Road.

Dr. Tarkanian's office was located upstairs in a nondescript two-story building on Glendale Avenue, near Los Feliz. I drove around the block a few times and parked a few doors down. The wooden stairs leading up to his offices creaked, and the air smelled of smoke and the great unwashed. The waiting room was half-full of elderly Armenian ladies, wearing the traditional head scarf, and long dark skirts.

The young receptionist was hardly more than a teenager, but her dark eyes were laced with cunning. I showed her a business card, *Law Offices of Brian Bellamy, LLP. Personal Injury and Accident.*

"I would like to see the doctor."

"Dr. Tarkanian is very busy."

Blocking her from view of the waiting patients, I slid a Franklin across the counter. She snaked the hundred dollar bill without changing expression.

"I'll see what I can do."

"Thank you."

She disappeared through a doorway behind her, reappearing seconds later. "The doctor will see you in ten minutes."

"Excellent."

I sat down near the ladies, who were watching the daytime soaps, oblivious to my bribe. Five minutes later there was a newsbreak. The Malibu fire was threatening palatial hillside homes, and was expected to only get worse.

The receptionist ushered me into Tarkanian's office. Sipping a Starbucks Latte, he had a refined, overly affected appearance.

"Dr. Tarkanian, I'm Brian Bellamy, Attorney at Law." I gave him a vigorous handshake, which he met with a limp wrist, wincing only slightly. "I have a thriving personal injury practice, and used to do a lot of work with Dr. Rufenkchyan back before, you know---" I let my words trail off.

"I don't know Dr. Rufenkchyan."

"Really? It's a damned shame what happened. We were settling four or five cases a month, real cases, and then he had to go and get greedy. There's nothing more dangerous than providing unnecessary procedures. I don't understand it. Why take the risk when there is so much legitimate work just staring you in the face?"

"Maybe he had financial problems," said Dr. Tarkanian. His voice had that sonorous musical quality that is common among Armenian-Americans.

"He's got more than financial problems now. He's overseas and the Feds are looking for him. They're like a contagious disease. Sooner or later you catch it, or rather in this case, they catch you."

"Where did you get my name?"

"Joey Abouchian recommended I talk to you."

He said nothing but his expression told me he was impressed. Joey is a legend among cappers.

"Joey's my guy. He's been working for me for three years now. Of course, as you know, he works for a lot of other attorneys too. No one guy can handle all of Joey's business. So, here's what I propose. You charge the standard rates and you don't have to kick anything back to me, if we settle at least three cases a month."

Tarkanian pursed his lips and thought it over. "I must say, that's a reasonable offer. Let me sleep on it and talk to a few people, and I'll get back to you in a day or two. Did you leave your card with my receptionist?"

"I did, but I really need an answer now. Joey's brought in three new cases already this morning. One severe whiplash over in Burbank, broken ribs and a cracked fibula up in Pacoima, and a grade two concussion in North Hollywood. If I can't handle these he'll just take them elsewhere."

"I'm sorry," he replied firmly, "but I don't make snap decisions."

I shrugged, reached into the manila envelope Halladay had given me, and took out Cicero's death certificate. I shoved it across his desk. "Perhaps this will help you make up your mind."

When he saw the certificate, he blanched. Not just a nervous start or a look of concern, but rather the paling of a man who's just seen a ghost.

"Just what the fuck is going on, Tarkanian? Level with me, or I'm gonna arrest you."

"What?"

"You ever been to Men's Central? You know what they do to people like you there? They cut your balls off and stuff them down your throat till you choke to death."

He tried to stand, but his legs had turned to jelly. He collapsed back into his chair. "Show me your badge," he said weakly, his breathing suddenly labored.

"I don't have a badge, but I've got a goddamned license. I'm a private investigator. I carry a pistol, two, actually, and I'm going to make a citizen's arrest and haul you down to the station."

He shook his head and stared down at his lab coat. "What do you want me to tell you?"

"The truth."

"All right. But if I do you have to promise to leave me alone."

"You don't get to make demands, but if you level with me, I'll get amnesia."

He nodded and paused to gather himself. "On the evening of August 16th, I got a call from Mrs. Lamont. She was frantic and asked me to come over immediately. I'd been caring for her husband for several years. He'd had four angioplasties, and had serious atherosclerosis. I called an ambulance and drove over and by the time I got there, he was in cardiac arrest. Massive myocardial infarction. I couldn't save him." He shook his head sadly.

"Good story," I said mildly. "Only one problem; they were separated and Mrs. Lamont was already living in San Francisco on August 16th."

Tarkanian wilted. It was as if I'd wrapped a noose around his neck and he was dangling over the trapdoor. Just to ease his decision, I extracted my Colt Commander, and idly pulled back the slide. Terror replaced fear and sweat leaked out of every pore. His whole body was shaking.

"I never saw the body. I just got the information from a man who said his name was Borders, Thomas Borders. I filled out the certificate and he gave me some cash."

"How much?"

"$5,000."

"You work cheap. What did Mr. Borders look like?"

"Not too tall, thin face, dark hair combed back, a little rough around the edges."

Fishburne.' I glared at the good doctor. "Are you in the habit of filling out death certificates without even seeing the body?"

He shook his head. "Would you please put that gun away?"

I put the safety on and placed it back in my belt. "You're an idiot. For 5 grand, you could be indicted for conspiracy, mail fraud, making a false statement, and money laundering. In short, you're looking at many long years at Club Fed which, while certainly not as unpleasant as Men's Central, is probably not the place you'd choose to spend your golden years. Now, suppose you start by telling me how much you were really paid."

His eyes shifted around the room and eventually settled on his shaking hands. "$15,000 and another $5,000 for arranging the service at Forest Grove."

By now his forehead was caked with sweat and he was very pale. His lips looked a little blue. I began to get worried. Although I was taking a certain perverse pleasure in scaring this prick, I didn't want him to die on me.

"You don't look so good. You don't happen to have a heart condition or high blood pressure, do you?"

"I have tachycardia and am prone to panic attacks," he said with a trace of self-pity.

"Relax then, goddamn it. You dying on me would complicate everything." I crossed to the water cooler, filled a paper cup and handed it to him. "You shouldn't drink so much coffee. It's bad for your heart."

He accepted the water and drank it gratefully. Bit-by-bit, the color returned to his face.

I leaned in on him. "Did you negotiate only with Borders?"

"There was his friend, too. A tall red-headed fellow with a tongue ring. He's the one who brought the money by."

"$20,000 for filling out a form and calling a funeral home. Not a bad payday, if you hadn't been caught."

"They still owe me $5,000."

"They goddamned better well pay up. Lot of nerve, ripping off a right guy like you." He looked like he wanted to shrivel up and crawl away. I laced my fingers behind my head and leaned back in my chair. "Here's what I want you to do. I need to have a talk with Borders and his red-headed buddy."

"But I can't get involved with--"

"--What do you really know about Lamont's death?"

"As far as I know, he died of a heart attack at his house on the afternoon of August 16th."

"Cut it out, Doc. We're both way smarter than that. If that was really the cause of death, they'd have no reason to kick you 20K to write up a bogus death certificate. This smells like Murder One. Of course, they might let you plead guilty to failing to report a capital crime, along with your conspiracy and mail fraud charges."

"They didn't tell me how he died," he said quietly, "and I didn't ask. I just looked the other way."

"Yeah."

I considered telling him to let Fishburne/Borders and Koncak know that their cover was blown, and that an investigation was underway. I decided against it, as I didn't want him killed. He was just a small-time fraudster, and the sad truth is that a large number of medical professionals in Los Angeles and Orange County are just like him. Small wonder the cost of health insurance keeps going up. Of course, the insurance companies are even bigger crooks, so you really can't win.

I sighed. "When are you gonna meet them to get the rest of the money?"

"Tomorrow afternoon."

"Where?"

"McDonald's on 3rd, on the edge of Koreatown, at 5:00 p.m."

"All right. I'll have one of my guys there. Just one other thing; how did you arrange to have Cicero Lamont interred at Forest Grove?"

"Mr. Borders told me that the family wanted the memorial service to take place there. It's a very nice cemetery."

"Why not Forest Lawn? That's where the folks with money usually like to be buried."

He shrugged. "I guess that's what the family wanted."

"That's the second time you said, 'the family.' What family?"

His fine upper lip curled into just the hint of a sneer. Then it clicked. If the bereaved loved ones contact the vampires at the cemetery, they take them to the cleaners. If somebody with an inside connection makes the arrangements, however, someone like Tarkanian, the family gets a discounted rate and the good doctor gets a kickback. The cemetery makes a little less money but they do a volume business. This scumbag was cleaning up.

"Just another way to game the system, 'eh? Who transported the corpse?"

"Borders and his friend. They drove it over in a flower van."

I stared at him incredulously. "A flower van?"

"You know, like florists use?" he smirked, his bravado returning.

"Careful." His smirk evaporated. "What's the name of the company?"

"Flowers for Every Occasion."

"I suppose you met them there with the death certificate?" He nodded. "And the family was there too?"

He leaned back in his chair. Perhaps it was because he was once again in the position of being the expert, but he was more composed. "I didn't see the family."

"And that was that."

"Yes," he said with a trace of bitterness, "until you came along."

Something had been bothering me about Tarkanian's face. Suddenly I realized that the right side of it was concave, just under his ear as if a piece of the cheekbone had been removed.

"Here's how this is gonna go; you keep your mouth shut about me. To you, I'm a ghost. You don't, I'll see you get banged up 'til they schlep you out in a box. We clear?"

"Yes."

I stood up, adjusted my gun and turned toward the door. "Oh yeah, one other thing. I'd be careful about slinging all that cash around. You don't want Federal tax evasion charges on top of everything else."

I walked down the hallway and back through the waiting room. The fires filled the TV and the ladies watched raptly. I didn't bother to say good-bye. A thin layer of soot had dusted across my forest green paint job. I got in and as I headed west on Los Feliz, toward the Hollywood Hills, I called Jade.

"Hey." She sounded forlorn.

"What's wrong?"

"I'd really like to step outside and interact with the goats."

"Any reason in particular?"

"I love animals."

"And has there been any street traffic?"

"No, and I'm going to get a dog, a rescue, when this is all over."

"Good idea and you should hang out on the back porch with the goats. They'll love you."

"Glad someone does."

Bobby called in on the other line. "Sorry, but I've gotta take this." She hung up.

"What's up?"

"We're in front of The Abbey, on Robertson. Seen three or four guys wearing stylish jogging outfits, but none of 'em were Arnold."

"How's Brad?"

"He's good at walking up to people and starting conversations. Word is the place to go for action is the Full Throttle, on Santa Monica. The doors open at 4:00. We'll be there."

"Be careful."

"Thanks, Dad."

I hung up and called Audrey. "Anything?"

"No. I'll hit the clubs tonight, Boss."

"Okay."

People were driving erratically as I made my way to Western Avenue. I took it north to Franklin where I hung a left and then right onto Beachwood, heading up into the Hills. The narrow streets wind through the canyons and the street signs are hard to spot. Finally, I found it, a very secluded section of Beachwood Drive, near the top, not far from the Hollywood sign. Arnold's house, a large, dark brown Tudor, with gables built into the roofline, stood well off the road to the right. I parked behind a gold Mercedes and scoured the area. An ornate, stone staircase angled up the hillside to the front door, and, of course, there was no driveway. That would be in back along with the servants' entrance. I sat there for several minutes mulling things over, then drove to the end of the street that doubles back sharply. When I came to Arnold's rear entrance I got out of the car and parked.

Starting up the hillside, I followed a footpath that cut through shrubbery and lodged grass. It was easy to imagine the wind whipping the fire up these tinder dry hillsides. Halfway up, the path spit me back onto what appeared to be a rarely used service road. Tufts of dun-colored grass pushed up through cracks in the asphalt. An almost vertical rock wall, overhung with manzanita and live oak, loomed to my left. Above, the smoke-rimmed sun, barely visible through the foliage, and to my right, the brushy hillside falling off sharply. There was complete silence, other than the wind and the rustling of shrubbery.

Near the top of the incline, I came to a padlocked sheet of stainless steel, built vertically into the rock wall. It reminded me of a ship's hatch, and I had the sense that there must be an underground storage area, or a bunker built into the hillside. I continued up the road sighting the house clearly now, the gables protruding against the blackened sky.

I spied a man standing at the top of the road, spying on me. He was supporting himself with a walking stick and although his posture seemed casual enough, I had the feeling he was more agile than he wanted me to believe.

"Hi," I shouted, giving him a cheerful wave and a smile.

He looked about 60, spare of build, and wore an earth-colored mesh jersey with European walking shorts and hiking boots. His crinkly white hair was brushed forward. "Hello there."

"Sorry for the intrusion."

"Not a problem, although I must say I wasn't expecting visitors."

"Nick Crane. Investigator."

"That's exciting, except I can't imagine why I'd be under investigation."

I let out a friendly chuckle. "No, no, not you, sir, unless you're Arnold Clipper?"

He studied me, rubbing the white stubble on his angular jaw, his green eyes hard as flint.

"Never heard of him."

"Not surprising as he's a bit of an enigma."

He nodded and I had the sense of a man with history. "As you've come this far and since I can't offer you Mr. Clipper, perhaps you'd like to come in for a glass of lemonade? I'm not sure I'll be much help, but I can tell you what I do know."

He gave a tentative cough as if testing the air, found it unsatisfactory, and turned and started back up the hill. I followed in his wake. His stride was slow but steady and in five minutes we were sitting in his living room, which was filled with fossils, the skeletons of small animals, and black lacquered edifices resembling forts or colonnades. He brought me a glass of lemonade, no ice, and sat across from me on an orange leather footstool.

"Mount," he said. "Reggie Mount."

"Wait a minute; I've heard your name somewhere. Weren't you--?"

"--I was," he said, smacking his lips with a dry popping sound. "I was an adventurer back when such a thing were still possible. I've studied the human mind, and I've written on a number of topics."

"That's what it is. Didn't you write a book about why people can't stay married?"

"I did." He ducked his head, his first sign of modesty. "*The Marriage Trap*. That was almost thirty years ago. It was a best seller and incurred the wrath of feminists everywhere."

"My wife read it. She said it was funny."

"I take it your wife's not a feminist?"

"I wouldn't say that. She has her tendencies. She does like men, however, doesn't blame us for her problems."

"Such wisdom, if I may quote Shakespeare, is honored more in the breach than the observance."

"This is great lemonade."

"Nothing to it. Fresh lemons, clean water, and just enough brown sugar to give it that touch of sweetness. I've long wanted to write a cookbook, but have never quite gotten around to it. It would be full of simple, tasty recipes that can be produced on a camp stove. I don't suppose you get out in the mountains that much, always skulking around in the city."

"Your backyard is about as close to the mountains as I usually get. I did take my daughter on a hike in the hills a few months ago. Got a tick."

"Infernal creatures. How did you remove it?"

"With tweezers. Grip and lift. When we met you said you've been working. A new book, I suppose?"

"Somehow, in recent years I've moved onto the eternal questions. Why is man evil and is there any way to stem the tide?"

"What do you think?"

"My working thesis, which is very radical, is that evil is a diversion and could perhaps be replaced by alternative diversions. Diversions are what keep us going -- sports, music, sex, empire building, books, movies, and, of course, cruelty. Anything to release us from our own inner emptiness."

"That's rather deep."

"Not really. It's really rather simple. What we fear more than anything is boredom. You hear kids say it all the time. 'I've got nothing to do.' It makes them miserable. Women tend to fill the void through social interaction. Men fill it through competition, striving and pastimes and when that fails, we bash one another's brains in, usually in the name of god and country."

"Yeah, I've seen a lot of violent xenophobia in the name of god and something or other."

He nodded, and his eyes probed mine as if he was scouring my brain. "The problem is that once we divert ourselves, or are diverted into evil, nothing else compares. In effect, we become addicted. That's why PTSD vets are so miserable. Nothing compares to the twisted thrill kill. It lurks there in the reptilian brain and once it's unleashed, it's hard to turn off. It becomes all-encompassing."

"I have a good friend who's a Vietnam vet."

"And?"

"He's miserable much of the time. The only time he's not is when he has something interesting going on."

"Which is probably rare. Killing is primordial. That's why serial killers can't control themselves. The rush, they say, is unbelievable. Nothing else comes close. And then, when blood lust gets all mixed up with sexuality, you've got a real fiend on your hands."

"Were you in Nam?"

"Yes, I certainly was. I was also in Cambodia. Bomber pilot. I started out flying for LBJ, and then I flew for Nixon. I was a patriot, in those days."

"And now?"

"I'm not so sure. I'm just an old man on a hilltop trying to make sense of it all. The only reason I'm not crazy is because I didn't see my victims. I was too far away and there was too much smoke in the air. Sometimes I look back on those days and wonder if they ever really happened. But of course, I know they did." He paused and his eyes drifted off to some ancient regret. He pulled himself back and smiled, "Can I get you a refill?"

"Delighted."

He brought me the lemonade and looked at me, intrigued. "So, Mr. Crane, here's what I can tell you." He spoke slowly, tapping his right index finger into the palm of his left hand as if to punctuate his points. "I rented this house through a management company. They were exceedingly circumspect and gave no hint as to the identity of the actual owner. All they said was that he had moved to another location. Didn't say where. The rent is high, but the lease was for two years. I just re-leased it last month for another two."

"Have you gotten to know your neighbors?"

"Does anyone, ever, in Los Angeles?"

I grinned. "I know what you mean."

"There is one peculiar condition in my lease. Back in the fifties, the owner of this house had made a fortune manufacturing shipping containers, but struggled with mental illness. He built an underground fortress extending from the basement, halfway down the hill. It is apparently terraced, to match the contours of the hillside. When fear struck, he would disappear down there for weeks at a time, or at least that's the way the story goes. Under the terms of my lease, I have no access to it. The door in my basement has been walled off with masonry. The leasing company was obligated to reveal the presence of the underground chamber for safety reasons, particularly as it could, in theory, undermine the house foundation if there was flooding or an earthquake. The structure is held up by steel columns and I-beams, and is thought to be of sound construction."

"So that explains the stainless steel door in the rock face."

"That's the other entrance, presumably what the owner would use if he wanted to get in. The structure is roughly in the shape of a large three dimensional "L," like the Knight's move in chess, only the board would be three-dimensional, descending in steps, like the Hanging Gardens of Babylon. I've actually got a copy of the blueprints, if you'd like to see them. I found them tucked up on a shelf in the basement when I was arranging my wine cellar."

"I'd love to. Thanks."

Reggie rose stiffly. "One moment." He took the open stairway to the second floor and returned a minute later, laying the blueprints out on the table.

"Amazing."

"Indeed. It's a bit of an engineering triumph," said Reggie. "There's enough concrete and steel down there to reinforce a good-sized building."

"Aren't you ever curious about what's there?"

"I was at first, but at my age I've learned not to torture myself with what I cannot change, unless, of course, I'm writing about it. The basement door is solid steel, six inches thick, apparently secured by steel crosspieces attached to the wall with huge lag bolts, and that's behind the masonry wall. No one's getting in there."

It crossed my mind that the other door could be breached with the right cutting tool, or maybe even a bump key, but I said nothing. "Does the owner ever enter by the other door?"

"Not that I know of."

"Interesting."

"Quite and now I must excuse myself. I've got to get back to work and as you may have noticed, evil waits for no man."

"Indeed. Thanks for the info and lemonade."

"You're very welcome."

On my way down the front steps, I was distracted by a set of curious inlaid tiles built into the staircase, apparently inscribed at the request of the same man who had built the underground shelter. They were scenes from the ancient world: Assyrians in battle garb, pharaohs lying in state, and beautiful Mycenaean wall paintings of colorful fish in the blue Mediterranean, the Levantine sun reflecting on the water.

Nearing the street, I noticed a runner heading east; whether by premonition or natural caution, I stepped back shielding myself. The shock of recognition was profound. It was James Halladay wearing blue shorts and a blue velour sweatshirt, intent on his workout. He passed the house without a glance, looking occasionally at what appeared to be a stopwatch in his right hand. I waited for a reasonable period to give him some distance, and walked back to my car.

Driving toward downtown, I kept one eye on my rear view mirror. I considered heading over to Forest Grove to see if William Jameson would corroborate Dr. Tarkanian's story, but decided against it. Fishburne/Borders and the ersatz Officer Koncak were right in the middle of Cicero's death. That was enough for now. I wanted to get on Merlin and do a search on Halladay, as my instinct was screaming that he might be connected to Cicero's death. I tempered myself with the thought that him jogging in Arnold's old neighborhood might be purely circumstantial; it could mean nothing, but it could also mean he lived nearby and had known Arnold for some time.

I called Bobby to check in but he didn't pick up, so I called Audrey.

"Hi, Boss."

"I need you to go down to the L.A. County Recorder's Office in Norwalk, to check on a grant deed for 3655 Beachwood Drive."

"Sure, but why?"

"Arnold Clipper owns it, but I need verification."

"I'll call you soon as I've got the info."

"Thanks."

I called Jade. She didn't pick up 'til the fourth ring and when she did she sounded distraught. "Nick, is that you? Nick!"

"Yeah. What's wrong?"

"Every time a car drives by, I think it's them."

"Relax. There's virtually no traffic there."

"I know. That's why I keep thinking they're sneaking up on me. I can't believe I was taken in by those creeps. They had the gall to sit in my living room, and lie to me about my father's death."

"Do you have the electricity on?"

"The fence? Yes, of course."

"They'd have a helluva time getting in."

"What if they shoot up the house? Nobody in this neighborhood would even notice."

"I'm on my way."

"Please hurry."

"Watch TV and try to calm down. Do you want me to bring you any take-out?"

"No. Just get here."

When I got back to the office, I parked two blocks north on 1st Street, east of Alameda. The neighborhood is gentrifying and condos are going up by the hundred. Construction guys wearing masks to protect them from the bad air worked steadily in the gray light. I threaded my way through the back streets and let myself in the side door. It was stuffy, so I turned on the air and skimmed my email -- nothing significant. I logged onto Merlin. James Halladay's current residence was on Linforth Drive, which intersects Beachwood half-a-mile below Arnold's house.

I was now certain that Fishburne and Koncak were involved in Cicero's death. The problem was Halladay. If he was, too, I was obviously compromised since I was now working for him. The motivation was the Lamont family fortune. Fishburne and Koncak could be employees, working for Halladay or Arnold or both. Halladay might be unaware of Arnold's more bizarre tendencies. His involvement, however, was made less likely by the fact he was going to a lot of trouble to see that Jade was protected. That, on the other hand, could be mere subterfuge.

I set the alarm and had barely hit the sidewalk when two LAPD detectives closed in.

"Nick Crane?"

I knew from their fine sense of dress they were dicks. "Who wants to know?" They pulled back their jackets revealing shields and guns. I grinned. "In that case, yes."

Officer Sanchez, all shaved head and glaring eyes, didn't like my sense of humor. He slammed me up against the side of their cruiser and snapped the cuffs on me. "Lemme know if they're too tight," he snarled.

He turned me around and his partner, Officer Tomito, yanked my Colt Commander. "Nice artillery."

"It does the job."

"You got a backup?"

"Right ankle."

He pulled up my trouser leg and took my Walther P22. Fortunately, I wasn't carrying lock picks or anything else that might be viewed as compromising. They opened the back door of the

84

cruiser and shoved me inside. Sanchez sat next to me. Tomito climbed behind the wheel.

The cop riding shotgun, who was casually dressed in street clothes, gave me a look that was seven-eighths contempt and one-eighth sympathy. I seriously doubted that Tarkanian would have had either the courage or just plain bad sense to lodge a complaint, which meant I had no idea what this was about.

"I'm Detective Jansen. You've already met Officers Sanchez and Tomito."

"Let's get this over with. I've got an appointment in 30."

Sanchez jabbed me hard in the ribs. "Shut the fuck up."

I grimaced, gritted my teeth and locked eyes with him. "You're real tough when I'm cuffed."

Sanchez opened his mouth to reply, but Jansen cut him off. "Tony Bott speaks highly of you. Says you're good people. Nonetheless, we've got us a little problem." He fixed me with a dead eye cop stare. "Murder One."

"I'm outta the hit business."

"Glad to hear that. Try to keep it that way."

"I will. Trust me."

"Never trust anyone who says 'trust me,'" added Officer Tomito.

This brought a round of laughter.

Detective Jansen looked at my .45, flexed his jaw muscles and said to Tomito, "Let's ride."

We pulled away from the curb, turned left on Central and right on 5th. When we got to Towne Street, we parked and got out.

Jansen looked at Sanchez. "Uncuff him."

I rubbed my wrists to get my circulation back. For years, Towne Street was the center of the Skid Row open air crack market, but in recent years it's moved down to 5th and San Carlos, near the missions. That way a basehead can get a fix on his way into rehab, and on his way out, without ever leaving the block.

Towne, between 5th and 6th was completely cordoned off. The only officials on the scene were the investigator, the coroner's investigator and the photographer. A few rubberneckers watched from behind sawhorses, as we ducked under the tape and headed down the block. The victim came gradually into focus: flat on its back, feet almost touching the rust-colored brick wall of what had once been a foundry. The body was nude and bloated and had been decapitated. The severed head rested on one cheek, facing north along the sidewalk. Its eyes stared lifelessly and what should have been hair was blood-smeared skull.

"At least the perp didn't cut his dick off," said Officer Tomito.

The cops wouldn't have brought me here unless they somehow connected me to the victim, which meant I must know him. It hit me like a sledgehammer. Ron Cera. My head started pounding. I turned and started walking back toward 5th Street. Officer Sanchez followed me and threw up just before we reached the sawhorses, thick gray bile that splattered across the already stained sidewalk. Tomito joined Jansen who yanked Sanchez to his feet. We walked back to the cruiser in silence.

When we got to the stationhouse, Sanchez and Tomito dispersed. Jansen ushered me into his office, and a homicide detective named Karsagian joined us. Mid-fifties, barrel-chested with sagging jowls, latticed with broken capillaries. He had a deep vertical cleft between his eyebrows and thick salt-and-pepper hair which he combed straight back. This guy looked like something straight out of an old black and white movie.

As we shook hands, he looked me right in the eye and chuckled. "Nick Crane. Private dick." He rolled his chair over until it was literally touching mine and glared at me, his face only inches from mine. "So how'd you meet Ron Cera?"

I made a disgusted face. "Your mouthwash ain't making it."

Karsagian frowned but didn't move away. Jansen tried not to smirk, lost that battle and instead cleared his throat.

I pushed my chair back a couple of feet. "If I'm a suspect I want my lawyer."

Karsagian balled up a fist that looked like a block of granite. "You got some balls."

"You think this is my first time around the block?"

"I don't give a goddamn."

"That makes two of us."

His face turned a nasty shade of red. He got to his feet, anger flashing across his eyes.

Jansen once again refereed. "Relax." Karsagian relaxed. "As of right now, you're a material witness."

I locked eyes with him. "All right then."

"On Wednesday morning you visited Ron Cera at his apartment in North Hollywood," growled Karsagian. "You drive a silver Toyota Camry XLE. This morning Ron Cera's mutilated corpse gets dumped on Towne Street out of a silver Japanese mid-size car. The two sets of eyeballs weren't sure if it was a Camry or not, but they were damned sure the car was silver and Japanese."

"What time was this?"

"Crackheads don't keep time too well, but they said it was about 4:00 a.m."

"At 4:00 a.m., I was home in bed with my wife."

"Is that a fact?"

"Last night my Camry was at Leo's Paint and Brake Shop, in East L.A., getting painted forest green. I picked it up this morning about 8:00."

"What color is your wife's car?" asked Jansen.

"Gold Altima."

"Why," said Karsagian, "were you having your Camry painted forest green?"

"Long story."

"I'm not gonna ask you again."

So I told them I'd been hired by Jade Lamont to find her brother, and that I'd talked to Ron Cera because he had recently been in touch with him. I explained that Ron was scared of Arnold Clipper and was in process of moving, and that I thought Cicero Lamont had been murdered.

Jansen glared at me. "Wait, you're working for *the* Cicero Lamont? The dope dealer?"

"Did you miss the part about him being dead?" The detective's eyes flashed hard. I grinned and added, "Again, it was his daughter who hired me."

"At least the son-of-a-bitch is dead."

"You're all heart, Jansen."

Karsagian asked, "You got any idea who killed him?"

"Could have been those two bogus cops, Fishburne and Koncak."

He nodded. "But what do we have to connect them to Cicero?"

I needed a minute to make sure I didn't spill too much. I got up and went over to the water cooler, took a paper cup and drank two of 'em down, slow and easy. In this business you learn to feign calmness. It's an art form and absolutely necessary. If I told them everything I knew about Fishburne and Koncak, even if I kept Halladay out of it, it could set in motion a chain of events that could end up with Arnold disappearing, and Richie right along with him. If the cops arrested the fake cops for the murder of Ron Cera, that was almost guaranteed. My plan was for Bobby to shadow them, assuming one or both of them showed up at McDonald's to meet Dr. Tarkanian, and to play it cool until they led us to Arnold.

I dumped the empty into the trashcan. "Those two clowns impersonating Fishburne and Koncak informed Jade Lamont that her father had been killed in a hit-and-run. They dressed like cops and showed her their badge numbers."

"How do you know they weren't police officers?" said Jansen.

"I contacted the county coroner's office. It turns out there was a hit-and-run fatality on Sepulveda, in Mission Hills, on the night of August 16th. Problem is, the deceased is not Cicero Lamont. It was a Mexican gangbanger, Mario Cantrell."

"One less asshole," said Jansen.

Karsagian said, "This is very interesting, but it doesn't prove squat. It's conjecture. You haven't offered any proof to go with your story."

"I've ordered Lamont's Death Certificate."

"So what? We can do that, assuming the son-of-a-bitch is dead," barked Jansen.

Suddenly he was now the surly one, with Karsagian relaxed and friendly. I was getting sick of their lame ass good cop, bad cop, switch-up routine.

"I'm not the jerk off here. I'm doing my job. There was absolutely no good reason to jack me. I would have been glad to answer any questions. All you had to do was ask."

"Relax yourself," snarled Jansen.

"You both know I'm not the murderer. The way I know that Cicero is dead is his kids attended his memorial service at Forest Grove. That's how it usually works when somebody dies."

Karsagian gave Jansen a look that said '*lay off*.'

"Look at it from our perspective," said Karsagian. "Grisly murder/mutilation. Body dumped on skid row. People panic. The victim was a regular middle class kid from a decent family. Not good."

"My client's been through hell. Her father's killed, her mom commits suicide and her brother disappears. It's not her fault that her father ran weight any more than it's mine."

"All right," said Karsagian. "But there's one part of this I don't understand. You told us that Ron was scared because Arnold had threatened him."

"He wanted Ron to set up a meet between him and Jade. He didn't want Richard involved because he didn't want him connected to the meeting. Ron wouldn't do it, so Arnold got pissed."

"We'll find him. In the meantime, I need the contact information for Ms. Lamont."

"You tell her about Ron's death and it's liable to push her over the edge. She and Ron were good friends."

"Good friends?" said Jansen.

"Very good friends," I said.

"That's tough," said Karsagian, "but given what we're up against, Ms. Lamont is gonna have to deal with it."

"For obvious reasons, Ms. Lamont is in hiding."

"Where?" asked Karsagian.

I glued my mouth shut.

"We can do this dance all night, if you want. Or, you can tell us where she is."

My mind was whirling but I managed to come up with some semblance of a plan. "All right. Let's meet at the Croatian Church on La Flora, in East L.A. Six o'clock tonight."

"Shit," said Jansen. "That's my cocktail hour."

"We'll be there," said Karsagian.

"I'm going to send her over with my investigator, Bobby Moore. Big husky guy. Vietnam vet. Walks with a limp. I don't want to be seen with Jade in public. She'll be disguised."

"Okay," said Karsagian, offering me his granite hand to shake. I did, then shook Jansen's and left.

PART TWO

CHAPTER I
Eyewitness

OFFICER TOMITO DROPPED ME OFF at my car on 1st Street. I drove slowly toward the river. Someone could have been following me for all I knew but I was too wrecked to care. The image of Ron Cera, big, good-natured pothead, full of wit and laughter, mutilated on Towne Street, seemed to blot out the whole horizon. The fires could have been raging down the city streets and I wouldn't have cared.

I stopped at a neighborhood dive around the corner from Abel's diner, and poured down some bourbon. The place was so low rent that it didn't even have television, just wall-to-wall drunks. I called Jade.

"Where the hell are you, Nick?"

"Sorry. I got hung up, but I'll be there soon."

"You okay? You sound exhausted."

"Yeah, I'm good. Later."

I didn't wait for her to respond and hung up. One old guy caught my eye and motioned for me to join him. I was in no mood for conversation. I paid up and slammed out of there.

Out front a skeletal and bearded homeless guy in a wheelchair, made me for some change. I gave him what I had; he rasped his thanks and scooted away quickly, hands working to propel his wheels. I watched him go, got in my car and headed for the freeway.

Cassady answered on the third ring.

"Hi, Baby," I said.

This time there was no 'How is your day going?' She could tell by my voice that something was wrong. "We're in danger, aren't we?"

"I dunno, but to be safe, you guys need to leave, tonight."

"I'm already packed. We'll catch the 6:50 flight out of Ontario."

"Good." I didn't know what else to say but I wanted to hear her voice, so I hesitated.

"I love you," she said.

"Me too," I mumbled.

"I'll call you when we touch down in Salt Lake."

"Okay."

"And if you fuck Miss Perfume, I guarantee you'll never fuck me again. And don't think I won't know."

She hung up and I pulled onto Highway 10. On my way to City Terrace, I swung by Leo's and temporarily exchanged my forest green Camry for a grey primered Chevy Yukon. I called Bobby.

"Nick, where you been?"

"Meet me at your place a.s.a.p."

"Brad found a guy who knows Arnold. We were in a dive bar, Gideon's Gamble. He approached this old guy drinking alone, bought him a Long Island Iced Tea and the old guy told him that Arnold hardly ever missed Thursday or Friday nights, cause that's when all the hot young trade make the scene. Said he would probably put in an appearance at Full Throttle tonight. Old guy invited him back to his apartment."

"He's not drinking, is he?"

"He knows I'll kick his ass if he even looks at a beer."

"Has the guy seen Richie?"

"He thought he has, but he's not sure. Said Arnold's arsenal of young men is the envy of half of Los Angeles. Word is Arnold's tossed everybody aside for the new boyfriend. It has to be him."

"I'm at your place. Have Brad come back with you. I don't want him working alone."

"Okay," replied Bobby.

When I got to his house, I parked and phoned Jade. "You here?"

"Right out in front, so turn off the juice."

A moment passed. I could hear her footsteps crossing the room. "It's off."

Her voice sounded flat, halting and I don't know why but I had the feeling she knew about Ron Cera. Maybe she saw it on the news. I greeted the goats as I climbed the hill. Jade was a mess. Her beautiful café con leche complexion was streaked with tears, and her eyes red and puffy. Her movements were wooden and she seemed tiny, lost inside her clothes. She couldn't meet my gaze, looked away and collapsed back on the couch.

"I've wrecked everything. Poor Ron. Poor good-hearted Ron." She was nearly hysterical, and I knew that nothing I could say would change what had happened.

"Listen, Jade, I'm up to my neck in this too, so stop feeling sorry for yourself. I'm late 'cause the cops held me for questioning. They tried to fit me up for killing Ron, but couldn't make it work. The cops aren't stupid; they did that because they know something is going on and they want to find whoever did do him."

She looked at me, her face a mask of despair, and whispered, "It's my fault."

"Don't be ridiculous. He knew how psychotic Arnold was, and could've gotten out of Dodge anytime. For some reason he didn't. It sucks, but that's on him."

She nodded as tears pooled in her eyes and started to tumble down her cheeks. I handed her a tissue.

"You know better than anyone that Richie's fucked up for a whole bunch of reasons that I'm not privy to, nor do I wanna be. Be pissed at Cicero. He's the one who let your brother down. Not you."

I watched the emotions play across Jade's mobile features. Her despair still held sway but there were ephemeral glimpses of something else, something stronger.

"You've got to meet with the cops in less than 2 hours. Pull yourself together and get your story straight, or you'll screw this up."

She nodded and was suddenly matter-of-fact. "I won't screw it up. I Promise." The change was remarkable, if not slightly disturbing. "I'm sorry I'm such a pussy."

"Bad choice of words," I smiled.

"You know what I mean. What do I tell the cops?"

"Very simple. Just describe your interaction with Fishburne and Koncak. Give them details. Their phone calls. Your meetings. They are going to want to take your cell phone to trace your calls. Give it to them. Tell 'em how Koncak was tailing us at the library. Do not mention Halladay. Pretend he doesn't exist."

Jade was genuinely surprised. "But he's the one who contacted me."

"Doesn't matter. That's what he wants."

Jade was incensed. "But he's my father's lawyer, for Chrissake! He's my fuckin' lawyer. Now he wants to stick his head in the sand?"

"For now, he's not the focus. Our whole game plan hinges on you convincing the cops that we really don't know very much."

"But you really know a lot more, don't you?" Jade looked hopeful and wary at the same time.

"Stay focused. I want you to cry real tears. Be helpless and pathetic."

"Why? Are they suspicious?"

"They're cops. What d'you think?"

"Yeah, sorry."

"They know I'm not telling them everything, so they're gonna press you, hard."

"Most men are suckers for a crying, helpless chick."

"Most." I smiled wryly. "You're smart, and strong. You'll be fine."

We looked at one another. I could see gratitude in her eyes, and something else that made me nervous. She could read me like a book and she reached out and closed her slim, warm hands over my wrist and started to pull me toward her. I shook my head almost imperceptibly, but it was enough for her to notice. She let go of my wrist and drifted past me, heading toward the kitchen. She made coffee and I tried to read Newsweek.

Audrey phoned and I was grateful for the distraction. "You were right. It's Arnold Clipper's name on the house deed."

"Meet up with Brad tonight at The Abbey, on Robertson, at 9:00 p.m."

No sooner had we signed off than Sheri Thomas, a skid row basehead, called. She's hit me up for money, on and off, over the last five years, but knows better than to call unless she's got something legit to sell me.

"Nicky, gotta to talk to you, Baby."

"Where are you?"

"Where do you think I am? On the street. Same old same old."

"I'll meet you in 15 at the convenience store on 4th, just east of the 60 turnoff. I'll be in a grey Yukon."

I took the back streets through East L.A. When I got to there, Sheri was waiting astride her old Schwinn bicycle, bundled up in a dirty orange ski parka. She glistened with sweat, and her eyes were big and dilated. I jumped out of my truck. "Let's put your bike in the back."

"Okay, yeah, cool. Let's book. Bad for my image to be seen with you."

Sixty seconds later we were tooling slowly down Boyle Avenue, past the tire recappers and miscellaneous businesses. "You gonna tell me, or not?"

She held her hand out. "Cash money."

"Don't waste my time, Sheri."

"Okay, chill, Dog." I opened my mouth to respond and she cut me off. "Just before I called you, I ran into a pipehead I know. It was luck. Good luck, for a change."

"Yeah? For who?"

"You, a'course."

Baseheads can conjure up any number of bullshit scenarios, especially when they're Jonesing. I was getting irritated and pulled over hard to the curb.

"What the fuck, Nicky?"

"Get out."

"Come on, man, I need money for my beauty products."

I tried not to smile, but I just couldn't help it. "Beauty products?"

"I know I ain't much to look at now, but I was a fine woman back in the day."

I'd hurt her feelings and although I hadn't meant to, the damage was done. Tears started popping out of her big brown eyes in discrete individual packages.

"Sorry, I didn't mean nothin' by it."

She nodded, sniffed and wiped her eyes with dirty fingers, calloused and dry from living on the street for all these years. I handed her a tissue and a Franklin. She looked at the C note with a surprising amount of disdain.

"That ain't enough."

"Give me something and if it's good, you'll get more."

"Why'd five-oh take you in today?"

I stared at her. "What're you, psychic?"

"Hell no. I don't believe in that witchcraft bullshit, but I peeped yo' ass in a cruiser, 'bout five o'clock this afternoon, over on 2nd and Central."

"It was about that body on Towne."

"Did you do it?"

"What'd you think?"

"Shit, Baby, I know you didn't, but I got a description of them that might have."

Sheri let that hang in the air and when it had become sufficiently weighted, I handed her another hundred. She looked at the 2 beans in her hand and bit the inside of her cheek.

"I don't have all day."

"Aw'ite." She slipped the folding money into her jeans. "When the body got dumped off, a friend of mine was asleep and the car woke him up. Not too many white people down there at night."

"Who was driving the car?"

"Uh-huh. Hang on, Baby. I'm gettin' there. Anyways, Drew, he was hid between these dumpsters in his raggedy ass sleeping bag, and he watched the whole thing go down. These two guys got out and dragged the other white boy outta the trunk. He said one dude was tall, real white, with red hair. Other dude was short with dark hair. The tall dude was laughing when he dumped the head on the sidewalk, sick motherfucka, and the other one came around and turned it this way and that. Then they split."

"Was there a driver?"

"Yeah, Drew said he didn't get a good look at 'im but said he was one of 'dem Hollywood types. You know, hair combed back, lookin' all cool."

"You did good."

"How good?"

I peeled off another 2 Franklins and pressed them into her hand. Her eyes widened and for a second, I thought she was going to cry again.

"Did Drew talk to the cops?"

"Hell no."

"Okay then."

She smiled; teeth yellow and chipped. "I'm a'get me a room for tonight."

I peeled off another Franklin. "I need your jacket."

"For reals?"

I held up the money. She handed me her dirty, worn ski parka, snapped her digits around the C note and climbed out. As I pulled her bicycle out of the back, she gave me a long, hard look and pursed her lips thoughtfully.

"Yo, Nicky, you gonna be aw'ite?"

I smiled. "Yeah, I'm gonna be alright. Make sure you are too."

Bobby arrived home a little after I did, followed by Brad ten minutes later. We sat in the living room, sipping coffee.

"I got pinched this morning and taken to see Ron Cera's corpse, over on Towne Street."

"Damn," said Brad.

"The cops couldn't make me for it, so here I am. They wanna interview Jade in about 30, at the Croatian church. Bobby, you have any warrants out?"

"I'm a patriot. I served this country. Only thing they want me for is to pin on the Congressional Medal of Honor."

"Good. You're gonna take her."

"Cool."

"Jade, put on the wig Audrey bought you and some of that pancake make-up."

"I don't wear pancake," she protested.

"You do today."

Ten minutes later she emerged from Bobby's spare bedroom -- stained, baggy chinos, an even baggier flannel shirt, a frizzed-out bleached-blonde wig and orange stage make-up.

"Wow," said Brad, "I'm impressed. You look ready for rehab."

"Not now. Not ever," she grinned.

Bobby clasped his hands in prayer and raised his eyes to heaven. "Lord, forgive these sinners that have come unto my house."

I pointed at his skintight jogging shorts, his muscular thighs bulging like a college fullback. "It's getting cold. How about you put on some long pants for your important meeting with law enforcement?"

"Why?"

"I want them to think you're halfway normal."

"I am. Just not all the way."

He went into his room and came back out wearing jeans, and a long-sleeved button down shirt, which made him look like a DEA agent showing up for sentencing in a Federal narcotics case.

"I grinned. "That wasn't so difficult, was it?"

"You owe me," he growled.

I handed Jade Sheri's ski parka. She pulled it over her flannel shirt, and was now a pretty good facsimile of a wigged-out bag lady.

"Okay, guys. Get to it."

They nodded and left.

I turned to Brad. "What's with the old guy at Gideon's Gamble?"

"I felt sorry for him. He had that hunger. I had the feeling he would be eternally grateful if I only gave him a little man love."

"Were you tempted?"

"Can't say I was. I gave him my cell number in case he heard anything. There's nothing sadder though than an old guy who still yearns for his restless youth."

"Let's hope we're not in that position one day."

"The rate we're going we'll be lucky if we live 'til next Thursday, much less middle age."

"I want you to meet Audrey at 9:00, in front of The Abbey, but don't take any unnecessary risks. I don't need either of you ending up like Ron Cera."

"Shit. Maybe I should be armed."

"Too risky. You guys might get patted down at some of those clubs."

"I could leave it in the car."

"And if you get pulled over, that's jail time for both of us."

"How?"

"Because all of my guns are registered and unless you're gonna say you stole it, which the cops most likely wouldn't believe anyway, it adds more fuel to the fire, which I don't need."

"At least there's Audrey's gun."

"She doesn't carry."

"Jesus, Nick, this isn't good."

"If you see Arnold, or get wind that something's not kosher, get outta there and call me."

He nodded and looked down at his feet. I felt as apprehensive as he did, but had no choice other than to trust that he wouldn't take any unnecessary chances. Audrey was a very experienced investigator, and I drew comfort from that. I hoped he did too.

Jade and Bobby were back by 6:45. As soon as they walked in, I breathed a sigh of relief. Bobby has two habitual expressions: a tight-lipped quasi-sneer in which the corners of his mouth point toward four and eight o'clock, and a lopsided grin which reveals his nicotine-stained teeth. He was wearing the latter. Jade looked relieved. It was obvious from the streaks in her make-up that she'd been crying again. She pulled off her wig and smoothed her hair.

"Beauty deserves an Oscar," said Bobby. "She had them eating out of her hand. Me too but that's a different story."

"I made them uncomfortable. They were embarrassed when they realized that the daughter of the notorious Cicero Lamont was a pathetic, teary bag lady. They did take my cell phone though."

"So they bought it?"

She nodded.

Bobby said, "You know how the cops are, though. They don't like to give anything up."

"Mostly they just kept going over two things. One, the time and place for my meetings and phone calls with Fishburne and Koncak and, two, my relationship with Ron. Since I hadn't seen him for some time and never met Arnold, I couldn't give them much. They didn't actually ask me much about Cicero. I tried to bring the conversation around to Richard, but they weren't interested."

"Soon as they mentioned Ron," said Bobby, "tears started bubbling and pretty soon she couldn't turn them off."

"They were shocked at how bad I looked. I told them I broke up with Ron because I didn't really love him. I know that they were thinking Ron must have been out of his mind to ever have anything to do with me."

Jade looked like she was going to cry again but controlled herself.

"Halladay was right," I said. "They don't give a damn about solving Cicero's murder or finding your brother."

"Cold hearted motherfuckers," snapped Bobby.

I nodded. "Yeah, they're only concerned with the fake cops and Ron's murder."

"They told me to be careful," said Jade.

"Big of 'em," said Bobby. "So, what's next?"

"Let's eat while I mull that over."

"Nothing in the house," said Bobby. "Let's go down to Rosario's on Cesar Chavez."

"We can't. At least Jade can't."

"Okay. I'll go get us some take-out. You guys wait here."

Bobby was back by 7:30 with a couple of roast chickens, coleslaw, potato salad and a half-gallon of milk. As we ate and drank, I envisioned my wife and daughter on the plane to Salt Lake. Maleah loves to fly and would be excited, wanting to walk up and down the aisle as soon as the seatbelt light went off. Cassady would watch her but at the same time would let her spread her wings.

I know I'm hardly the best father, and having been brought up cockeyed with a psychotic old man, know next to nothing about raising kids, but Cassady has the touch. From the day she was handed Maleah by a weeping nurse in a lead-infested South China orphanage, she has dedicated her existence to making that little girl's life a thing of joy.

I walked out to the back porch. The air was still smoky, there were no stars, and a faint smell of gas seemed to emanate from the hillside. I could hear the freeway traffic off in the distance. My mind kept coming back to Ron. I could still see his head lying on the sidewalk, staring blindly at nothing. His life finished before it had even really begun, and now he would never get that good role he yearned for. I wondered who his mother was and what she must be feeling. I felt I ought to contact her, tell her I knew her son and that he was a good guy, somebody people liked and enjoyed being around. I thought maybe I would if I had the chance.

My thoughts turned to the people inside. Bobby, whom I loved in the casual way of brothers before the sword, and Brad, my good friend whose eyes lit up when he got excited and who never failed to make me laugh. Then there was Jade. Everyone liked being around her, but it was the comfort of moths drawn to flame. She burned with pure female heat and everyone, whether they knew it or not, could smell her scent.

I went back inside and their small talk drifted away. I guess it was my expression, but suddenly the air became charged.

"Bobby, tomorrow I need you to shadow Koncak or Fishburne, or whoever shows up to pay off Tarkanian at the McDonald's in Koreatown."

Bobby's eyes lit up. I could tell he'd had enough of West Hollywood for a while and that he liked the idea of tailing real people rather than phantoms.

"Consider it done. What are you gonna do?"

"Jade and I are flying to Frisco."

"We are?"

"I want to get you out of town for a day or two, and we've got to try and find out what really happened to your mom."

She tried to look composed, but it was obvious to all of us that she was only moments away from leaking tears. "Then you don't believe it was suicide."

"Normally, I wouldn't have an opinion either way, but under the circumstance, we need to be sure."

She nodded, tried to smile and went into the bathroom. We all knew why.

Bobby turned to me. "You better be careful. No one knows you up there."

"I'll be armed."

"Wish I was going with you."

"You're more valuable here. Koncak saw me at the library. He won't recognize you."

"Unless he's seen me in West Hollywood."

"Even if he has, he won't necessarily put the pieces together."

He grinned. "I do look like a guy who spends my afternoons in McDonald's, eating French fries, and staring at married women."

We all laughed.

Bobby clapped his hand on my shoulder. "Let's roll."

CHAPTER II
San Francisco

JADE AND I DECIDED TO catch a San Francisco late night flight out of LAX. First I doubled back to my house to pick-up my luggage and the hard case for my Colt 45, while Bobby swung out to Jade's condo on Wilshire to pack for her. I left the Yukon in long-term parking at LAX and we took the shuttle bus to the Southwest terminal. Nothing seemed out of the ordinary, other than flights were delayed because of the fires. Bleary-eyed passengers milled around. I checked my gun and luggage and called Bobby on his cell. Thirty minutes later we met him at the curb.

He was grinning. "That's a nice place you have there, Beauty. I think I'm moving in. My goats will make short work of your carpet."

"Did they give you any trouble at the desk?" Jade was curious.

"Just the usual. Terror. Astonishment. I gave them the 1000 yard stare. It's a good thing you phoned in advance. Otherwise, they would never have let me in. As it was, I had to show them my I.D. and give them my phone number."

Jade thanked him. We all shook hands and watched him nose back into traffic.

I was painfully aware of Jade's presence as we worked our way through security, and finally took our seats. Once we were on the plane, I closed my eyes and tilted back my seat, feigning drowsiness in order to collect my thoughts. Jade thumbed through the flight magazines. She had that old lady's habit of dampening her index finger before turning the pages. I actually did doze for a few moments as the flight attendant gave pre-flight instructions, and then we accelerated up the runway.

It was even worse once we were in the air. The cabin was dim, most of the passengers were either asleep or reading, and Jade and I had an empty seat to our left. She had freshened up while we were waiting to board, and wore a light perfume that reminded me, for all the world, of the pink and yellow roses in my backyard that bloom every November. Once we'd reached 30,000 feet and the seatbelt light went off, Jade placed her magazine back in the rack and turned to me.

"What a day. I guess I lost it there for a while."

"You did good. Nobody said this was gonna be easy."

"Detective Karsagian and his chunky buddy, the Sergeant, had I looked like this instead of an insane bag lady, would've kept questioning me. As it was, they couldn't wait to get it over with." She shrugged, her disappointment in the male gender, obvious. "For once I'd like to be surprised."

"We're not all stereotypes."

"There are exceptions -- you, Ron. But you're few and far between. He didn't take himself too seriously, except for his acting, of course. He was a funny, gentle guy. Made me laugh a lot."

She choked on her emotion and fell silent, looking out of the window at the moonlit sky. I gently patted her left hand. She looked at me, her green eyes liquid in the dim light. As a single tear trickled down her left cheek, she wiped at it impatiently, placed her head on my chest and began to sob quietly. I put my arms around her. Anyone would have done the same. The world seemed to compress until all that was left was her fragrant hair, her quiet tears, and a pounding in my heart that rose and fell to the rhythm of her pain.

After what seemed an eternity, she disentangled herself and sat up straight, taking a Kleenex out of her purse, wiping her eyes.

"I'm a wreck." She balled up the damp tissue and looked at me curiously. "How come your heart was pounding so hard?"

"It was?"

She smiled at me knowingly, and ran her pink tongue across her bottom lip. I was already horny, and this turned the spark of desire into a flame. She leaned in, her mouth almost caressing mine. I started to sweat as my heart pounded on the inside of my rib cage, begging for release. Her eyes closed, her mouth opened and our lips touched. Soft, warm and wet. Her tongue slid into my mouth and suddenly I realized what I was doing and quickly pulled back. She opened her eyes, more bemused than angry and frowned her question.

"I've a family."

"I wanna fuck you, not marry you."

I wiped a shaking hand across my mouth and leaned back out of harm's way. "Oh, you don't make this easy."

"I couldn't make it any easier."

"I appreciate it, I really do, I mean, jeez, but I love my wife."

"That's very gallant, Nick. Actually, it's refreshing."

Regret was gnawing the inside of my thigh, and gallantry started to feel like a fool's errand. The flight attendant wheeled her trolley next to us.

"Can I get you something to drink?"

"I'll have a double bourbon, up, and Jade?"

"Same, please. Water back."

"Sure."

She handed each of us 2 miniatures of Woodford Reserve with plastic cups, and another for Jade's water.

"Thanks. How much?"

"$32 even, please."

I handed her $40. "Keep the change."

"Wow, thanks. Here," she smiled and handed me another small bottle of water.

"Appreciate it."

She moved off and we poured our bourbon into the plastic cups. I slugged half of it, and was grateful for the instant warmth as it spread through me, calming me down.

Jade sipped hers and asked, "Feeling better?"

"Yeah."

"Is she pretty?"

"Who?"

"Your wife."

"Very, and she's got personality. Lots of it."

"Show me a picture. I want to see her."

"Don't have one with me." I lied. It would have felt like an act of betrayal.

"No picture? For shame."

"Yeah, I guess."

We arrived at SFO shortly after 2:00 a.m. I had to go through extra screening to retrieve my gun, and it was 3:00 by the time we pulled out of the Avis parking lot, in a rented Chevy Impala. We were both exhausted and as soon as we hit the freeway, Jade slumped over against the passenger door and slept.

40 minutes later, I checked us into a two-story Best Western on Van Ness. I half-carried her up the stairs to her second floor room, steered her toward the bed, and went back down for our luggage. When I came back up, she was asleep on top of the covers, her skirt hiked part way up her thighs. I forced myself to look away, loaded and holstered my gun, and went down to the lobby. It was empty except for the deskman; in another hour they would be bringing out the coffee. I found a chair near the fireplace, leaned back and closed my eyes.

One by one, the players from the past few days appeared. Reggie Mount constructed a corral out of the bleached white bones of small animals, and Arnold looked at me with smug complacency. Ron's head lay on Towne Street, his eyes staring mute reproach, and Richie, his eyes big from chemicals, mumbled something. Finally, I drifted into oblivion. I was roused a few hours later by the voices of guests pouring their complimentary coffee, and making their selections from the tired array of English muffins, plastic-wrapped Danishes and bright-hued herbal teas. I looked at my phone, 7:00 a.m.

Pulling myself to my feet, I staggered outside. The Van Ness traffic was in full force, three lanes churning in both directions. I smiled. It was good to be back in the City. This was where I had seduced Cassady, in her Noe Valley Victorian flat, the day my life changed forever. This was also where Brad and I had a thousand conversations over beer, at his apartment and mine, talking about crime, women, guns, books and our aspirations. Where he had met Keri, and where I had first met Bobby in sociology class.

Like any city, for all its beauty and warm, fuzzy memories, it also has its cold, dark side. Dominique Dominguez Lamont had either sucked the end of the gun barrel, or someone had shoved it in her mouth for her. This could be a rough day for Jade, but every day had been that way lately. I glanced at the Chronicle headlines: WILDFIRES RAVAGE SOCAL. It made me feel right at home. I went back inside, grabbed two coffees, two Danishes and went upstairs. I knocked and announced myself. Jade didn't answer, so I let myself in. She was in the shower, the door ajar.

"I'm back."

"Thank God." She turned off the spray. "Could you hand me my bathrobe? It's right on top of my suitcase."

It was white pique with blue piping and felt expensive; I hung it on the inside of the bathroom door.

"Thanks."

I turned on the news and drank my coffee. Ten minutes later, she came out, her robe belted loosely around her waist, exposing the top of her café con leche breasts. I imagined that her nipples were more brown than pink, swallowed hard and pointed to her coffee on the table.

"That's yours."

"I need it."

She sipped and paced, stopped and stared at me. "Nice of you to tell me you were going out. I was scared, you know."

"Sorry. I needed to think and fell asleep in the lobby."

Jade nodded and frowned, deep in thought. She crossed to the door and retraced her steps. "Halladay knows I depend on him. I can't believe he's so involved in this mess."

"How well do you know him?"

"I was there in the office with him and Daddy when they set up the trust. He told me that Halladay was like my honorary uncle, and that I could always count on him."

"What did Halladay say?"

"He was flattered."

"But--"

"--But it didn't stop him from devouring me with his eyes. It was creepy."

"But 'til now, he's done right by you. Yeah?"

She nodded. "He thanked Cicero for placing so much faith in him, and told me he would always do his best for me."

"Money's killed a lotta friendships."

"What about loyalty? Cicero made him a very rich man."

'Cold world,' I thought, but said nothing.

"Or maybe he has ulterior motives. After all, he's the one who phoned me in Austria."

"That'd be my guess."

"And the money's his motive."

"How much control over the trust does he have?"

"Power of attorney, but only if both of us are deceased or incapable of managing our own estates."

I locked eyes with her and she nodded her understanding.

"Jesus."

I bit the inside of my cheek, breathed out through my nose and replied, "Doesn't mean he killed him."

"No, but one day Daddy told me that Halladay was jealous of him, because he was richer than he was. That's the only time he ever said anything negative about him."

"It provides motive, but that's all."

"A few years ago, Cicero started talking to me about money, and how to manage it. He had tried to teach Richard, but he showed no interest and, I guess out of frustration, he turned to me."

"Was Halladay privy to this?"

"Yes."

"Did Cicero tell you how he made all his money?"

"He was very proud that he'd made millions in the refrigeration business. Proved he was a sharp guy, and not just another drug dealer."

I finished my coffee.

Her eyes flashed hard. "How much is he paying you?"

"Six figures. On the nose."

"What?"

I shrugged. "Like I said, he made it very clear that I was to keep him out of this."

Jade collapsed on the edge of the bed. She leaned forward, placed her elbows on her knees and her palms to her temples, and rocked back and forth. Then she sat up straight.

"Would we be better off if the police were more involved?"

"Ordinarily, I'd say yes. The problem is your brother, and Arnold strikes me as one of those controlling psychotics who likes to interact, but only on his terms. If he finds out the cops are involved, he'll get skittish and who knows what he could do to Richard. No, we're better off without them."

"You're right. I don't want to do anything that puts Richard in more danger."

"If Halladay is involved, that makes it all the tougher." I spoke softly but my words were still audible. "When I met him, he struck me as a callous bastard, and what I've heard about Arnold is that he marches to a particularly cruel drummer."

Thinking out loud can get you in trouble. I immediately regretted my last statement, but it was too late. Her shoulders slumped forward and emotion closed her throat.

"I just don't understand what Richard sees in him."

"Jade, without him, Arnold has no game. He's not gonna hurt him."

"If he does, I'll give you a million dollars to kill him."

I sighed and looked at her steadily. "You say that to the wrong person, and you're gonna be doing a 20 year bid for conspiracy."

"Then lucky I said it to the right one."

"No you didn't and please, I don't wanna hear it again."

It was a crisp, Indian summer morning. We headed south on Van Ness through the Tenderloin. A short while later, we crossed Market and headed into SOMA, where signs of gentrification were everywhere, not unlike the L.A. warehouse district, east of Alameda. But there were still plenty of pockets of decay. Every big city seems broken if you look in the wrong places.

Brad called. "Hey, Boss. How's San Fran?"

"Still here."

"No news, I'm afraid. We closed the bars, but they never showed."

"Where are you now?"

"At your house. You want us back in the clubs tonight?"

"Let's wait and see what happens with Bobby."

"Okay," said Brad and hung up.

Our first stop was the Hall of Justice on Bryant Street. This is the new cop shop; the striking old Hall of Justice on Kearny Street, near Chinatown, was torn down in 1968. The new building is boxy, made of glass and steel, a soulless edifice promising little other than efficiency. We parked and headed for the Office of the Medical Examiner.

The dignitary behind the counter was a plain-looking woman with wide hips, tight red curls and a mouth that looked like she'd sucked a lot of lemons. She gave us the once over, barely able to hide her disapproval.

"Yes?"

"We'd like to see the AR on a decedent, Dominique Lamont."

"You are?"

I flipped my PR license. "Nick Crane."

"You have no authority here."

"She does."

Jade stepped forward and showed lemon mouth her driver's license. Her mouth puckered. She snorted and trundled off to do our bidding. I grinned at Jade and a moment later, the woman returned, handing it over. The Office was kind enough to supply tables in an adjoining viewing room; Jade and I sat side-by-side and read the Autopsy Report.

Witnesses:

SFPD-Northern Police District Detectives Franco and Moskowitz were present at the autopsy.

Opinion:

The cause of death is a single shot from a Heckler & Koch HK4 semi-automatic pistol to the right temple. The gun in question was legally registered to decedent. The bullet passed entirely through the skull of the decedent exiting from the left side of the skull just above the hairline. The bullet traveled at an approximate 20% upward trajectory. Toxicology tests revealed no illicit substances. The decedent had taken a therapeutic dose of alprazolam approximately two hours before her death as well as a standard dose of aspirin. Trace amounts of Wellbutrin (bupropion) were also found in her system. The amount of alprazolam appears insufficient to have altered decedent's ability to think or reason at the time of the fatal incident.

The mode of death would appear to be suicide. Decedent's medical records show that she had been depressed for several months at the time of the incident and had been in therapy with June Iverson, Ph.D. Although Dr. Iverson, when contacted, chose not to release decedent's confidential information, she did state that decedent had suffered from moderate to severe depression and had been prescribed Wellbutrin in addition to alprazolam by her M.D. Dr. Iverson did state that decedent had discontinued her therapeutic dose of Wellbutrin because it gave her "splitting headaches."

Powder burns were evident at the star-like aperture where the bullet entered decedent's skull. In addition, there was gunpowder residue on decedent's right hand. These facts are consistent with suicide. In addition, only one shot was fired which is also typical of suicides. The bullet followed the upward trajectory consistent with suicide and was fired at point-blank range as evidenced by the star-like wound formation and the gunpowder residue. Had this been homicide, the shot would most likely have been fired from a distance of at least 12 inches resulting in minimal star-like formation and little if any gunpowder residue. Furthermore, had this been homicide, there would be no powder residue on decedent's right hand.

The theory of suicide is further supported by the fact that decedent had old knife cuts across her wrists suggesting an earlier suicide attempt at some point, perhaps two or three months before her death, as well as minor knife wounds in her chest area, suggesting aborted suicide attempts and apparent suicidal ideation.

Inasmuch as there is no evidence of any sort consistent with homicide, the inescapable conclusion is that decedent's death was self-inflicted and was caused by the single pistol shot.

Lisa Gavin, M.D.

Deputy Medical Examiner

We then read the Investigator's Narrative, which, while exhaustive, revealed no information inconsistent with the theory of suicide. Dominique's roommate, Alexandra Snow, had discovered the body upon returning home from lunch with a client at 2:30 in the afternoon, on August 28, 2007. She confirmed that Dominique had been quite depressed, and stated that she'd been worried about her. She also stated that Dominique had broken up with her boyfriend, Anthony Romano, a few weeks before her death.

There was no evidence that anyone suspicious had entered the Pacific Heights duplex between 11:00 a.m., when Alexandra had left for her lunch date, and 2:30 p.m., when she returned. Both the house phone and Dominique's cell had been checked. The only incoming calls to the house were business calls for Alexandra. Dominique had received no calls during this period, although she had called 310/555-2257 repeatedly, once at 11:30, once at 11:54, and three more times between 1:00 and 2:15. 310/555-2257 had not answered and Dominique had left no messages.

"My God, that's Richard's old number."

I looked at her. "She was trying to reach him."

"Shit. Why didn't he pick up? It might've--"

"--You don't know that, so knock it off."

She nodded and bit her lower lip. "Dominique was left-handed, yet according to this, she did it with her right hand. Why?"

"Maybe she was holding her phone in her left hand. There's no evidence that this was murder, so the real question is, why was your mother depressed enough to take her life?"

Jade stood up and moved woodenly toward the door. I quickly gathered the documents, gave them to the red-haired clerk, and followed Jade outside.

We got in the Chevy, and as if by reflex, I headed toward Pacific Heights. Jade sat with furrowed brow, deep in thought. She opened her purse and thumbed through a small address book.

I glanced at the ink filled pages. "Didn't know they still made 'em."

She closed it and put it back into her purse. "I screwed up. I was so upset over Cicero's death that I didn't consider the effect it had on Mother."

"How was she at the funeral?"

"Stricken. She came alone and left immediately afterward to catch her flight. Richard was crying and he never cries. It was weird, too, because we were the only family members. Nearly everybody else were Cicero's guys. I remember thinking that his people were dressed way too sharp for a funeral."

"Sound like nice guys."

"If you like thugs, but that was his world."

"Did you speak to her after that?"

"Uh-huh, a couple of times over the next week. She seemed okay, but was good at hiding her feelings. I guess it was all part of being in a loveless marriage for so long, and being a mom at too young an age."

"She was from the Islands?"

"Yeah and sometimes I think she left her soul there and never went back to reclaim it. Her mother was a housekeeper and her father a janitor at one of the hotels. Mother, Richard and I flew to the islands when I was 11 and I met them, only once, though." She fell silent and looked wistfully out of the window. Close to tears, talking was obviously cathartic for her. "My grandfather called me his little California *florita*, and would give me rides on his shoulders. I missed him when we left."

"Did you ever write?"

"No. You know how thoughtless children are. I don't believe he could read or write anyway."

"What was your grandmother like?"

"Emilia, she was broken, having been endlessly abused at the big house where she worked. They were rich people from Baltimore and by all accounts, had wild parties. God only knows what went on. Anyway, when I met her, she was mostly silent. I look like her though, more so than Mother did.

"She's still alive?"

"They both are, and don't know Mother's dead."

Pacific Heights is probably the most affluent neighborhood in San Francisco. It was originally mostly small Victorians, but was largely rebuilt after the great earthquake. Today it is a mix of Edwardian and Chateau-style homes, interspersed with lovely blocks of Queen Anne Victorians.

"Trust Mother," said Jade, "to find the trendiest neighborhood in the trendiest city in the western hemisphere." She studied her address book. "She lived on the top floor of an Edwardian mansion, on Jackson Street, sharing the flat with Alexandra Snow."

"How did they meet?"

"I don't know. Maybe it was through her boyfriend, Anthony Romano, who I believe runs delicatessens. I've got his number."

"Good, 'cause we're gonna talk to everybody."

"What about the cops?"

"They won't tell us anything that's not in the coroner's report."

Alexander Snow's phone number turned out to be her answering service. She was apparently some kind of personal adviser. I didn't leave a message.

Jade was despondent. "Guess we'll try her later."

"Not answering and not being in are two different things."

Parking on Jackson Street was non-existent, so we resorted to a small, overpriced lot on Fillmore. Ms. Snow's Edwardian was on the northeast corner of Jackson and Divisadero. We studied the nameplates. Snow's was silver calligraphy on ebony backing: *Alexandra Snow, Advisor.* We rang the doorbell and waited, but there was no answer, so I rang long and hard. Finally, a reluctant, irritated voice said, "I'm not expecting visitors. Please call if you want to make an appointment."

"I'm Dominique Lamont's daughter."

"Come again?"

"Jade Lamont, Dominique Lamont's daughter."

A moment trudged by and finally the buzzer sounded. "Fourth floor."

Despite the elevator sounding like it could use a good oiling, we were deposited, without incident, directly into Ms. Snow's foyer. A thin-faced, timid looking maid, wearing a long apron, peered at us.

"Hello," she said, in heavily accented English. "Come with me, *por favor*." She led us into a drawing room, which looked out over Jackson Street, and was flooded with natural light. It was NorCal hip, tastefully New Age. Copies of Psychic Reporter and Psychology Today filled a magazine rack next to the door. A graceful tiffany table lamp topped a cherry wood table standing next to an antique settee, and a leaded glass mirror hung on the wall opposite the window. Apparently, the New Age approach was good for business.

A few minutes later, Alexandra Snow swept into the room wearing a Romanian peasant blouse, her long, thick hair spread about her shoulders like a fan.

"Hello," she smarmed, looking at us curiously. "You are Ms. Lamont, no doubt. Your friend?"

"Nick--"

"--Crane," I smarmed back.

"Dreadful business."

"We're trying to come to grips with Dominique's death," I said helpfully. "We've been to the coroner's office and are convinced it was suicide. We're hoping to understand why."

"Ah yes, of course," said Ms. Snow. "It's very upsetting when a loved one turns their hand against themselves." She gave us both a keen look, with eyes that were rather small, bright blue and wide-set. "If I might ask, Mr. Crane, where do you live and what do you do?"

"Private investigator from Los Angeles."

"I see."

"You're a psychic advisor?"

"I help people make decisions and find their correct path."

"Then you may have a unique insight into Dominique's state of mind."

Ms. Snow hesitated, weighing her response. "Although I did spend a lot of time with her, she was hard to get close to."

This struck a chord with Jade and she nodded in agreement. "You're right about that."

"I've spent a lot of time thinking about that dreadful day I found your mother," turning to Jade, "dead in her bedroom."

The words slammed into Jade; she sat there, fighting back tears. I wanted to reach over and choke the New Age bitch for her callous remark. Ms. Snow sensed my anger and slapped on a peacenik smile.

"Are you alright, my dear?" she inquired gently.

Jade nodded and choked down her emotion.

"It must have been a horrible shock," I said.

"It was. Fortunately, I don't scare easily, although for a time I considered moving, but decided it was unnecessary. I'm not aware of your mother's spirit having remained at this address, or even in San Francisco, for that matter. She wasn't here long enough to grow that type of attachment."

I was struggling to remain calm and was tiring of her pretentious mumbo jumbo. "What type of attachment is that, exactly?"

"Spirits or ghosts, if you prefer, develop an attachment to their physical surroundings. That's how hauntings occur."

She was irritating the piss out of me, though for all I knew she was right about the ghosts. "So you don't think she's here?"

"I'm almost certain she's not. What I do know is that Dominique was a divided soul. We met in a grocery store on Webster, when she was new to the City and staying at the Drisco Hotel on Pacific. Her boyfriend lived in Seacliff, I believe, and she wanted her own place."

Jade asked quietly, "Was he nice to her?"

"I couldn't say, but the first thing I noticed about her were your emerald eyes." This made Jade smile and Ms. Snow reciprocated, this time with sincerity. "Your mother was genuine, a rare commodity in this neighborhood. On a whim I told her that I had a spare room, actually an entire spare wing, and that she was welcome to take a look if she wanted to. She didn't squabble about the rent. I appreciated that. I don't like to argue about money."

"One thing about Mother is that she spent freely."

"You alluded to not being close to her. Was Richard?"

"He was, yes."

"She was matter-of-fact when she talked about you, but for him she had overwhelming love and sadness, as if she'd betrayed him somehow."

"I feel that way too."

"You can only be responsible for yourself, my dear."

Jade couldn't hold back. Her tears fell, big and wet. Ms. Snow handed her a box of tissues. She blew her nose, wiped her eyes and took a deep breath.

"We all felt abandoned but it was never clear who was abandoning whom."

"Yes. I'm sure that was very hard."

"Any thoughts on the boyfriend you never met?"

Ms. Snow locked her gaze on me. The faintest of smiles creased the corners of her mouth. "Although you might not put any substance in what I do, Mr. Crane, I could tell you a lot about yourself."

"Yeah?"

"You have a fascination with evil, although you're not particularly evil yourself, but you're not entirely good either. You're comfortable in the fallen world you inhabit and if you weren't a private investigator, you might be a policeman, which would be inconvenient because you don't like the police. You prefer outlaws as long as they follow the code."

"Which is?"

"I don't know, but it's something you intuit, isn't it?"

"I'm impressed. You nailed me."

"We're both investigators, in our own way and like you, I'm intuitive. You have kind eyes, which is why people are drawn to you. You suffered a fair amount during your childhood, so you try to help people, yet curiously, you're addicted to pain and that's what keeps you connected to your work. At some level, you're aware of all this but you don't really like to go too deep which, ultimately, could be your undoing."

"Thank you, Doctor. How much do I owe you?"

Ms. Snow laughed. "It's what you owe yourself, my dear. I am merely the facilitator."

I let out a long deliberate sigh. "Let's get back on topic."

Alexandra turned to Jade. "Your mother felt abandoned by your brother. She used to phone him constantly, and would be very sad when she couldn't reach him."

"That afternoon, she called him five times."

"Codependency is a deadly addiction."

"Ms. Snow," I said, "what was the problem in their relationship?"

She shrugged, took a moment and replied. "She was racked with guilt over something, only I don't know what."

Jade listened intently, her long fingers fussing with the buttons on her blouse. "A couple of months before Richard got arrested for the home invasion, his attitude toward mother completely changed. He'd always been the one to defend her when I'd complain, and, of course, I'd been the one to defend Cicero when Richard claimed he was a lousy father. Then suddenly, he started calling Dominique a bitch, giving her the cold shoulder when she'd try and talk to him."

"How was he after his release?" asked Ms. Snow.

"He never talked about being locked up and at first, he seemed okay. He went to school, dated girls and hung out with his friends, but that faded and he slowly became withdrawn."

"Where is he now?"

"He's with his unsavory new boyfriend."

Ms. Snow mulled this over and replied. "One last thing, and then we have to bring this to a close."

"Okay," I said.

"Are you aware that she met with your brother after the funeral?"

Jade, stunned, shook her head. "I thought she flew straight back."

"Yes, but only after the meeting. When she got back here, she was devastated. All I could gather was that it hadn't gone well. After that, she mostly stayed in her room and a week later, she shot herself."

Jade, trembling, asked, "And you've no idea what happened between her and Richard?"

Ms. Snow shook her head. "Did you know she was seeing a therapist?"

I nodded. "Yeah, it was in the coroner's report, a woman named June Iverson."

"She's a sharp lady. I'll call her and tell her you're on your way over."

"Thank you," said Jade and hugged the older woman whose robin's-egg blue eyes were suddenly teary.

I didn't buy it and I knew why. The key piece was still missing. We still didn't know what drove the stake between Richard and Dominique. On our way down in the elevator, Jade was silent. I put my arm around her and gently kissed the top of her head.

CHAPTER III
Caught Red Handed

WHILE WE WERE TALKING TO Ms. Snow, I'd turned my phone off. Now, standing in the sunshine, I listened to my messages. Bobby said he was all set for the afternoon, and Brad said that he was bored and needed some action. Audrey had a good lead on one of her adultery cases, and Tony wanted me to call him immediately.

"Where are you?"

"Pacific Heights. Why?"

"I've been asking around. Karsagian isn't overly suspicious of you."

"Cuz he's a freakin' prince."

"He did say his boys fucked with you."

"They shoved me around a little, but apart from Sergeant Jansen having a hard-on for me, that was it."

"Don't mind him, he hates the world."

"And?"

"The shit's running real deep on this one, so let's get together when you get back."

"You've heard something?"

"I hear a lotta things, Nick. Just watch your ass."

"Always do."

He hung up and I called Cassady.

"Hi, Baby," she said. "Everything okay?"

"Yeah. How's Maleah?"

"They're cool with her staying for a few weeks 'til this blows over."

"Okay, good."

"It is going to, right?"

"It always does, eventually."

She hesitated and I could sense her fear. "Relax. It's gonna be fine."

"She's with you, isn't she?"

"Yeah."

"Just remember, I'm the one that loves you."

"I know, Honey."

She hung up and a sudden swirl of emotion rippled through me. Even though I held it in, Jade sensed it as we headed for the car.

"That was your wife, wasn't it?"

"Yeah."

"You really love her, don't you?" Her eyes seared into me.

"Of course I love her."

"Does she know I'm with you?"

"She knows."

"Is she threatened?"

"She has confidence."

"I'll say."

Jade shook her head and we got in the car. Despite my attraction, her arrogance was beginning to gnaw at me.

June Iverson's office was about ten blocks away on Fillmore, near Green Street. We were starving and stopped at a frankfurter place near Union, and ordered Polish dogs and coffee. The food was delicious and we sat outside and watched the world go by. It was mid-afternoon and already there was a chill in the air. At ten to three we arrived at June Iverson's office and entered the waiting room that she shared with two other psychologists. Three patients looked up as we entered, but really didn't want to acknowledge us, much less each other, or, presumably, themselves.

Three o'clock signaled the changing of the guard; patients emerged from three directions in various states of distress followed by their doctors, two of whom were women.

"Excuse me," I said, "we're looking for June Iverson."

"Then you're looking for me," said a middle-aged woman with hard facial angles and a shock of bone white hair. "I assume you're the people Ms. Snow called about?"

Before I could answer, she turned quickly to a freckled woman, who seemed agitated. "I'll be right with you, Heidi."

Heidi looked worried.

"This is certainly inconvenient," said Dr. Iverson. "I have to see my patient now, and I have another at four. After that I go to the gym."

"It's very important, which is why we flew up from Los Angeles."

Irritated, she reached up and pushed her white hair off her forehead. "All right, I'll give you exactly fifteen minutes, so please be back here at the stroke of five."

"Thank you."

Her patient looked relieved and followed Dr. Iverson back to her office.

"Intense woman," said Jade as we walked downstairs.

"Indeed."

Next we contacted Dominique's former boyfriend Anthony Romano. Jade, using my cellphone, left a message. Within seconds, he called back.

"Jade?"

"Yes."

"Your mom spoke about you a lot. Such a damn tragedy."

"Can we meet?"

"Where are you?"

"Near Union."

"You're in my neighborhood. There's a really good frankfurter place. I'll meet you there in about half an hour."

"Thanks."

Back at the frankfurter joint, we sipped coffee and waited.

Anthony Romano appeared to be in his late 50's. He was one of those jumpsuit guys, swarthy with wavy gray hair, and a thick unibrow. His eyes lit up at the sight of Jade, but dimmed when he realized she was not alone. He recovered quickly, though, and I bought him an Espresso.

"Your mother, she was a good woman," he said sipping from his cup. "We were in love. I offered her my house, my heart, everything." He choked up and stared down into his coffee.

Jade felt for this guy, and reached out, gently touching his hand. He looked up at her, smiled through his embarrassment and continued.

"I couldn't believe it when she broke up with me. I thought I had finally met the woman with whom I could share my golden years. I still don't understand what went wrong. Maybe it was her roommate, Alexandra Snow," he said bitterly.

"Why do you think that?" I asked.

"When Dominique first moved here, we spent three glorious weeks together at my house. We swam, went to the opera and even did the City cable car bit, like we were youngsters. Then all of a sudden she decided she needed to have her own place. I know that too much too soon can kill a relationship, so I was reasonable and said I would help her find a place, but she moved into a hotel and, within a week, met Ms. Snow. Through all this we were fine and then, sorry, but then your father happens. It was incomprehensible and a terrible shock to Dominique. From that moment everything went sideways. Although I don't know for certain, I believe that this Snow woman told her she needed time by herself."

Jade smiled warmly. "Did you continue to talk, at least?"

"I tried but it was no good."

"Did she ever talk about my brother?"

"Sometimes, but mostly she would gaze at a photo of him that she had." Mr. Romano took a final sip from his cup, set it down and his eyes drifted to a distant memory. "I still love her." His voice quavered and as he stood up, there were tears in his eyes. "If you need anything else, you have my number." He wiped his eyes with his sleeve.

"Thanks."

Sadness had taken its toll on this man. He nodded and headed south along the sidewalk.

When we got back to June Iverson's building, the waiting room was deserted. I closed my eyes and rested. Five o'clock rolled around and two patients exited. Five minutes later, June Iverson appeared and ushered us back to her office. Jade and I sat side-by-side on her broad comfortable couch; she sat across from us in a straight-backed chair. The afternoon light streamed in through plantation shutters that faced onto Fillmore Street.

"So," she said, "first of all, I'm very uncomfortable with this entire situation."

"I realize there may be issues of confidentiality, but Jade here is Ms. Lamont's only daughter. The family estate is basically in her hands."

June Iverson looked long and hard at her. "Although the next of kin has certain rights, the right to disclosure of the deceased's therapeutic confidences, I believe, are not among them."

"Ms. Iverson, I'm a detective and fully understand client confidentiality. We wouldn't be asking unless it was absolutely necessary. Richard, her son--"

Jade cut me off. "--My brother is in grave danger and we believe that you may have knowledge that can help us save him."

Ms. Iverson frowned. "From what?"

"From a really bad guy that he's involved with."

"You're referring to Arnold Clipper."

"Yes."

"Your mom told me about him. She'd met him on her last trip to Los Angeles."

I was getting tired of her coy act. "So you understand the urgency?"

No doubt my tone of voice betrayed my growing impatience. She looked at me as her ego had a brief and losing argument with fear and the desire to be done with it. Her nimble digits fiddled with each other and she cleared her throat. "One day when Richard was fifteen, he came home from school unexpectedly and heard sounds of passion coming from your mother's bedroom. He went in and saw her having sex with a man that he recognized." She looked at us both. I didn't dare look at Jade. "He was," she said deliberately, "your father's attorney, James Halladay."

Jade sat there, the blood draining out of her face. Rage replaced hurt and her lips pulled back into a nasty sneer, not unlike a rabid dog. If I had scared Ms. Iverson, Jade terrified her as she stood up quickly and fighting to control herself, hissed, "I have to go. Now."

Jade left without looking at her. I followed her out.

It was cold and the October evening had the feel of winter. Jade was pale as we got into the car. I was about to turn the key when her fingers gripped my forearm.

"Five! Five million!"

I locked eyes with her, but didn't respond.

"If you won't kill him, I will." Her heart-shaped face was hard, her sculpted lips, bloodless.

"You can't kill him for sleeping with your mother."

"You're wrong. That piece of shit is responsible for her suicide, for Richard being so fucked up and, I'd bet every last penny I have, for killing my father." Her eyes were daggers of scorn, and I felt myself flinch. "I never took you for a coward."

I let that go and waited for her to finish.

"The islanders have a saying: A veces se dice vice que se debe matar al hombre. Sometimes a man needs killing. Halladay's that man, and I'm going to do it." Saying anything was pointless. We drove in silence toward the airport, through heavy rush hour traffic. We'd passed Candlestick Park before she spoke again. "Cicero would have done anything for that man."

"I understand how you feel and yeah, some people do need killing. But if we can prove Halladay murdered your father, the state'll do it for you. He won't fare well on Death Row."

She stared out of the window, and hatred pushed the breath out of her. "We have to find Richard. He's all I have left."

My phone rang. It was Brad and he was shouting.

"Nick, I need a fucking gun. Two hard looking dudes rolled up in a flower van, and they're walking this way."

"That's got to be Fishburne and Koncak."

"Gun!"

"Bedroom closet. Cassady's Beretta."

I could hear him pound up the stairs, find the box and grab the gun. "Those fuckers come in here and--"

"--Leave out the back and go next door to our friends, the Montez family. They'll hide you."

"Fuck that. I ain't going anywhere."

Our bedroom window faces the street and I could envision him folding himself against the wall, aiming through the curtains. "Brad, get out!"

"They're ringing the doorbell," he whispered hoarsely.

There was a long silence. I had to brake behind a Chrysler 300 that stopped suddenly. Someone else honked. "Brad! Are you all right?"

"They're leaving."

"Can you get their license?"

"No but the van's sky blue, with a sea of flowers."

The relief in Brad's voice was audible. My knuckles were white on the steering wheel. Jade's green eyes were huge, her face taut with worry.

"Are they gone?"

"Yeah, just like my nerves."

"Okay, wait a minute, then see if they left anything. Be careful."

Another long silence while Brad walked downstairs. "Shit," he said, "It's an envelope addressed to you. Should I open it?"

"No, you better wait, just in case."

"Hell, I'll take my chances. Those guys didn't look smart enough to have anthrax on hand or anything real exotic."

There was silence. Then Brad's voice came back on. "Oh, man. You won't believe this. It's a drawing of a dismembered nude body. Got a round hole right through the middle, with a pile of what looks like intestines, stacked up next to it. Jack the Ripper stuff. Separate head. No eyes. Just sockets with a caption underneath: 'I'm looking through you.'"

It seemed to take forever, but we finally got a flight out of S.F.O and landed in L.A. around midnight. Jade was exhausted and slept with her head on my shoulder, her breathing soft and slow. I put my arm around her, and thought about how physical beauty and fortune had brought her and her brother nothing but pain and misery.

We got to Bobby's around 1:00 a.m. I phoned and waited.

"Nick?"

"We're here."

"I'll kill the juice."

We went through the gate and the goats, like phantoms on the hill, paid us only the slightest attention as we headed to the front door. Once inside, Jade staggered off to the guest room. Brad was sleeping, his elongated frame stretched out across the sofa.

"He's kind'a freaked out," said Bobby. "He insisted on falling asleep with the piece across his chest."

"Where is it?"

"On top of the fridge."

"Did he show you the picture?"

He went into the kitchen and came out carrying the envelope and two cans of Bud Lite. Bobby's room is like a teenager's fantasy palace. Beautiful women occupy his wall space along with posters of sports heroes. An ancient poster of Dr. J palming a basketball occupies the place of honor above his bed. We sat down and drank our beers as I looked at the picture. I've never tried to draw internal body parts, but this guy had nailed it. It looked like an anatomical drawing from a medical textbook. The eyeless head was an almost precise likeness of Ron Cera.

"'I'm looking through you,'" I read out loud.

"What the hell does that mean?"

"I dunno. Clipper knows I'm looking for Richie. Maybe he's trying to tell me that he's one step ahead."

"I can't wait to meet this asshole," growled Bobby, his jaw flexing angrily.

"What happened at McDonald's?"

"The very nervous doctor was sitting in back when I arrived. I ordered coffee and sat down a few tables away and about ten after five, the messenger arrived. It obviously wasn't Fishburne or Koncak; I guess they were busy terrorizing Brad. This guy was about five-three, chubby, middle-eastern. They made the exchange and the dude booked outta there. I followed him."

"What about the doc?"

"I dunno. He just sat there looking worried. I guess."

"And the other guy?"

"He was walking toward Alvarado and when he realized I was following him, he picked up his pace."

"And then?"

"When he knew I wasn't going anywhere, he stopped and waited for me." Our beers were now dead soldiers. "I need another one."

Asking him to wait and finish the story was pointless, so I nodded and he disappeared, returning a moment later with two new brews. He sat and continued, "I told him I was a PI and needed to ask him some questions."

"Was he scared?"

"Yeah, but the forty dollars relaxed him. He told me his name's Mamdouh and that he'd been hired to drop off the money by a tall, red-headed man named Ernie. He'd shown up yesterday and paid him $200 to deliver the envelope."

"Did he say what was in it?"

"No, it was sealed, but he said it felt like a grip'a money."

"You think he was telling the truth?"

Bobby nodded. "I took $500 out of my wallet and said it was his if he could lead me to Ernie. He stared longingly at it but shook his head. I doubled it and still he didn't bite."

"Money, still the best lubricant in the world."

"I gave him another $100 and split."

It was about 2:00 a.m., our beers were finished and I was beat. "I'm gonna hit the sack."

"What are we gonna do with Brad?"

"I dunno, but we've got a war on our hands."

"Have him stay here and keep an eye on Jade."

"Yes, I guess so." I stretched and headed for the door. "Good night."

"If this goes sideways, I'm gonna kill every one of those motherfuckas."

It was late, we were buzzed and the gathering danger was pressing in on us.

CHAPTER IV
Body Bags

A SLEEPING BAG ON A kitchen floor's not the most accommodating of beds. I woke up a few times, jarred awake by the noise of the refrigerator, but managed to get back to sleep. In the morning my friends' voices eased me back into consciousness.

"Sleeping beauty needs to get his ass up," teased Bobby.

"The boss is on strike."

"He does his best thinking on his back," offered Jade, winking at me.

Bobby and Brad looked at her, then at me, then at each other. She laughed, sounding refreshed compared to yesterday and wiggled away. I crawled out of the sleeping bag and staggered to the living room couch, but couldn't get back to sleep, and after a while someone brought me coffee. I took a sip and tried to shake out the cobwebs.

"Cassady called, bro," said Bobby, handing me my cell.

"Thanks." I dialed her.

"Bobby said you were asleep."

"Long night. Are you flying back today?"

"In a couple of hours."

"When you get here, don't go to our house. Come straight here instead."

"Why?"

"'Cause we've got your gun here."

"That bad?"

"Worse. They came to our place yesterday afternoon. Scared Brad half to death."

"Any damage?"

"Nada."

"Okay, good."

"I don't want anyone following you here. When you get to Ontario airport, don't pick up your car, but get a rental instead. Something dark colored, nondescript."

"You realize I've gotta teach Monday."

"Sorry, Baby, that's on hold for a while."

She sighed. "Really?"

"Yeah."

"See you soon."

I took my coffee, went out and sat on the back porch. The air was still brown, but showed signs of clearing, and as the winds had died down, I figured the worst was over. I phoned Audrey.

"Hey, Boss, I'm trying to get my daughter to eat breakfast. Can you call back?"

"No. Be very careful. Arnold and his crew are on to us and out for blood. Don't go by the office 'til I give you the all clear. Understand?"

"What can I do?"

"Work from home and do what you can."

"Do they know where I live?"

"No way for me to know."

"Jesus."

Halladay beeped in, but I let it go to voicemail.

"If you guys wanna split for a hotel, I'll cover it. No worries."

"I'll talk to Tim."

"Just in case, if you do, don't give me the address."

"Understood."

She hung up and I checked my voicemail. Halladay's voice was crisp, cool, authoritative.

"Nick, call me immediately."

I finished my coffee and went inside for another. Everyone was eating eggs and toast. The blonde women on the Fox morning show were laughing.

"Get some eggs, boss," said Bobby.

I went back outside with the food and another cup of coffee. I ate methodically. The goats discovered I had food, and came nuzzling up. I threw them bits of egg and let one lick the plate. Sometimes a criminal's psychological make-up can lead you to the facts, rather than the other way around.

Arnold, a psychotic and sadistic killer, was certainly the artist who drew the picture of Ron's corpse. He's wouldn't be concerned about Richie and Jade's fortune. No. His motivation would be to feed his ego, control his victims, and have an audience to marvel at his exploits.

The fake Fishburne and Koncak were just garden variety scum, but dangerous. Their pleasure in meting out death was not the almost rarified joy Arnold would experience, not the product of some inexplicable aberration, but was simply mundane. Theirs was the banal pleasure of sub-humans with a basic inability to cope with life's everyday frustrations, striking out randomly. And now they were getting paid for it.

The problem was Halladay. Why was I so reluctant to tie him to the cover-up? He was the enigma. Jade had been quick to doubt him and she had known him for years. Was it merely coincidence that I had seen him in his running togs right in front of Arnold's old house?

I went back over my conversation with Halladay at his office. He'd worked hard to make himself seem worldly, yet jaded, but for what purpose? And why had he been so insistent on my loyalty? I took a sip of coffee and stirred what was left with my index finger.

Maybe he'd invested in Cicero's drug deals. It was certainly possible. Maybe they'd had a falling out and Cicero was now a liability. Maybe Halladay was broke. Maybe he'd been struggling for years to keep up the charade. Maybe he'd lost his fortune in the tech crash in 2000. A handful of maybes were all I had right now. Anything was possible.

To top it off, he'd slept with his best friend's wife. It's obviously not unknown for a client's wife to have a love affair with the attorney, but in her house in the middle of the afternoon? That was notably reckless, not the pattern of a prudent man. But the key point, the one I had rationalized away, was that Halladay was so insistent no one be made aware of the cover-up. Even if he was innocent, he was taking a huge risk. Concealing a capital crime is a very serious offense, and all the more if it turned out that you were involved in it. Which, viewed in a certain light, was a damned good reason to keep it on the down-low.

Halladay answered on the fourth ring. "Took your time."

"Busy."

I could hear him chewing his teeth as he fought for control. "How're things going?"

"Jade's doing as well as can be expected, and we're zeroing in on Richard."

"Is that right?"

"Have you ever run across Arnold Clipper?"

I waited in the burgeoning silence. He cleared his throat. "I don't think so, Nick, though the name sounds slightly familiar. Why?" His voice, smooth as a pickpocket lifting your wallet.

"Clipper's connected with the two clowns impersonating the cops. They murdered a young actor, either late Wednesday, or early Thursday morning, dumping the body near Skid Row."

"Yeah, it was on the news. Anyway, why would I know Clipper?"

"You both live on Beachwood."

"You investigating me, to know where I live?"

"Star Maps. Everybody knows where the celebrities live."

"Didn't know I was listed there."

I managed not to laugh as I thought about Halladay, his ego leading the way as he purchased a Star Map from one of the many street corner hustlers.

"Wait a minute. I have heard that name and, in fact, if memory serves, I met him at one of the neighborhood watch meetings."

"Is that right?"

"Yes, yes it is."

"This isn't good, Mr. Halladay. He knows what you look like."

"But why would he want to hurt me?"

"Connect the dots. Cicero's millions, Richie, Jade and you."

"Oh my."

"He tried to get Ron Cera to set up a meet with Jade. He wouldn't and now he's dead. We need to reconsider not going to the cops."

"Good Lord."

"They even delivered a hand drawn image of the decedent to my house, the bastards."

"They've contacted you?" Halladay sounded genuinely surprised.

"Yeah, it's a good thing my wife and daughter weren't there."

I could hear Halladay breathing hard as he considered this new information. The long silence only served to agitate my growing unease.

"We maybe should go to the police, but before we do, I want to meet and explain my reasons for the secrecy."

"Okay. Your office?"

"No, too public. Where do you live?"

"Whittier."

"Text me your address and I'll see you in an hour. Does that work?"

"Sure."

"It'll be nice to meet your wife and daughter."

"They left for Mallorca, Friday afternoon."

"I love Mallorca. It's my second favorite place after Ibiza. Shouldn't your daughter be in school, though?"

"We home school her. My wife insists on exercising considerable control over her education."

"Very smart. Anyway, I better get moving. Later, Nick."

"See you in a bit."

As I called Tony I was laughing. Home school Maleah? Fat chance. Tony didn't answer. Bobby and I left in the Yukon. I was carrying my Colt and my Walther. Bobby had his nine, but also brought his fully auto M14, made all the nastier by the black silencer. I pulled up on my driveway, let him into the house and parked on the next street over, hotfooting it back to the house. Bobby was down in the den, attaching the bayonet to the M14. The intimidation factor was off the charts. Bobby handled it with practiced ease.

He grinned at me. "Haven't touched this baby in a while." He was chewing the inside of his mouth, a holdover from his drug days. The TV was on mute, and he looked completely at home and completely relaxed.

"I assume he'll be alone, but just in case, be ready."

"I'm ready. Feel like shit, I always do when I drink, but I'm ready." He leaned his rifle up against an end table and stretched out on the bed. I had the feeling he'd be asleep in about 60 seconds but wasn't too concerned. Any double-cross from Halladay would almost certainly be by proxy.

I went back upstairs and turned on the coffee pot. Then I waited. By the time Halladay arrived, I had a pot of Colombian dark roast waiting on the coffee table, plus two mugs and cream and sugar.

"Come in, Mr. Halladay."

He was in his workout outfit and smiled warmly as we shook hands. "Thanks."

"Please, have a seat."

We entered the living room, sitting opposite each other. "Coffee?"

"Black."

I poured him a cup and handed it to him. He took a sip and seemed friendly enough, but my instinct was telling me to be careful. "We appear to be sitting on at least two murders, Cicero's and that goddamned actor's."

"Actually, that's not quite accurate."

"How do you figure?"

"Because it's you that's sitting on two murders."

He looked at me curiously as his friendly vibe began to evaporate.

"Our constabulary, as you call them, jacked me up Thursday afternoon. They were laboring under the misapprehension that I had killed that goddamned actor."

"Really?"

"I was home here in bed with my wife when he was beheaded and dumped. I gave them my theory, which they were very interested in."

All ears, he gripped the mug so tightly, I thought it might explode. "Which is what, exactly?"

"Cicero's death was a cover-up, and he was probably whacked by the two assholes that're impersonating cops, per Arnold Clipper's orders. They also talked to Jade and now, in their own peculiar way, LAPD has a real fucking hard-on."

"Why didn't you tell me?" said Halladay quietly.

I was surprised. His normal dominant personality was momentarily blunted, which made me all the more suspicious. "Not the sort of thing I like to talk about on the phone."

"You didn't even contact me." His eyes, suddenly glistening and hard, bored into me.

"You wanted me to take care of this on the D.L, so you could distance yourself as much as possible. Am I wrong?"

"No."

"I didn't think you paid me 100 G's to call you every five minutes."

Halladay nodded as he mulled this over. "What should we do?"

"I'm no lawyer but if I were you, I'd inform the police you had your paralegal run a Vital Records check and to your surprise, it turns out Cicero wasn't killed in a hit-and-run after all. All you risk is embarrassment."

"Sounds messy."

"Yeah but you clear yourself on any possible misprision of felony charges."

"Maybe you're right." He put down his coffee cup and rubbed his hands together to get the circulation back that he'd squeezed out. He looked at me and sighed. "Me and Cicero were making so much money, it was ridiculous. I mean cash was flowing in like Scarface. Then the idiot stopped selling Persian Brown and switched to blow. Cut our profit margin in half because we didn't have the same fantastic connections as we did with the brown. And then Cicero got bored and quit. One day, out of the blue, he phones me up and tells me we're out of business. I suppose I should have been relieved but I'd gotten very used to the money. You know how that goes?"

I nodded and deliberated. "You shouldn't really be telling me this."

Halladay shook his head. "Without even asking me. I could never understand why."

As I listened to his confession, I felt like I was having an out of body experience. "Mr. Halladay, I--"

"--Have you ever seen, I mean physically, how big of a stack 300 million dollars is?"

"No."

"It's the most amazing sight. You feel like you own the world and it gives you the biggest hard-on of your life."

He fell silent and we looked at each other. I was fascinated but acutely aware that he wouldn't be telling me this unless he had ulterior motives. I had an opening and took it.

"Why were you sleeping with his wife?"

The blood drained out of his face. He opened his mouth to say something, but changed his mind and sat there in the telling silence.

"You know it was bound to come out sooner or later."

He sucked in his top lip and sighed out of his nose. "Prison changes a man."

"He came out Cindy instead of Cicero? Is that what you're saying?"

"Dominique had a voracious appetite that he no longer wanted to satisfy."

"So you served her?"

"Yes, but with his complete knowledge and permission."

"Did Jade know?"

He shook his head. I wanted to twist it right off his pompous neck. "We were discreet."

"Not discreet enough."

"I'm sorry?"

My coffee had gone cold, but I drank it down anyway. "You remember the day Richard came home unexpectedly and caught you two?"

He blanched and licked his dry lips. "How do you know about that?"

"Dominique had a therapist. Jade and I met her in San Francisco."

"Oh my God."

"Richard never forgave her. It broke her heart and she cracked, and pulled the trigger."

Halladay seemed genuinely moved. Then again, I've been wrong before.

"That's why she did it?" he asked.

"Uh-huh."

"Stupid whore."

"Sorry?"

"She did this to get back at me."

"I don't follow."

"It's not my fault that Richard, the waste of skin, wouldn't speak to her anymore."

"You knew?"

"Yes, of course. She would call me, begging me to take her back."

He was either delusional or a consummate liar. Either way I didn't care and regretted not listening to Cassady when she advised me to give him the retainer back.

He shrugged. "Anyway, what's done is done."

"As simple as that?"

"Yeah, simple as that."

Regret became a fleeting memory as he looked at his watch. "It's been illuminating."

"Very."

"Sorry, but I have to send a text." I watched fascinated as this arrogant prick, without waiting for me to reply, took out his cell and sent the text. He put his phone away and headed for the front door. "I'll be in touch."

I held it open for him and he stepped outside without so much as a backwards glance. I watched as he drove away. I went back into the living room and was about to sit down, when the patio doors exploded as two Latino bikers burst through. Jagged shards of glass flew through the air and I stumbled backward, falling on my ass. Before I could even get my Colt out, the fat one was smashing me across the face with his gun. I covered up as best I could, and he jumped on top of me, sitting his 280 pound frame on my chest, pinning me down. He began systematically punching me in the face and the world went dark. I heard voices swirling around and felt myself being lifted up. I opened my eyes just as I was dropped onto the sofa. My two assailants were looking down at me. I tried to focus, but the ringing in my ears had me flailing.

The larger one grinned revealing a gold tongue stud that nicely complimented his black gang tattoos. "Wake up, motherfucka!"

The skinny one, dressed in jeans, motorcycle boots, and a tee-shirt under his denim vest, glared down at me. I looked at his 1% patch and the Los Muertos insignia on the other side of his vest. He grinned, revealing a gleaming row of gold teeth, sucked noisily on them and knelt down next to me; his fetid breath almost made me puke.

"Where's your money, bitch?"

"What?"

He looked at his partner. "Go see what this motherfucka got upstairs."

I was so happy when the big one got up off me and headed toward the stairs. He wasn't happy though when the bayonet on Bobby's M14 stopped him dead in his tracks. He looked incredulously at the Vietnam vet, who was in full kill mode. All men of violence recognize that look and the consequence of ignoring it.

"Back the fuck up," snarled Bobby.

Skinny, caught off guard, recovered and went to raise his gun.

"Hey, fuckhead, this is fully auto. I can spray right through him and blow you out the front door."

"Bullshit."

Bobby pressed the bayonet into fat man's gut, piercing his tee-shirt, drawing blood. "Put the gun down, and I ain't gonna tell ya again."

"This dude got me cold, man!"

Skinny looked at me and started to raise his gun. I grabbed it with my left and hit him hard in the balls. He screamed and doubled over in agony.

"How you like me now, asshole!" I yelled just before I smashed him on the back of his head. He passed out and crashed to the floor.

Bobby grinned his approval and forced the other biker to back up. "Sit down."

He sat down.

I was feeling crappy, but adrenaline had kicked in and was keeping me on my feet. I aimed the gun at him. "You're Los Muertos. What the fuck do you want with me?"

"Fuck you," he snarled.

"Arnold sent you?"

"Who?"

I slapped him hard across his face. Humiliation reddened it. "You want another, ya fat fuck?"

He shook his head and kept his mouth clamped shut.

"I'm gonna ask you again, and if you don't tell me, I'm gonna let him go to work on you."

Bobby's eyes lit up at the prospect. He put down the rifle and flipped open his razor sharp Spyderco knife. The biker eyeballed it, sweat oozing out of his pores.

"Naw, man, it wasn't him," he said.

"He's all yours."

I stepped back as Bobby stepped forward, the knife gleaming in his hands.

"Wait, man, wait!" he pleaded.

"Nick, get a roll of paper towels for the blood."

"Okay." I took a step toward the kitchen.

Fatso looked like he was about to start frothing. "Please, I can't tell you. He'll kill me."

Bobby's thousand yard death stare was blazing into him.

I said, "What do you think my partner's gonna do to you?"

He opened his mouth just as Bobby wrapped a massive hand around his throat, bringing the edge of the blade toward his left eye. This was all too much for the no longer tough guy. Urine darkened his crotch.

"Jesus, bro," chuckled Bobby, stepping back instinctively.

Humiliated, he blurted out, "It was the lawyer dude! He paid us to fuck you up, man!"

"Halladay?"

"Yeah."

Although I'd suspected as much, the confirmation still took my breath away. "Shit," I said quietly.

Bobby looked at me and shook his head. I glared at the biker.

"What's your name?"

"Gordo."

"You got ID, Gordo?"

He handed me his wallet. I pulled out his license, looked at it and gave it to Bobby. "Hand him Sleeping Beauty's there."

Gordo pulled Skinny's wallet out of his back pocket and gave it to Bobby, who extracted the license and tossed the wallet back to him.

I considered him for a long, tense moment. "Now we know who you clowns are, and where you live."

"What're you gonna do?" he asked.

"Was this gonna be a beat down, or were you supposed to whack me?"

"Naw, just a beat down."

Bobby voiced what I was thinking. "Doesn't make sense."

"Unless it was to get me outta the way for a couple'a weeks 'til he and Clipper could complete whatever it is they're up to."

Bobby nodded. "Yeah, maybe."

"And Clipper didn't know?"

Gordo shook his head.

"So you do know him?"

"We do shit for him, you know, when he need us."

"I don't get that," said Bobby.

Gordo shrugged. "He ain't tight with the lawyer. They don't like each other."

Skinny, A.K.A. Flaco, began to regain consciousness.

"Lean Piss Boy against the sofa, but not on it," I said.

Gordo helped him and sat next to him. Bobby picked up his rifle, fingering the trigger. This wasn't lost on them.

"You did the hit-and-run?"

Gordo looked at me and shook his head. "Naw."

Each bad answer infuriated me more. I stepped forward and cracked him hard in the nose. His head snapped back. "I ain't gonna ask you again."

Flaco glared at me. "You a bad motherfucka with that nine in your grip."

I cracked him across his face, almost knocking him out. I turned to Gordo, pressed my boot into his crotch and applied a little pressure. He moaned and paled and I eased off.

"It was you two, wasn't it?"

The fat fuck nodded. I stood up and glanced at Bobby, who shook his head as anger coursed through him.

I said, "Who ordered it, the lawyer?"

Gordo nodded.

"Who went to the doctor for the Death Certificate?"

"Them other two fools."

"The white dudes?"

"Yeah."

"How do you know this?"

"We was all getting twisted one night, and he got pissed."

"Who did?"

"The lawyer, Halladay, 'cause he wanted a straight coroner's report, to make it legit."

"These white dudes, what're their names?"

"Ernie and Tom."

"Did you kill Cicero?"

They glanced at each other, sharing a knowing half-smirk. I wanted to smash in their faces. Bobby beat me to it and cracked Flaco in the mouth with the rifle butt. He spat blood and teeth, his eyes rolling up into his head as he slumped back into semi-consciousness. Bobby turned to Gordo.

"Stop beating on us, bro!"

I motioned Bobby to stop. "Then tell us what's so funny."

"You dunno what you up against, puta."

"I know all about Arnold Clipper."

"No, you don't. He ain't just crazy, he Satan, bro."

"I don't give a shit about him, you or the devil. I wanna know if Cicero's alive."

"We didn't smoke him, but that don't mean he ain't dead."

I was tired of the runaround and looked at Bobby. "Convince him."

Bobby raised the rifle butt and drew back to smash him in the face again. "You can grind me into hamburger, motherfucka, but I ain't saying no more."

Again I motioned Bobby to stop. Again he looked disappointed. "What about Richie?"

"We don't see him too much, but Halladay told us Clipper treats him like a chavala."

"Chavala?"

Gordo nodded and smirked. "A bitch, just like his father."

"What?"

The biker smiled but didn't elaborate. "Where does he live?"

"He moves from hotel to hotel. We don't even know how to contact him."

"So how'd Halladay find you?"

Flaco opened his eyes, wiped the blood away and said, "He sends us a text, cabron."

"Is that right?"

He nodded and cast a quick, fearful glance at Bobby, who was still fingering the trigger on his fully auto rifle.

"Bobby. Bobby!" He looked at me with seeming reluctance. "Give 'em a garbage bag and broom."

He lightly tapped the trigger, flexed his jaw muscles and went into the kitchen.

Flaco snarled. "You better finish this, motherfucka!"

"You've got more balls than brains, pendejo."

He looked at the blood on the back of his hand and grinned. "You the pendejo, 'cause you still don't get it."

"Mira," hissed Gordo.

Flaco ignored him, locking eyes with me.

"Then enlighten me."

Flaco shook his head.

"That means--"

"--I know what it means, cabron. You gonna find out yourself, sooner or later."

Bobby returned with the garbage bag and broom, and dropped them on the floor in front of them.

"Fuck you, man. I ain't your maid," growled Flaco.

"You made the mess, you clean it up."

"No."

"Or I can let Bobby here finish what he's itching to do."

They looked at the M14 in his paws, slowly got to their feet and started to clean up the broken glass and wood.

"What do you think?" I asked Bobby quietly.

"As I see it, you've got two choices; bury 'em, or turn 'em in."

"No. I mean what he said about Cicero."

Bobby shrugged. "I dunno, bro. It's kind'a weird."

The uncanny revelation was crawling through my mind. I took a breath and said quietly, "If I'm right, Clipper killed Cicero because they were lovers, and then for whatever reason, Cicero wanted to break it off. I guess Arnold didn't like the rejection."

"What?"

"So the ultimate 'fuck you' to Cicero was for him to get close to his son, Richie."

"Bro, that's too fuckin' dark."

"Yeah, but everything we've heard about Clipper is that he's in love with Richie, so it sort of makes sense."

"Jade, she can't ever know that."

I nodded. "Yeah, I agree and if Halladay's using Clipper to get to the trust, popping Richie's the only way to do it, which Clipper won't let him do. He could, I guess, get him to sign it over, but as that would also hurt Richie, again I can't see Clipper allowing that."

"What I don't get is why stage the hit-and-run on Cicero?"

"I dunno either."

Bobby said, "If you're gonna disappear someone, you just do it. Either way, according to those two clowns, Cicero's dead. How he died doesn't really matter."

"Yeah, but I'm missing the bigger picture here and have no idea what it is."

"We need another bag."

I looked at Gordo. "What?"

"This one's full," he replied.

"I'll get it," said Bobby.

He went into the kitchen, retrieved a new bag and handed it to them. He placed his M14 by the now missing French doors, grabbed the full one and placed it outside. They continued to clean up the last pieces of wood and glass.

Bobby reappeared, picked up his rifle and came over to me. "So what're you gonna do?"

I shrugged. "Halladay wants the money. I get that. What I don't understand is what Clipper wants."

"He's a psycho. Who the hell knows or cares what his motive is?"

"I do, 'cause it's the key to this whole situation."

They had done a good job and were sweeping up the dusty remains.

I studied them and switched my pistol to the other hand. "Who cut the actor's head off?"

Flaco glanced at Gordo, frowned and replied, "How're we supposed to know?"

"'Cause I have an eyewitness that'll testify that you two, along with Clipper, dumped the body.

Fatso took an aggressive step forward, blocking the skinny biker from view. "Yeah, cabron? Then you better--"

The crack of pistol fire at close range is all I heard as the bullets from Flaco's hidden .32 seared past my head. In times of extreme stress, everything can seem as if it's happening in blurred slow motion. Bobby and I fired simultaneously, our bullets slammed into them, spraying blood and gore up the wall. His M14 had almost cut them in half. We stood there, our ears ringing. The stench of cordite, blood and piss filling the air. I lowered my gun and looked at Bobby. He went over and nudged the bodies with his boot.

"Dead and gone."

The weight of what had just happened was beginning to press in on me. "Jesus Christ."

"What d'you wanna do, Nick?"

"Do?" I replied. My voice sounding strange, thin, distant.

Bobby came over and took the nine millie out of my hand. "Bro, get a grip."

I looked at the blood and bits of tattooed flesh slowly dripping off the mantelpiece, the spray pattern across the wall. I desperately wanted to feel something, anything, but all I felt was numb.

He said quietly, "We call this in, the cops'll be all over us like flies on shit. We'll beat it; I mean it's clearly self-defense, but who knows how long they'll detain us. Clipper'll be alerted. So will Halladay. But the real problem is that Jade and Richie'll be vulnerable, and fuck knows what'll happen to 'em."

He was right and we both knew it. The desire to protect them was overwhelming, even though it could cost me my liberty. "I guess we have to bury these bastards."

He looked at them with utter contempt and shook his head. "Fuck 'em. They were gonna kill us."

I shrugged. "So what do we do?"

"I have a compadre who runs a hog farm."

"Oh, man, I dunno."

"Why not? Hogs gotta eat too."

I realized I'd been holding my breath and let it out. "No, that's just wrong."

"Are you high?"

"No, but I could a use a few shots'a bourbon."

"We'll do that after we dump the guns and feed the porkers."

I hesitated and Bobby grew anxious. "Make your mind up, bro. We don't have time for any weak shit."

Even though it felt wrong, I knew that he was right. "I'll get the body bags." Years ago when we were first becoming pals, Tony Bott gave me half-a-dozen body bags as a gag. Figuring you never know, I'd always held onto them, hiding them up in the garage where Cassady wasn't likely to spot them.

When I came back in with two bags, Bobby was pulling a pair of rubber utility gloves over his massive hands and stuffed what remained of the bikers into the bags. I sliced open several black garbage bags and taped them over the entrance where the French doors used to be. Next, we wiped up all the blood, shoving the blood-stained rags into one of the bags. We washed the wall and floor with a mixture of hot water, bleach and disinfectant. It wouldn't stand up to a UV blood scan, but on first blush it would pass. I retrieved the Yukon from around the corner and backed it up to the garage. We piled in the body bags and dismantled their guns, putting them in an old shoebox. Before we took off, Bobby stashed his M14 up in the attic. Cops take a real dim view of fully automatic guns, particularly when they're fitted with a silencer. They're not fond of bodies full of bullet holes in body bags either, but if our luck held, that would be only a passing concern.

As Bobby drove, I looked at myself in the side mirror. My left eye was nearly closed and there was a bruise extending from it clear to my chin. It was painful, but fortunately, nothing seemed to be broken, and I could still see after a fashion.

Bobby wore a more relaxed version of his 1000 yard stare, and was silent as we cruised at a smooth 60, heading north on the 605 freeway. I was still trying to get my head around how we were about to dispose of the bodies, and was grateful for the silence, no matter how brooding. I got a chill as we passed the Santa Fe Dam recreation area; the geography was like some strange lunar landscape. The earth is gashed by a series of stone quarries and heavy equipment lines both sides of the highway. Huge power poles stand guard over the terrain, with random billboards advertising graveyards and cancer cures. In the distance, the stone mountains shimmer.

We rolled east onto the old Route 66 and after another few miles, turned north on a soothingly deserted Route 39. This is the only access road leading to Morris Reservoir and a couple of miles further on, our destination, the San Gabriel Reservoir. As we climbed into the foothills, the smoke seemed to have dissipated, and the snow shimmered on the distant mountains. It was nearly 5:00 and the quarry was completely deserted when we pulled off the road. We parked in front of the locked chain link gate and got out of the Yukon, stashed our guns, and clambered over the gate. The smell of oil lingered in the air as we passed a bulldozer and stacks of sawhorses.

"My old man used to be into these machines," said Bobby, pointing at the bulldozer. "Big gravel industry outside of Mobile."

"I never knew that."

"I never told you."

We worked our way around the perimeter, taking a trail that overlooked the deepest part of the reservoir. When we reached the top, half-shielded from the road by scrub oak, we stood gazing down into the water, a good 200 feet below. I opened the shoebox and we each grabbed pieces of the dismantled guns and threw them are far we could, watching as they hit the surface before sinking to the bottom.

Back on the road, on the way to the pig farm, we were both silent. The traffic was light to non-existent and we made good time, finally pulling onto a hidden driveway that led to Bobby's friend's spread. We stopped in front of the main house, a run-down affair made of quarry stone. The stench from the pigs was overpowering, but not as bad as their constant squealing.

Bobby was scanning the area. "Stay in the car 'til I've spoken to Porky."

"Porky?"

Bobby looked at me. "What?"

"That's his name?"

"Yeah."

"And he runs a pig farm."

"Is that a problem?"

'Nada. Just kind'a weird, that's all."

Bobby shrugged. "Okay and, like I said, stay in the car 'til I give you the word. Porky gets real touchy about strangers."

I nodded and he got out. As he headed for the main house, a huge mountain man, complete with a shock of red hair and ZZ Top beard, wearing bib-and-brace overalls and carrying a 12 gauge pump, exited the front door. Bobby stopped and waited for Porky, who was now accompanied by three pissed off looking dogs of indeterminate breed and lineage. They greeted each other like long lost comrades and walked over to the Yukon.

"Nick, this is Porky."

His huge shovel of a hand wrapped itself around mine and felt like a steel press as he squeezed the blood out of it.

"Wha'sup, bro?" asked Porky, all smiles, not many teeth, more or less Bobby's age.

"I've been better."

"Heard that."

He released my hand and I rubbed it, waiting for the feeling to return. As I climbed out of the truck and joined them, the dogs eyed me suspiciously, but refrained from ripping my throat out.

"You want the bags in the pen?" asked Bobby.

"Yeah."

I unlocked the back of the Yukon and we grabbed the body bags and carried them over to the nearest pigpen. Inside, the smell was even more rancid and the pigs, perhaps sensing that it might be feeding time, squealed eagerly.

"Here's good," smiled Porky.

We dropped the bags, opened them and his smile evaporated.

"What's wrong?" I asked.

He ignored me and turned to Bobby. "You didn't tell me they was Los Muertos."

"So what if they are?"

"It's a problem."

"Why?"

"If they ever find out I disposed of some of their crew, they'll feed me to my own hogs."

"But how would they know?" I asked.

"'Cause I did some work for 'em yesterday."

Bobby shrugged. "So what?"

"So they could show up anytime with more business for me."

"Then you best get to it, bro."

"I can't, man, too risky."

Bobby frowned, his growing irritation clear to anyone who wasn't blind. I wondered how well this hog farmer knew him.

"I'll double your normal price." Porky looked at me, clearly swayed. "How much?"

"Twenty."

"Done."

Bobby was now glaring at him, his muscles coiled and ready.

"You have it with you?"

"I've gotta go to the bank, so tomorrow."

"Then bring the garbage when you come back."

"But we can't drive around with that in the truck."

"Not my problem."

Bobby bit the inside of his cheek, and spat out blood. "Nick, wait in the car."

I knew that look and the tone in his voice all too well. I headed for the door.

Suddenly Porky looked scared. "Relax, bro, I'll do it."

"You sure?" growled Bobby quietly, looking like a mountain lion, ready to pounce and rip him to shreds.

"Yeah. Did you remove the teeth?"

"For twenty large, you fuckin' do it."

"Okay, yeah, sure. No problem."

Bobby stomped past me and got in the truck. I gave Porky a small wave without really looking at him and got in next to him. We drove off in silence.

CHAPTER V
Jailhouse Rock

ONE BLOCK FROM BOBBY'S HOUSE, four black-and-whites closed in from all directions.

"What the hell?" I said as Bobby pulled over and cut the engine.

Officer Jansen climbed out of the cruiser that was across our bow, swaggered over to my side and smirked. "Out."

All my favorite officers were there: Sanchez, Tomito, Jansen, Detective Karsagian, and a host of others.

I grinned. "Nice to see you all again."

"You're an asshole," said Jansen.

Bobby and I got out and they cuffed and searched us. "I guess you're not so smart after all," said Karsagian.

I shrugged. "I have my moments and this ain't yours."

The cop searching me found my .45 and looked at it appreciatively. "Dirty Harry, huh?"

I ignored him and said to Karsagian, "To what do I owe the pleasure?"

"You're under arrest for the murder of Doctor Tarkanian."

Bobby and I looked at each other and grinned.

"What's so funny, dick?" hissed Officer Sanchez.

"You gonna read us rights or not?"

"Put 'em in a car and let's go," snarled Karsagian.

This time there was no unnecessary roughness, as they ushered us to the back seats of two separate cruisers.

Once again I had Officer Sanchez riding beside me. "You look like shit, Crane."

"Everybody's a comedian."

"Only you won't be laughing very much longer."

I ignored him and addressed Karsagian who was riding shotgun. "When was he killed?"

"Late Friday night."

"Wasn't me."

"Got an alibi, I suppose?"

"Ironclad."

He frowned and I knew it was pointless to tell him I was in San Francisco. He was intent on seeing this through and I had no choice but to let him make his pitch. My time would come.

"How'd he die?"

"Don't play games with me."

"Indulge me, please."

"You don't remember burning his face off with a blowtorch?"

I clammed up as we were transported to the Parker Center at 1st and Los Angeles Street, just around the corner from the Roybal Federal Courthouse. The Center is a nine story glass-and-concrete structure built in the nondescript style of the 50's. It appeared frequently on the late '60's version of Dragnet, and is where they house the newly arrested until they're either released, or arraigned and transferred to L.A. Men's Central.

In this case, however, they didn't take us inside immediately. Instead, I was escorted to the car holding Bobby. Officer Sanchez shoved me inside and we were left alone. It was after six with just a hint of lingering smoke in the dusty air.

This is an old police trick, leaving two suspects together in a patrol car with a live microphone in the hope they'll make incriminating remarks. Bobby and I were hip to their game and sat there in silence. I dozed off, falling into a half-lucid dream state. Bloody limbs, eyeless decapitated heads, smoke and gunfire, cops and hogs side-by-side munching on body parts. I woke up shuddering, drenched in sweat. Bobby was sound asleep.

I tried to slow my breathing. My wife and daughter materialized in my mind's eye and then they were gone. I missed them terribly and suddenly felt emotion sweeping over me. I pushed it to one side and replayed the scene in Dr. Tarkanian's office. He'd been shifty and thoroughly corrupt. Still, his sins didn't seem of a magnitude to justify murder. I had the feeling that this time it was purely Tom and Ernie; Arnold had given the order but had not even bothered to attend. This murder had obviously occurred sometime before Gordo and Flaco jacked us at my house. When I'd been questioned downtown on Thursday afternoon, I told Detective Karsagian what I knew about Tom and Ernie. Jade had done the same when she and Bobby had met the cops at the Croatian church in East L.A. At that time, I'd had no more sense of how to find them than the police did. The key thing I'd held back was that Tarkanian had been scheduled to meet with Tom or Ernie at the McDonald's on 3rd Street, to receive the last $5,000. Since the Egyptian taxi driver had showed up instead, our anticipated straight path to Arnold had gone up in smoke.

Bobby finally woke up, looked at me and blinked rapidly several times.

"Man, I could do with some chow."

"Yeah, me too."

"Maybe these pigs'll get us a bacon sandwich?"

"I wouldn't hold my breath."

He grinned and made obnoxious oinking sounds.

I knew exactly what he was referring to and shook my head. I was about to respond when Officers Tomito and Sanchez opened the back doors.

"Out," said the latter.

We climbed out and they started to lead us toward the entrance.

"Any chance of some In-N-Out?"

"Shut up, Crane," hissed Sanchez.

"What about a Starbucks latte and a blueberry muffin?"

Sanchez stopped, spun around and yanked down hard on my cuffs, causing me intense pain. "Open your fucking mouth again, and I'll burn your goddamn eyes out," he snarled, placing his hand on the can of mace on his belt.

We locked eyes. "Take my cuffs off and give it a shot."

His lips curled back like an angry dog as he pulled out the mace. Officer Tomito got in between us.

"Relax, Sanchez."

"Get outta the way!"

Detective Karsagian came out of the lobby. "Sanchez!" The cop let me go and turned to the detective. "Escort the prisoners inside. Now!"

This time Sanchez led me by my arm, watched closely by the senior officer.

I've been in Parker Center many times with attorneys to meet with clients, and am actually rather fond of the place. A great old African-American officer, Samuel Thomas, holds down the front desk, Wednesday through Sunday evenings, from 2:00 to 10:00. He is knowledgeable on a host of arcane topics such as spelunking, and lapidary, and always has time for a cheery greeting. This time we weren't brought in by the front desk but were escorted through the rear entrance, where we were fingerprinted and booked. Like many private investigators, I've been detained a few times over the years, but it had been at least a decade since I'd been hauled in here. The desk officers at Parker are as friendly as the guards at L.A. Men's Central are hostile.

There's an old underworld saying that there's no worse place on earth to spend the night than in a South Georgia jail, but L.A. Men's

Central can't be far behind. A sprawling stone edifice, it was built back in the 60's when confinement allegedly wasn't as cruel as it is today, and guards and inmates apparently cooperated to a reasonable degree to keep the ship afloat. Today, Men's Central is run by gangbangers who decide which inmates are housed together, and have carte blanche to "regulate" troublesome convicts whenever the spirit moves them.

Parker Center, on the other hand, offers reasonable overnight accommodations, that is, if you don't mind the likelihood of sleeping on a mattress on the floor. Of course, things go wrong at any jail and it's a good idea to keep your wits about you. Bobby and I were booked and finger-printed by Officer Trujillo, an elderly Filipino officer with a ready smile and a great head of thick, black hair. He's been booking fresh arrivals since the mid-80s, and maintains a pleasing calm that cannot fail to soothe the inflamed mind of the newly arrested man.

"Nick, what's going on?"

"Beats me."

Trujillo scanned my bruised face and gave Sanchez a disgusted look. "Looks like they already did."

"Your friend," said Officer Sanchez, who was crowding me from behind, "brutally murdered an Armenian doctor."

Officer Trujillo digested this bit of unexpected information with a raised eyebrow. "You didn't, did you?"

"Not that I recall."

"I believe you have the wrong man," said Trujillo.

I smiled and shrugged. Sanchez didn't.

"I've pinched a lotta assholes, Crane, and I really want some alone time with you."

Trujillo glanced at Sanchez and placed my thumb firmly down on his inkpad. "I'll bet you a free trip to Santa Anita, Nick gets sprung before you get any alone time."

"We'll see."

Trujillo smiled at me. "Good luck, Nick."

"Thanks and if you don't mind, please ask Mrs. Trujillo to burn a few candles for me."

"Sure, my friend."

It was Bobby's turn and Officer Tomito shoved him up to Trujillo's desk.

Once we'd both been processed, we were turned over to the guards, who escorted us up to a dormitory on the sixth floor. Parker Center boasts a few wings of two and four man cells, but mostly houses its detainees in dormitories. Depending on how business has been, these dorms are either half-full, full or bursting at the seams. Right at the moment ours held only six other guys, but the evening was young and Saturday night is usually rocking. There are six sets of bunk beds occupying two walls, and a stack of mattresses in one corner. Urinals, sinks and latrines painted institutional green, occupy the opposite wall. The showers are down the hall. Generally speaking, short-term residents have others things on their minds besides trying to keep clean. There are no bars, simply a steel door with a meshed steel window, through which an inmate could see out into the corridor and, of course, Parker Center's fabled, pneumatic tube delivery system for legal documents. When a document arrives, a bell rings and an inmate walks over, slides open a curved plastic door and extracts the paperwork.

Our fellow prisoners, predominantly Latino and black, looked at us curiously as Bobby and I claimed 2 primo bunks while they were still available. He took the lower and settled in as I clambered to the upper. I stretched out and tried to relax, but there was such a cacophony, it was all but impossible.

"What's our next move?" said Bobby, his voice weary.

I jumped down off my bunk and sat next to him on his. "They're trying to sweat us. That's why we're in here."

He nodded. "Yeah."

"They know we didn't kill the doc, but suspect we know who did."

"Why not just ask?"

"Because shit rolls downhill and right now, we're at the bottom."

"I don't understand."

"Karsagian didn't make detective 'cause he's stupid. He knows there's a lot more to this and, I guess, he figures I'm the key. So he'll bide his time, leaving us in here to ripen."

"How long can they hold us?"

"Until arraignment court on Tuesday."

"Shit, bro, who's gonna look after my goats?"

I lowered my voice. "We have another problem."

"What?"

"I was supposed to drop off the package for pig boy tomorrow."

"Why's that a problem?"

"If he doesn't hear from us, will he run his mouth?"

Bobby grinned and shook his head. "No."

"How can you be sure?"

"Because he knows that I'll feed him to his fucking hogs if he does."

I looked around to make sure no one was within earshot. Inmates will trade the smallest scrap of info for reduced time, or if it's valuable enough, although this is quite rare, immunity for their own crimes.

I nodded and whispered, "If they question you, which they might not after talking to me, don't say a word about Los Muertos, and tell 'em the only thing we were expecting at the McDonald's was for someone to slip the five large to the doctor."

"What about me tailing him?"

"Negative, and leave Brad out of everything."

He nodded and began chewing the inside of his cheek.

"If you don't like the way the questioning is going, stonewall. Tell them you're not saying another word until you consult with your attorney."

"I don't have an attorney."

"Sure you do. Bill Boxer. I'll take care of it."

"Man, the shit's getting so thick it would drown an alligator."

"Just so it doesn't drown us."

Bobby glanced around the room. "I could use a beer."

"I'm covered for Friday night, so they can't hang Tarkanian on me. Where were you?"

He grinned. "After McDonald's, on the way home I stopped in at Leo's a little after 7, and we went to a pescado restaurant at Boyle and Olympic."

"What time did you bail?"

"About 11:00. When I got home, Brad was already there and I had to shout for him to even let me in the house 'cause he was still freaked out over the picture."

"Okay, good."

"These pigs are just fucking with us. Didn't you once tell me that about 40% of arrests end up going uncharged?"

"Yeah, something like that."

Jail is usually the single most boring place in the world. If nobody's trying to kill or extort you, there's very little to do, and now that they don't allow smoking, it's a nightmare.

I stood up and surveyed the room that was filling up fast. Groups of new arrivals, mostly head-shaved, tat-covered gangbangers, and their "distant cousins", non-gang affiliated pisas, were huddled together, claiming their little piece of concrete as a continuation of their neighborhoods. A couple of white guys that looked like cons were making their way toward us, safety in numbers. Bobby is one of the only guys I know that doesn't play games with anyone of any race, color or creed. Like a junkyard dog, his face turned harder and his muscles steeled. The cons got the message, gave us a curt nod, and turned away.

"I'm gonna see if they'll let me make a call."

"Want me to watch your back?" asked Bobby.

"Stay here and guard the bunks."

He nodded and I made my way toward the guard. Several hard looking inmates eyeballed me, and I knew there was going to be a problem. In lockup, you're either a warrior or a victim, and mamma didn't raise no pussy.

"I'd like to make a call."

A group of 5 gangbangers were watching me with great interest. The guard, a white guy with a mashed face who could easily have been one of them, glanced over at their leader, a nasty, head-shaved specimen: 5'8", trunk like a gorilla and a brow ridge that out-Neanderthaled the Neanderthal. And, of course, the black tats. Neanderthal nodded almost imperceptibly and the guard pointed at the payphone.

"Collect only."

"I know the drill."

He didn't like my reply and his eyes narrowed as he mulled over an appropriate response. I didn't have time to wait and headed over to the phone.

I dialed Bobby's home number.

"Hello?" It was Brad.

"I'm in jail."

"What the fuck happened?"

"Not now. Later. Get me Cassady."

"Okay, sure."

Cassady was on the phone in a flash. "You okay? What the hell's going on?"

"They're holding me and Bobby here at Parker Center."

"What's the charge?" she asked, all business.

"Murder One."

"Jesus."

"They're claiming we killed an Armenian doctor, but it's all circumstantial and it's totally weak. I don't want to be here 'til Tuesday, so tell Bill to work something out."

"I'm on it."

The guard came over. "Time's up."

"What?"

"You heard me motherfucka, time's up."

"Gotta go."

"I love you," she said quickly, worry propelling her words.

The guard reached over and snatched the phone out of my hand. I glared at him. "What the hell, bro?"

"Get the fuck back in there."

His attitude assured me that something was about to go down. As I walked through the door, the already tense atmosphere amped up about 1000 per cent, and I could feel the heat from the gaze of the gang of five, searing into my back. I made my way over to Bobby, using every part of my peripheral vision to watch for the inevitable. He had sensed it, too, and got to his feet, scanning the crowd for any sudden movement.

I sat next to him and spoke quietly, "Cassady's getting the lawyer."

"Won't be soon enough."

"I know."

"When it goes down, keep your back to the wall."

I nodded and readied myself for the coming battle. The gang of five were facing us now, their eyes steely lights in a gunmetal world. Suddenly the main door opened, and a new batch of detainees shuffled in. Yep, it was Saturday night and humanity was displaying its warts. This group was mostly black and Latino with one thin, good-looking white guy with Mediterranean features. He definitely thought he was riding in the black car. He didn't even glance at

Bobby and me, instead started jawing with some black guys, his voice rising shrilly.

"Motherfucking PoPo, fuck dem bitches!"

The blacks looked dubious but made a half-hearted effort to listen.

"I was getting my grip on, feel me? And they jacked me fo' nuttin'. Sheeit, dawg, me and my boy, we was riding on Crenshaw and the fuckers pulled us over, and planted 2 eight balls on us. Motherfuckas."

Nobody responded; in fact, the black guys turned their backs on him. Humiliated, he stood there as inconspicuous as a rattlesnake smoking a cigarello. He turned away, grabbed a thin, plastic-covered mattress, and sat on the floor fuming and muttering. A wave of intense emotion swept over his thin, intelligent face and he looked like he was about to cry, alerting the predators who are always vigilant for a sucker. I hoped no one had noticed, but knew that he was already marked. When it happened, no one would come to his aid, just as no one was going to help us.

It was time and the five gangbangers made their way through the crowd, which parted without resistance and folded back in behind them, shielding the impending violence from prying eyes. Not that it made any difference anyway as the cameras, most likely, were already turned off. The two white cons glanced at us and melted away, so much for safety in numbers.

With our backs to the wall, we waited -- muscles coiled, adrenaline pumping. They oozed out of the crowd and fanned into a line. Everyone watched and waited for blood. Their Neanderthal leader had a ring of black skulls tattooed all the way around his neck. He gave us the once over, then settled his gaze on me.

"You remember me, Holmes?"

"No."

"You snatched my brother in Dago."

I shrugged. "Yeah?"

"He was almost to TJ. Now he's doing 15 to life." His voice shrill; odd in such a gorilla of a man.

The penny dropped. "Jose Torres."

"Si, cabrón."

"So what d'you want?"

"You, motherfuc--"

I didn't wait for him to finish and stepped forward, kicking him fast and hard in the balls. He screamed and dropped to his knees. Bobby was airborne, and slammed his knees into the second dude's chest, knocking him back, out cold. The third gangbanger cracked me hard in the face, I rolled with the punch and spun a 360, jacking him in the side of his neck with a back elbow. Bobby had the last two in headlocks, one in each of his burly arms, squeezing the life out of them. The leader was still trying to force air back into his lungs when I grabbed his throat, and punched him multiple times, as hard as I could in the face. Flesh split, blood sprayed out and he was out for the count. No one stopped the beating. No one said a word. No one looked away. Breathing hard, I looked at Bobby. The two gangbangers were fading.

"Let 'em go."

He was enjoying himself a little too much, squeezing out whatever life these assholes had left in them. His trademark 1000 yard stare bore into me.

"Bobby!"

His eyes cleared and he let them go. They slumped to the ground.

Suddenly the emergency buzzer sounded and several guards came running in. Everyone backed away as they pushed their way through, bursting onto the five beaten bangers. The lead guard glared at me.

"Get on the ground, asshole!"

"What took you so long?"

"Shut the fuck up!" was the last thing I remembered.

I woke up in isolation. My mouth felt raw and tasted like putrid blood. More of it crusted the corners of my mouth and now the pounding in my head exploded, irritated at being ignored while I was unconscious and now determined to make up for it. I tried to stand but felt dizzy and broke out into a cold sweat, so I lay back down and closed my eyes.

At around 8:00 a.m., the steel door was yanked open and a screw stepped inside with a breakfast tray. He handed it to me and left. I sat there contemplating the cold scrambled eggs, greasy bacon, dry toast and lukewarm coffee. Still, I was hungry and tried to suck down a few bites but my mouth hurt too much, so I sipped the coffee and sat back, feening for some aspirin. About 20 minutes later, Detective Karsagian and Officer Jansen stood in the doorway.

Karsaigian looked grim, and his suit looked as tired as he did. He locked eyes with me, scratching at his five o'clock shadow, his shirt open at the collar revealing tufts of coarse gray hair.

"Crane, what happened to your face?"

"I got jumped."

"By whom?"

I nodded. "As if you don't know."

"You have a habit of pissing people off," smirked Jansen.

"Only your mother."

Jansen gritted his teeth, balled up his fists and took a step toward me.

Karsagian almost cracked a smile. "Back off, Detective."

He backed off.

"Cut the crap, Nick," said Karsagian.

"Now we're on a first name basis?"

Jensen was busily chewing his bottom lip and from his expression, he wanted nothing better than to work me over.

"So what do you want, Detective?"

"We've got a witness who says you killed Dr. Tarkanian," replied Karsagian.

"So why should I even talk to you without my lawyer here?"

"You know how this goes; cooperate and we can make it much easier for you."

"Who's the eyewitness?"

"I don't have to tell you that."

"'Cause you don't have one, do you?"

"Now listen--"

"--No, you listen; you've got nothing to hold me on. You know I didn't kill anybody and you sure as hell don't have this mystery witness 'cause if you did, you'd have already charged me and doofus over there would be working me over."

There was a long, pregnant pause. Karsagian nodded, took a deep breath and said, "We had to take you in. The witness says it was you."

"Obviously she didn't witness the murder 'cause if she had she'd be dead too."

"She said you were at Tarkanian's office on Thursday morning and that you and he had an altercation."

"But that doesn't mean I killed him."

"She also said you said you were a personal injury lawyer named Brian Bellamy. She gave me a business card with his name and your fingerprints."

"So what? You ever watch the Rockford Files?"

"I don't get you."

"He had all kinds of business cards. It goes with the territory."

"And?"

"Yeah, I gave his receptionist the card, but that doesn't make her a murder witness, unless she actually saw me doing it, which she didn't, 'cause I didn't do it."

"But you know who did."

"And that would make me an accessory, wouldn't it?"

Karsagian nodded and sat on the other end of the bunk. "We rousted you 'cause we figured you knew more than you were telling."

"All you had to do was ask."

"Okay, I'm asking now."

"First of all, I flew to San Francisco late Thursday night with Ms. Lamont. I got back around 1:00 a.m. Saturday morning, and went straight to Bobby's house in City Terrace."

"So why did you hold back on Thursday?"

"Would you have believed me?"

"Not 'til we'd checked it out, no."

"So either way we'd have landed in here."

"Yeah, I guess."

"You guess?" They looked at me without expression. "And can you guess where Bobby is?"

Jansen said, "Next door."

"Is he okay?"

He snickered. "About the same as you."

I nodded and wanted nothing more than to knock the smirk off his face. I put that thought on hold and continued, "We drank a few beers and went to sleep. The only time I'd ever seen Tarkanian was Thursday morning."

"Why'd you think he'd be interested in personal injury cases?"

I sighed inwardly. I knew where this was heading and unless I revealed Halladay's involvement, which I was avoiding like grim death, this could be a very slippery slope. Right at the moment the death certificate was sitting in the glove compartment in my Camry.

"I was tipped off that he might be involved in Cicero's death, and used that as a ruse to get in to see him because I felt he was the guy who signed the death certificate."

"How in hell did you figure out that this dead doctor, the same guy who had his face burned off with a blowtorch, was the one who signed the death certificate? Unless you already had it, in which case, you should've also told us that on Thursday afternoon."

"After I realized Cicero wasn't killed in a hit-and-run, one of my contacts told me to check out Tarkanian."

"Crane," said Jansen, "you're not getting out of here until you produce that contact."

I ignored Jansen and continued to address Karsagian. "I tell sawbones I have evidence he signed Cicero's death warrant. He looks like he's about to have a heart attack and he tells me that the family called him, and he went over to their house. It turns out that Cicero's had a massive myocardial infarction and that his gig's up."

"Wow, you're really quite the detective," said Jansen.

"Yeah, I am. Thanks."

"It wasn't a compliment, asshole."

"Knock it off!" snapped Karsagian. "Finish what you were saying."

"I happen to know that nobody in Cicero's family was around when he got whacked, so I knew the doctor's lying. I threaten to make a citizen's arrest and this time I really thought he was gonna stroke out. He says that Koncak and Fishburne, you know, the two fake cops you still haven't found?" They looked at me like I was a freshly laid turd. I grinned and continued, "He told me they still owed him 5 large and were sending someone to pay him off Friday, at the McDonald's on 3rd, in Koreatown. I send Bobby to tail whoever makes the drop, and he confronts him. The dude tells him that Koncak used to live in his building and that his name is Ernie, but that's all he knows."

"You should've told us this on Thursday," said Karsagian.

"Yeah, except Bobby didn't witness the exchange 'til late Friday afternoon."

"So why didn't you tell us on Thursday that they were gonna pay him off on Friday?"

"I didn't think it really much mattered. Turns out I was right."

"Wrong. You concealed key evidence concerning a capital crime," barked Jansen. "You, Crane, are a true asshole."

"I know this might be difficult for you, Jansen, but try and think it through. If you'd have arrested Tarkanian, he'd have been sprung in five minutes. We all know that. You're not gonna hold a guy for signing a phony death certificate. You'd release him and give him a date. And you might tip off the medical board to start proceedings to get his license pulled. But that's it. Tarkanian got in bed with the wrong snake and got bit. He knew too much, so they smoked him."

"Is that supposed to be funny?"

"You made it very clear you weren't interested in solving Cicero's murder. You wanted to pinch the fake cops. Had you done it, the doc might still be alive."

Jansen was incredulous. "You're blaming us?"

"Why not? It's as ridiculous as blaming me."

He looked at Karsagian. "I need some quality alone time with the prisoner."

The detective ignored him and said quietly, "We haven't been able to find 'em. Can you?"

I sighed. "Maybe."

Karsagian stood up and paced around as best he could, given the limited space of my cell.

I watched him and said, "Arnold's the key to all this."

"Why do you think that?"

"The guy's a psycho. Everything's a game to him."

"How so?" asked Jansen.

"I'm working for Ms. Lamont. Clipper's already got his fingers into Richard and his money; now he wants her and her money. But, what's more important to him, is how he plays the game."

There was a weighty silence and when Karsagian spoke again, it was with immense gravity.

"We don't have much to connect Clipper to the actor's death. Just because he had an altercation with him, doesn't mean he was involved in his murder."

I grinned and shook my head in disbelief. "Wait, isn't that exactly what I said to you when you accused me of murdering Tarkanian, because I'd argued with him?"

Trapped, the cops glanced at each other. Then Jansen said, "So what?"

"I know thinking is a struggle for him, but I'm surprised at you, Karsagian."

Instead of lunging at me, or sniping back, Jansen just stared. I locked eyes with him, and we both knew that a reckoning was coming.

Karsagian said, "I don't buy your story about getting tipped off that Tarkanian could be dirty, and I don't believe you can produce your contact."

"I never said I would."

"I'm real tired of your shell game. Now either you tell me what you've been leaving out, or I'll find probable cause to transport you to Men's Central, and put you in K10 with Mario and Sergio and Bustamante. You feel me?"

Jansen finally looked happy. "You're gonna end up with your ass in the air."

"How could I have whacked the doc when I was in San Francisco?"

"Don't know and don't care," hissed Jansen. "But unless you tell us everything, you're gonna get well and truly fucked."

"I want my attorney."

The atmosphere changed as they exchanged concerned glances.

"You can't deny me. You do, and it'll go even worse for you when it comes out that a licensed detective, an innocent licensed detective, was arrested, incarcerated, beaten and denied legal counsel."

They looked at each other and although a lot of bad things happen to prisoners, they knew that this was one problem that could blow up in their faces.

Karsagian said, "We'll get you your phone call."

"Thanks."

"Fuck you," snarled Jansen.

"I will tell you this; I didn't whack the doc, didn't have anything to do with it directly or indirectly and you both know that. Right?"

"Go on," the detective said.

"While Clipper's the key, there's someone even bigger to be had, who, I believe, is directly involved and, is pulling most, if not all the strings."

The tension in the cell was palpable. "Who?" asked Karsagian.

"James Halladay."

"*The* James Halladay?"

"No other."

"Jesus fucking Christ."

The cops were salivating like two starving dogs at a banquet. I told them how he'd insisted that his involvement be hushed up, how he'd produced the phony death certificate and how he'd said that if I didn't play ball, I'd never work again. They listened in silence and I could feel their wheels churning.

"Are you willing," said Karsagian, "to testify before the grand jury?"

"In return for immunity."

"Jesus," said Karsagian, "you want a lot, don't you?"

"It's my ass on the line, not yours."

He nodded. "All right."

Jansen was livid. "You're not seriously gonna give this asshole immunity?"

"Relax yourself."

"This is bullshit."

"You can leave, Jansen," I quipped.

It was too much for him and he flailed with a wild left. I swept the blow away and hit him hard in the left kidney. He screamed and went down like the sack of shit he is.

As Karsagian yanked him to his feet, he wrenched his arm away. "Get the fuck off'a me!"

He guided him to the door. "You deserved that."

"I hate that son of a bitch!"

"I don't want this collar screwed up. Get out and stay out."

I wiggled my fingers at Jansen and smiled.

He said, "I'll see you soon enough."

"Anytime, bro."

His glare was unadulterated hatred. Then he left.

Karsagian got on the phone. "I want James Halladay picked up and brought down to Parker for questioning…yeah that's right, him…okay."

There's nothing the law loves more than going after a dirty, powerful, high-priced lawyer.

The detective hung up and turned to me. "I'm gonna let you and your buddy go, but, and you hear me now, Nick, if it turns out that your fingers are dirty, in any way, I'll let Jansen take over the case. We clear?"

I nodded solemnly.

They gave us back our personal effects and guns, and we took a taxi out to an impound lot in Culver City to retrieve Leo's Yukon. Why they stashed it way out in Culver City when there were three lots nearby is beyond me, but I suspect it had something to do with Mr. Green. When we got there, it was obvious that the vehicle had been searched. On the drive back, as we sat in traffic on Interstate 10, Bobby, feening for CNN, snapped on the radio. The newscaster announced a breaking story about a prominent Los Angeles defense attorney who had been abducted from his Hollywood Hills mansion. LAPD had found signs of a break-in and struggle; the living room was trashed.

I glanced at Bobby. "I almost feel sorry for him."

"Screw that asshole."

"I said, 'almost.'"

Bobby nodded and we fell silent. Then a few minutes later he spoke up. "Dude, we gotta talk about something. The silence is killing me."

"Relax, bro. We're almost home."

"I wanna tell you this story."

I could tell that it was important to him, so I smiled and replied, "Okay, sure."

His words came slowly, cryptically, like they held both question and answer. "It was maybe five years after I'd got back from Nam and by then, I'd pretty much reached the end of my rope. I couldn't get Charlie out of my mind. Dude was haunting me. I was in San Francisco and had discovered some caves at a beach, near Half Moon Bay, south of the City. So I drive down there late one afternoon. I'm wearing fatigues and carrying my Bowie knife. "The caves are like dark triangles in the rock face, and I sit down below them on the beach, facing the water, watching the tide come in. The sun's going down so I take off my prosthesis, bury it in the sand, and just sit there, deliberately waiting. The tide comes in and pretty soon the water's up to my neck."

He looked at me and although I wanted to acknowledge him, I kept my eyes on the road.

"Anyway, the undertow was powerful and started pulling me out to sea. It's completely dark, no stars, just blackness everywhere. I spent half my boyhood in Mobile in the water, and I'm a damned good swimmer, so I decide to strike out for those caves, but each wave is bigger than the one before, and the harder I fight, the more I'm being sucked out to sea. I'm fighting for my life now, don't know how I did it but somehow I reach the headland. Had to be half a mile out. Waves as big as mountains. Suddenly the undertow hits some type of cross current and propels me back in toward those caves."

"Jesus, bro."

"With each wave, I'm carried closer to the caves, but there's rocks and the waves are bursting like napalm. There's nothing I can do. So I don't."

"You don't fight it?"

"No point. I wasn't afraid anymore. I felt peaceful. It was great. The Vietnamese have this old saying, 'water will always find the easiest path,' and it did. A wave picked me up and surfed me right between the rocks and suddenly I was in one of the caves. It seemed like it happened instantly but it must've really taken ten minutes or so. I'm inside the cave and it's pitch black, and I know Charlie's in there too. I killed those gook tunnel fuckers more times than I can remember, but--"

Bobby paused and his eyes glistened. I wanted to say something but knew better and kept my mouth shut.

"--But he took my soul." He fell silent and dragged one of his rough, massive hands across his eyes. He sighed deeply and continued. "With each wave, the water gets higher. If I stay there, I'll drown. If I go deeper in the tunnel, Charlie'll kill me. Fucked if I do. Fucked if I don't. The tunnel's almost full and the water's ice cold. I found a spot, like an indent in the rocks and wedged myself in. I pulled my blade and for some damn reason I still can't figure out, I ran my thumb across it. I'm bleeding like a stuck pig and my blood's mixing with the water and I know that soon enough some fucking shark's gonna smell it and I'm dead, if Charlie don't get me first."

"You once told me that the enemy could smell you in the tunnels."

He nodded, his jaw set tight, the muscles flexing rapidly. "We could smell each other. Each other's fear."

We were finally off the freeway, getting close to Bobby's house, so I pulled over and parked to give him time to finish his story

"Then I see him."

"Who?"

"Charlie."

"You hallucinated?"

"No. Only he wasn't a gook with an AK, he was a shark. A Great White, I guess. It was massive and just cruised right past me."

"Fuck, bro."

"It freaked me. I suddenly realized that Charlie was in Nam, dead and buried, where I'd left him and where he wanted to be. But the shark was real. You understand?"

"Not really."

"It was the physical manifestation of my own fear."

"Physical manifestation?"

"That's what my therapist said."

"I didn't know you had a therapist."

"Fuck, yeah. Why d'ya think I'm still alive?

"Okay. Got it."

"It sucks being alone. You've got Cassady. It's the loneliness that's killing me now."

"I didn't know, bro. You always told me you liked being alone, with your goats." I knew it was a lie and felt instantly guilty.

Bobby gave me a strange look. "I do, mostly."

I nodded and waited for him to finish his story.

"Anyway, the shark smelled blood and I knew it was only a matter of time before he figured out where I was."

"How did you see it? I mean, you said it was really dark?"

"Full moon that's reflecting off the water."

I nodded.

"What I didn't know was that an injured seal was also hiding in the cave. It tried to make a run for it, but it was no good. The shark snapped down on him and bit him in half. Man, I've never seen so much blood in the water. The shark eats what he wants and leaves. There's bits of meat and blubber and blood floating around me. But I was damned glad it was him and not me. I put the knife away and try to hang on. I'm freezing and can't stop trembling and my teeth chatter so hard, I think I'm gonna bite my tongue off. At times I prayed and at times I screamed, and some of the time I sang those fucking marching songs that we all knew. Finally the water recedes. Even the longest night has to end."

I looked at him and I was proud to know the man.

"The tide goes out, and I follow it stomping through the sand into a cold, grey dawn. You know how it gets on the California coast up north. Earth and sky are a sheet of gray mist. I dig up my prosthesis and get out of there. I had a good breakfast that morning."

"What did you eat?"

"You know, the heart attack stuff -- eggs and bacon and hash browns and blueberry pancakes with gobs of butter and three or four cups of coffee. All the while I was shivering and my clothes are still wet. The waitress is looking at me like I'm crazy, but keeps filling my cup. I tipped her a five and drove back to San Francisco."

"That's why I respect you."

"Because I left her a five?"

"No, because you've made it this far. You decided to live."

"You know what, bubba, that's why I respect myself."

PART THREE

CHAPTER I
Ladies Love Outlaws

IT WAS SUNDAY AFTERNOON AND the air was clear. People thronged the open-air markets. We stopped at a burrito stand near a park and watched the Aztec dancers go through their paces while we ate.

Bobby slathered hot sauce onto his burrito and washed it down with Diet Coke. "What do we do now?"

"We wait while LAPD look for Ernie and Tom--"

"--The fake cops?"

"Yeah and come all over themselves trying to find Halladay."

"Clipper, that motherfucka, must be in ecstasy."

"He might be. Halladay sure isn't." I finished my burrito and swigged the rest of my Sprite.

"I never saw that coming, him snatching the lawyer."

"All that's left now is for him to get his hands on Jade. Then it's mission accomplished."

"Not exactly."

"What d'you mean?"

"Clipper wants you along with everybody else."

"Then let the fucker come get me."

Bobby finished his diet coke and dumped the can into the blue recycle bin. "You know your Revolutionary War history, right?"

"Pretty well."

"How did we turn it around?"

"Nathaniel Greene and the Swamp Fox, Francis Marion. Guerrilla tactics. Strike fast, hit hard, lose the battle, win the war."

"Very good. Most Americans have no idea how we won. They may not even know that there was a war."

"Sad but true."

"You know what made the Vietnam conflict so difficult?"

"We faced a better enemy."

"They haunted us. Our command did everything possible to adjust to their guerilla tactics, and never succeeded. But that wasn't the real reason."

"They were fanatics. Willing to die for their cause."

"Bingo."

"You're talking about Clipper."

"Yep. From what you've told me, you're right, this is all a game to him and he's exactly as crazy as the Cong was."

"Then we better make sure that we find him before he finds us."

Bobby nodded and burped. It smelled like beans and guacamole. We waited while the wind wafted it away. "Sorry, bro."

I shrugged.

"You know, the Vietcong had their own way of inflicting ultimate fear. It was more terrifying than death itself."

I looked at him. The sun went behind a cloud and I shivered.

"They'd cut their victims into three pieces. Buddhists believe that robs you of your soul. To our South Vietnamese allies, that was 1000 times worse than any torture or death."

"That's why Clipper had them cut Ron Cera's head off."

"Imagine what he'll do to Jade if he gets hold of her."

When we got to Bobby's house, the television was off and the radio was blasting hip-hop. Cassady, who was wearing a tight-fitting pullover jersey, was teaching Jade dance moves. She had tied her floral blouse above her waist displaying the firmest, tautest belly anyone had ever seen complete with the ubiquitous belly piercing that the girls of today favor. Brad was sitting on the sofa with a look of wonder, taking it all in. Cassady, Jade and Brad weren't aware that Bobby and I were watching them.

"This is the America I adore," Brad said. "Hot chicks with no morals. The world knows we're bound to fall but can't wait to fall with us."

"This isn't hot," said Cassady. "This is lukewarm. If I showed you hot, it would--" She saw my face and gasped. "Oh, God!"

She fell into my arms, her chest crushed against me, and I knew why I had fallen in love that night in San Francisco in 1984.

Jade and Brad were stunned.

Cassady led me down the hall into the spare room. She swept a few of Jade's garments off the bed and we lay down.

"Who did that to you?"

"Doesn't matter."

She gently kissed my swollen face, struggling to hold back her tears.

"Did you give as good as you got?"

"Better."

"So what's gonna happen now?"

"We all need to lay low and let five-oh do their thing. In the meantime, let's get out of here."

Cassady stood up, pulling me to my feet. "And where are we going?"

"You'll see."

We went back to the living room where the music was still playing, but now no one was dancing. I turned it off and the silence crushed us.

I said, "Have a seat, Jade." Cassady took her by the hand and steered her toward the sofa. She looked bewildered and very young. "Halladay's been kidnapped. Those two fake cops, Fishburne and Koncak, snatched him. We still don't know what their real names are but we do know they work for Clipper. They're also the ones that abducted your father."

Cassady held her hands, but Jade was wooden and didn't react. The shock was starting to penetrate. "They killed him, didn't they?" Her voice, low.

"Halladay wanted him dead. They grabbed him but turned him over to Clipper instead. I don't know what happened after that."

I'd seen Jade sink before but this time it was downright scary. Fifteen minutes before her face had been bright and vibrant. Now it was like a death-mask, something you'd find painted on a sarcophagus. When she finally spoke her voice was flat, toneless, which was somehow worse than hysteria. "They tortured Daddy, just like Ron."

"No way to know for sure."

"Don't bullshit me." There was no venom in her voice, just resignation.

There was nothing any of us could say. This path she had to walk alone.

"Probably."

"And now they're going to torture Halladay."

I shrugged. "I guess so."

Her tears flowed silent and nameless.

"Cassady, grab some of our things and let's go."

She nodded, looked at Jade and headed for the spare room.

Brad said, "Where are you going?"

"To spend some time with my wife." He nodded and fear drifted into his eyes. "Bobby's staying here?"

"Bet your ass I am." Bobby answered for me.

Jade went to the bathroom and closed the door. We could hear her crying.

I said quietly, "Watch her."

"Can I keep Cassady's Beretta?" asked Brad.

"I've got plenty of weapons, Sport," said Bobby, a gleam in his eyes.

We exchanged glances. "Be ready to move fast if I call you."

Bobby nodded and Cassady returned with a flight bag. "Let's go," she said, placing her pistol in its hard case, putting it in her bag.

I drove the Yukon to Leo's, with Cassady following in the Impala. The place was deserted, so I parked next to my Camry and dropped the keys in the mailbox. Then we drove south into Orange County, armed to the teeth. Cassady nuzzled over against me as Waylon Jennings sang "Ladies Love Outlaws" on the radio.

We stopped in Westminster where we had Vietnamese food and drank several glasses of sweet Thai iced tea. Then we found a nondescript Motel 6 in Garden Grove, off Beach Boulevard. Cassady tenderly washed and cleaned my damaged face and put drops in my bloodshot eye. She placed her Beretta on the nightstand and we made love. Then we slept and woke up around seven the next morning.

"Maybe we'll just stay here for a while," murmured Cassady. "If you really think we can't go back to the house."

"When this is over, we'll call Tomas and have him replace the French doors."

"I loved them," she sighed. "I hope you shot those bastards."

I said nothing but I think she felt me tense up. She started to speak and stopped.

"I'm gonna hit the shower," I said and started to get up.

"Not before you fuck me."

"Can I pee first?"

After that we slept some more, got up around 10 and showered. Clean clothes can feel so damn good. We checked our guns, dropped off the keycard with reception and split. We drove around aimlessly for a while looking at nothing in particular and when we'd worked up an appetite we stopped and had an amazing Vietnamese lunch, then got back on the road. Cassady drove and I called Maleah.

Stephanie, Cassady's sister, answered, serious and dour as ever. "Are you guys okay?"

"Why wouldn't we be?"

"Because my sister didn't look too good when I dropped her off at the airport."

"She's great and sitting right next to me. Now let me speak to Maleah, please."

"Fine."

Maleah, excited, blurted with that childish enthusiasm I love so much, "I'm going to beat Sam, Dad. I already took his queen."

"Good work. Now do you remember how to do a checkmate the easy way?"

"How many times are you gonna tell me?"

"Got it."

"Are you with Mom?"

"Yep and we just had Vietnamese food for lunch."

"No fair!"

"It was delicious," I said with an emphasis on the "Dee" and laughed.

"I thought you were chasing the bad guys."

"I am. We're just taking a little break."

"Hurry up, Dad, I had trouble sleeping last night."

"Did you leave the light on?"

"Yeah, but I was still scared. I had to watch a video to get to sleep."

"Which one?"

"Some dumb romance. Stephanie doesn't have the kind of comedies I like."

"Okay, gotta go."

"Can I speak to mom?"

"She's driving."

"Okay. Love ya, Dad."

"Love ya too."

I called Tony but he didn't pick up. On our way back to the motel, we stopped at a Blockbuster and rented some videos. Back to our room, we took a shower together, stretched out on the bed, and watched "The Quiet American" with Michael Caine. When it was over, I stepped outside and called Bobby.

"Nick, we're all starting to go stir crazy."

"Then it's lucky I got a job for you."

"Tonight?" His excitement was obvious at the prospect of something dangerous.

"You got it."

"I'm waitin', Boss."

"Go to Home Depot and pick up a portable reciprocating saw, and a couple of vanadium blades."

"Okay."

"Bring a striker, and I'll meet you at 11:30 on the corner of Franklin and Beachwood. Use the van."

"Got it."

"Wear dark clothes and bring the bullet-proof vests, helmets and some heavy artillery."

Bobby chuckled. "Nice."

"Did you talk to pig boy?"

"Not exactly. I grunted at him. We're cool."

"You sure?"

What did I just say, bro?"

"You're the man."

"Best damn believe it."

"Later, Bobby."

I hung up and went back inside. Cassady threw me a dazzling but enigmatic smile and went back to reading. I flicked on the TV and watched *Family Guy*, my favorite. I felt kind of bad because Maleah wasn't there to watch it with me.

CHAPTER II
Church of the Poisoned Mind

Around 10:15 I phoned a taxi service and 15 minutes later a bearded, middle-eastern Yellow Cab driver knocked on our door.

"You called a cab, Sir?"

"I did. I'll be right out."

"Okay," he replied and went back to his cab.

I closed the door, holstered my guns and slipped on a jacket.

Cassady tried to pretend that she wasn't worried, but we both knew better. I kissed her, first her left eye and then her right and walked out, closing the door firmly. I got into the back seat and made eye contact with the driver.

"Hollywood Hills."

He sensed I didn't want to talk and nodded. It was a cloudy night with a nip in the air, and he drove smoothly. The fare came to $80. I handed him a Franklin.

"Keep it."

"Thank you, Sir."

I was a few minutes early so I walked down the block to an Exxon Mobil, grabbed a coffee and waited outside sipping slowly. At a little before 11:30, I went back to the corner. Bobby pulled up in his blue, 1990, Ford E-series van and I jumped in the passenger side. It's fitted out with double-decker storage cabinets, a small sink, refrigerator and enormous Captain's chairs. It's always reminded me of the Scooby Doo van. We were carrying an arsenal -- pump shotguns, handguns, fully auto machine pistols and an AK-47.

"Where to?"

"Take a right up the hill and park in front of the apartment building."

We were both tense and drove in silence. He parked and I clambered into the back. There were two Kevlar vests, and a couple of big-pocketed, safari bush jackets, with matching cargo pants. Although Kevlar is bullet-proof, it's a misnomer because a 9 millimeter bullet will still result in a hellacious bruise, and some blunt trauma organ damage, but it's a big step up from no protection. I handed one to Bobby and got changed, strapping on a vest and matching groin protector. I inserted a steel trauma pad into the front of the vest, buttoned up my jacket and pulled on my pants. Bobby did the same and looked like even more the Neanderthal than usual.

"Which sidearms?" I asked.

"Where are we going?"

"Underground."

"A bomb shelter?"

"No. A labyrinth type bunker that extends all the way up a hillside, and is apparently terraced into separate floors."

"Where is this place?"

"Up by the Hollywood Reservoir. Belongs to Clipper."

"This should be interesting."

"He doesn't live there now, it's rented out. But under the lease he still has access to the bunker. I don't know what's in it or if he's even using it."

"So why are we going in?"

"Dunno, bro, just a feeling I have."

"You and your hunches, Nick."

I shrugged. He looked grim.

"It was built by an eccentric millionaire in the '50s who apparently feared the Russians."

"Smart man. I still fear the Russians."

"I've got my Colt and my Walther."

"I've got two nines and that reciprocating saw."

"Let's do it."

On the drive up, two LAPD cruisers passed us, probably on their way back from Halladay's house. One slowed down and took a long look, but didn't stop us. Bobby drove slowly and carefully up the small, winding roads that get narrower and twistier the higher you go. The streets were all but deserted and lights from the houses cut thinly through the overcast night. We turned west onto Beachwood and drove slowly 'til we came to the front of Clipper's old home. Then we drove around back and started up the access road. We parked off the road at the base of the steep incline, near some shrubbery that partially concealed the van. After locking up the front, we climbed in the back. We strapped on buck knives, put on our Kevlar, military style helmets, grabbed flashlights, locked up the back and started trudging up the hillside.

The moonless night gave us some cover and the city lights were distant, swallowed by the greater darkness. We would be hard to spot from either the road below or from the house above, should Reggie Mount be peering out of his back windows. I imagined him working steadily in an upstairs study, musing on the nature of evil. We came to the rock wall as a sudden wind moaned through the foliage. I could make out the grain lines in the stainless steel door, and flicked my flashlight to low beam. The padlock was gone and the hasp was closed but unlocked. Fear that tasted like gunmetal started at the base of my throat and moved down through my chest. Sweating, my breath coming in short rasps, I shivered and stepped back to control myself.

We stood shoulder to shoulder and Bobby gave me a grim look. "Almost like they're expecting us."

I stashed the flight bag containing the saw in some brush. Bobby pulled his Beretta and screwed on the silencer. Sliding my Colt out of its holster, I carefully opened the hasp on the door. I turned sideways trying to be invisible as Bobby flattened out on the road, gripping his pistol with both hands, aiming into where the darkness would rush out to meet us when I opened the door. I exhaled and pulled it open. Nothing. Dead silence except for the low whisper of the nighttime wind. We inched forward and the beams from our flashlights dissolved into what seemed an immense blackness. Cement steps descended, matching the angle of the ceiling. Had my heart not been doing its best to bang its way out of my chest, I would've had vertigo.

Bobby peered down into the gloom. "How come the freakin' steps go down, but the hillside goes up?"

"Bizarre sense of humor. Makes it creepier."

He nodded grimly and gestured impatiently with his pistol. Bobby led the way, and I tried to count the steps but immediately lost track. At the base of the staircase, we came to a landing enclosed by two by fours with insulation nailed between the ribs. The ceiling was cracked and discolored, and the drip of moisture sounded loud in the stillness. To our right, an opening ran into a low corridor. We looked at each other and entered. It was maybe 30 feet long, ending in an ascending staircase, which led to another similar landing, only this time the connecting passageway was finished. The walls were painted with Mediterranean designs, similar to the tiled steps I'd been descending when I saw Halladay jogging the first time I came here.

There was no sign of anyone having recently passed through, but, we proceeded with great caution. As we threaded our way through the maze, I was struck by the horrifying thought that we could be locked in by someone simply attaching a new padlock to the outer door. If Bobby shared my thoughts, he kept it to himself. He was in his element, securing each passageway, guiding us deeper into this underground riddle. Although he's not my equal when it comes to pure investigation, he's a superb scout and if anyone could lead us to the heart of this labyrinth and back out to the world above, Bobby was the guy.

After 20 minutes of slow progress, we came to a corridor which sloped down at a 30-degree angle and narrowed as we descended. There was a round hatch at the bottom, not unlike the door to an old furnace. Bobby took a deep breath, grabbed the handle and swung it open. Our beams barely cut the blackness as we descended down a wide ladder staircase, shoulder to shoulder. Halfway down, we triggered a motion detector and I shuddered as the dark was replaced by an overwhelming brightness.

Steel support columns had been sprayed with an orange, furry, soundproofing material, giving the cavernous room an industrial feel. Nickel-plated art deco chandeliers hung in silence. The walls were painted with party scenes, in which attractive young men and eyeless servants carrying trays of drugs and delicacies posed and mingled.

"I don't like this guy," said Bobby. "He's way too modern and efficient. Give me an old school psycho any time. Somebody I can relate too."

"Look for the control panel for the motion detector."

As we searched around, Bobby said, "It's as hidden as the light switches."

"Yeah. Not good." Unease was crawling up my spine. I had the distinct feeling we were being watched.

It was beyond disturbing. At the back of the room, three staircases threaded upward. Black leather furniture contrasted with an ornate Persian rug. Speaker cabinets were mounted on the wall. Flat screen TVs and a state-of-the-art sound system threatened to display things that few had ever seen, and sounds that could never be unheard. Lawyers' bookshelves held a small library. I opened one volume, men and boys and animals engaged in vile practices. My hands shook and I felt sick as I replaced it on the shelf.

"What is it?"

"You don't wanna know."

His eyes narrowed and he reached to pick it up. I didn't try to stop him. Some things you have to find out for yourself. He turned a page and rage creased his big face. He replaced the book and took out a block of C4 from one of his cargo pockets.

I was stunned. "What the fuck?"

"There's only one way to cure this disease. He held up the C4. "With this."

"I get it, bro, but first we have to find out what's down here."

He nodded and put the C4 away.

"What's this thing that Clipper has about eyes?"

I shrugged. "See no evil. Feel no evil?"

"This fucker's pure evil."

Bobby led the way and we mounted the right hand staircase. The area in front of us illuminated, while the main room behind us went dark. The stairs led directly into a galley-style kitchen and again, lights flickered to life as we stepped inside. It was all ultra-modern and very expensive stainless steel appliances and upscale cookware, but without any signs of recent use.

I checked behind a Norman Rockwell calendar hanging on the wall just inside the kitchen door, and found the control panel. I pressed the dimmer and the lights faded. Bobby grabbed his flashlight and I flipped off the lights completely, plunging the room into total darkness and then brought them back up.

"Detectors for every room. But why?"

Bobby shrugged. "Dunno. I get using dimmers, for mood an' all, but not the whole motion thing."

"Unless it's for security?"

We descended back into the main room. Using my flashlight, I searched above the light fixtures and found what I was looking for. Just below the ceiling, in each corner, were tiny, recessed security cameras. I pointed to them.

"Shit," said Bobby. "You think they've made us?"

"Guess we'll find out soon enough."

Stepping it up, we took the left hand staircase. When we reached the top, we stepped onto a large landing, furnished with antiques. The walls were painted yellow in a contemporary scroll style, and a single step led to a flat panel door made of dark hardwood. A stainless steel sign with letters in black calligraphy hung at eye level: Abandon All Hope, Ye Who Enter Here.

"I've seen that before," I said.

"*Dante's Inferno.*"

"Yeah. You've read it?"

"Several times."

"That's amazing? When I read it in college, it freaked me out. I had to force myself to finish it."

"When I got back from Nam, it somehow seemed fitting. The only thing I could find that helped me make sense of the horror of it all."

I nodded and grabbed the door handle. Bobby moved to the right, and I pushed it open. Soft, moody light flooded a well-furnished, high-ceilinged bedroom. In the middle, lacy lavender curtains surrounded a four-poster bed. Saloon style swinging doors led into an exotically tiled bathroom with recessed lighting. It was divided into sections with two wooden toilets sitting side-by-side in a separate cubicle, finished in Asian black lacquer with gold designs. An entire wall of the bedroom was dedicated to what had to be Clipper's intricate, precise, and very disturbing artwork. Pen and ink in the hands of a madman can be terrifying. Horrific creatures, twisted and deformed, tortured, raped, and devoured each other.

"It's the nine circles of Hell, with his own twist."

"Fucking weird, bro."

It was unnerving. That someone as evil as Clipper was a first-rate artist was troubling. I'd been staring at the wall for some time when Bobby shook me out of it.

"We gotta keep moving."

He yanked me away and we walked out of that nightmare. We descended back to the main room and immediately started up the center staircase, which was carpeted in black with ebony handrails. Halfway up we were plunged into darkness.

"No motion detectors," whispered Bobby.

"I feel safer this way."

Our flashlights probed the darkness and at the top of the stairs we came to a landing where a second staircase intersected it and angled sharply downward. There were no handrails and the walls had been sprayed with black powder paint.

"Jesus," said Bobby. "Feels like we're stepping deeper into hell."

We continued on and, after about 100 feet, the tunnel forked.

"Left or right?" I asked.

He said nothing and I followed as he stomped off down the left hand tributary. After about a minute, we came to a barrier made of flat-stacked rock. It too was painted black.

Bobby looked at me, his eyes narrowing, "What's the point of this? A tunnel that goes nowhere?"

"Maybe that is the point."

He turned and I caught a glimpse of his face, his square jaw set, his sad eyes hooded. He muttered something under his breath and started back up the corridor. When we reached the other branch he picked up the pace, striding rapidly forward. To my surprise, a dim light shone in the distance. We came to a large landing with the ceiling supported by four thick cylindrical pillars. This time the walls were painted to resemble a winter forest scene -- snow on the ground, pine trees, their needleless branches extending toward a thin sky, a family of white foxes hurrying toward their hillside burrow. The work was painstaking and precise.

"Glad to see him do something in color," said Bobby.

Twenty feet in front of us, twin inlaid wooden doors topped by a stained glass archway suggested a church or sanctuary. Low curved steps in natural granite led up to the doors. Guns drawn, we moved forward. I turned the knob, pulled the door open and we crossed the threshold. The air was thick and a putrid stench, one we both instantly recognized, wrapped itself around us. I had the odd thought that somebody should open a window. I played my flashlight across the ceiling and walls of a huge rectangular space with a beamed cathedral ceiling. Rows of wooden pews faced forward, above which chandeliers hung at intervals, but offered no light. At the front, a thick burgundy velvet stage curtain hanging ceiling to floor extended from one wall to the other. Nativity scenes that might normally have been inspiring made me shudder. Men and young boys in naked undress mingled with goats, sheep and donkeys.

"I can't take much more of this shit," growled Bobby.

We climbed the five small steps up to the stage, pulled aside the velvet curtain and stood as still as the body that was strapped across a rough, plank table. The victim had apparently starved to death. The emaciation was absolute and the remains, what were left of them, looked like something out of a horror movie. The flesh, blackening and putrefied, was covered with maggots and nocturnal beetles. The clothes had been removed and stacked on an altar next to piles of mold-covered cakes, cheese, bread, rotten milk, bottled water and wrinkled fruit. Above that hung a plain wooden cross. It was undoubtedly Cicero and he was very dead. A single, straight-backed chair sat near the body, with a red oak pulpit completing the arrangement.

Bobby, his eyes glazed, said, "Is that him, Cicero?"

"Yeah, I guess it is."

BANG! The slug seared the air right in between us, slamming into Cicero's skull, spraying congealed blood, brain matter and maggots through the air. The room erupted with light from the overhead inset fixtures. Reggie Mount, his green eyes ablaze with fury, aimed his .38 at us.

"How dare you enter this church and invade the sanctity of this man's death?" His voice, shrill with excitement, laced with insanity. I took a step away from Bobby in the hopes of distracting Mount, so that Bobby could get the drop on him. But Reggie Mount was cunning, and not to be so easily outsmarted. He grinned and jacked back the hammer on his gun. "You're gonna have to do better than that."

I nodded and smiled. "No harm in trying."

"Your weapons? Put 'em on the altar."

We complied, carefully placing them as far away from things that crawled as possible.

He flicked his gun at me. "Grab the rope and tie up Hulk Hogan."

"Where's Clipper?"

"Don't be in such a rush to meet the devil," he grinned.

"And what's he to you, Reggie?"

"My nephew." A shiver raced down my spine. He must have sensed it and smiled, but it was completely without warmth. "Amusing that you didn't make the connection."

"I'll get over it."

"You know this guy?" Bobby was astonished.

"Met him last Thursday when I came looking for Clipper."

Agitated, Reggie gritted his teeth. "I said tie him up."

"Did he bring Richie here, to watch his dad die?"

"He most certainly did not."

"But wouldn't that have been the ultimate way to demonstrate his power over him, to get him to do exactly what he wants?"

"He already has total control over Richard."

"Then what does he want with Jade?"

"He'll be here soon. You can ask him yourself."

Bobby, the muscles in his body rippling as he prepared for combat, announced as if to an unseen moderator, "I can't wait to meet him."

Reggie was growing more arrogant by the second, Bobby more dangerous. Explosion time. I started laughing. Bobby remained coiled, ready to leap at the precise right millisecond.

Reggie, perplexed, stared at me. "What the hell's so damn funny?"

"Why'd you murder him?"

"Because he had it coming."

"You'll have to expound on that."

Reggie sighed and looked at me like I was a moron. "Mr. Lamont was no babe in the woods. During the course of our long vigil, he revealed that he was responsible for multiple homicides. Admittedly they were drug dealers and other types of criminals, but still, you get the point."

"But that doesn't give you the right to murder him."

"The right? The world doesn't run on who has the right. It runs on who has the power."

"So then what's the difference between you and him?"

"What about the hundreds, perhaps thousands, who overdosed on his product?"

"That's not for you to judge. And certainly not for you to--"

"--Hold on, Nick," said Bobby. "Maybe he's got a point."

"What?" The shock coursed through me.

"I fucking hate drug dealers. You know that."

"So what? You're not buying his bullshit, are you?"

Reggie was bemused by this sudden turn in events. His eyes darted from Bobby to me.

"A lotta Vietnamese and GIs died 'cause'a drugs."

I nodded, fully aware of why Bobby hated drugs so much.

Reggie's eyes narrowed. "You were In Country?"

"What?" said Bobby, pissed.

"Nam. You were in Nam?"

"Yeah. Tunnel rat."

Reggie Mount lowered his gun. "Jesus. You guys were crazy."

"1st Recon. 9th Cavalry," he smiled. "All in a day's work."

"I was a door gunner on a rescue chopper. Three tours. Almost 500 missions."

Bobby grinned. "And you call me crazy?"

They looked at each other, a mutual admiration society. I felt like I was watching a Monty Python sketch, but I let it play out.

"One of your guys saved my life," offered Reggie.

"Is that right?"

He nodded. "We'd just taken off from a hot zone, north of Saigon and the NVA opened up with a 50 cal. Blew me right out of the Huey. I dropped like a stone into a paddy field. Next thing I know, I'm being dragged into a tunnel."

Bobby's mouth fell open. "Where, where did it happen?"

"Why?" glared Reggie, suspiciously.

"Duc Ho, Quang Nai Province?"

"So what if it was?"

"You were cut up pretty bad."

"Uh-uh. I'm not falling for that."

"The Huey went down. No one but you survived."

A curious mixture of shock and disbelief spread across Reggie's face. "I don't know you. I'd remember."

"In the tunnel, there was a firefight. You got shot. Left forearm if my memory serves me well."

He stared blankly. "How could you know that?"

"Simple. I dragged you into the tunnel. Your arm, can I see it?"

Reggie's hard green eyes turned soft. Trembling, he began rolling up his sleeve. "Are you…I mean, it's not possible."

Bobby, 225 pounds of pure fighting mad, adrenaline-coiled muscle, nodded almost imperceptibly.

There it was, an old bullet wound, thick with white scar tissue, staring up at Reggie. "Shit." His tone was half-incredulous, half fait accompli.

Bobby smiled. "Long time no see, bro."

Looking down at his arm, Reggie licked his suddenly dry lips. "I dunno, I dunno what to say."

"Small world."

"Yeah." He looked sad, embarrassed and sighed, "SNAFU."

"Copy that."

They stared at each other in the charged silence.

Reggie looked down at his gun, then at me, then at Bobby. "I wish we'd met under different circumstances."

"Me too."

"I'd be KIA if it wasn't for you."

"Don't suppose you can let us sky out?"

Reggie's face creased with what might've passed for real emotion. "No. Sorry, I really am."

Bobby nodded. "A handshake then, after all these years."

"I can do better. You wanna go first? Your choice."

Bobby nodded and Reggie slipped the .38 into his left hand. He held out his right and took two steps forward, jacking back the hammer. Bobby stiffened and saluted. They were like marionettes on some infernal stage. Reggie came to attention and returned the salute. Bobby sprang, turning sideways, grabbing the .38 with his right, chopping him across the throat with his left. Sinking to his knees, Reggie's hands flew up to try and massage air back into his crushed larynx. Faster than I thought possible, Bobby wrapped his paws around his head, slamming him down on to the concrete floor. Now in full kill mode, enraged, he smashed his head so hard it made a hollow, cracking sound, like a coconut being broken open. Blood and pink brain matter oozed out of his skull. Reggie Mount twitched several times, his eyes glazed over and he died. Bobby stood up, breathing hard, eyes wild with blood lust.

The adrenaline was like a hurricane. "Let's get the fuck outta here."

He didn't move.

"Bobby!"

He looked at me and slowly, deliberately, pulled out the C4. "It's time."

"No. We can't go blowing up the Hollywood Hills."

"Cicero's dead and Jade doesn't need to see or know how much he suffered."

"Yeah, I get that but still."

"Plus our prints are all over the place."

"It doesn't matter. As much as I'd like to blow these bastards to hell, we can't."

Bobby nodded and sighed. "What about me?"

"What about you?"

"I just killed him."

"It was self-defense." Bobby looked skeptical. "Besides, they'll spend years analyzing Clipper's paintings, and who knows how many others he and his crew have murdered. There's probably DNA all over this place."

"I don't like it, but you're the boss."

I inwardly sighed with relief. "Ironic, huh, that you saved his life? I mean, what're the chances, right?"

"I didn't." He shrugged.

"What? But I thought--"

"--I'd heard about it from one of the grunts in my unit, who knew the guy that actually did save him." I didn't know what to say. I looked at him in amazement. "I figured we were screwed anyway, so there was nothing to lose."

The blood from Reggie Mount's head was oozing out and spreading across the concrete floor. I took a step to one side and grabbed my guns off the altar. "Get your guns and let's go."

Bobby picked his up, deliberately blowing off a maggot. "Bye, asshole." Then he turned to me, "You gonna call this in?"

"At some point."

He looked around. "This place is huge and I'll bet that we haven't explored half of it."

"I don't care. There's too much evil here."

"Heard that."

"Let it stay here."

He nodded and we got out like the house was on fire. Ten minutes later we passed through the stainless steel door and stepped out onto the windswept hillside.

"You see the bag?" I asked and played my flashlight over the brush.

"There."

I retrieved it and that's when it hit me. "Shit."

"What?"

"The surveillance tapes have to be in the main house somewhere."

I could barely keep up with Bobby, as he hammered up the access road to the back door. He reached for the handle and froze. "Wait. What if it's wired?"

"I dunno. I'm guessing there's a way into the labyrinth from the house. If I'm right, then it figures that the system's on."

"We need to get those tapes."

"The only way to not trip the alarm is to go back, through there." I pointed at the steel door.

"SNAFU," he said.

"Yep."

We headed back down the hill, pulled open the door and retraced our steps. We didn't speak. It was nasty. Sweat drenched us as the unknown chilled our bones. We've both seen our fair share of dead people, in my case mostly lying on cold mortuary slabs, but the vibe in there was as foreboding as anything I've ever experienced. Eventually, we reentered the perversity of Clipper's church. I almost expected Reggie to greet us, looking like Nosferatu, but he was as dead as the cold concrete he lay on. We sidestepped the spreading red ooze of his death, traversed the stage, past the crawling scavengers feasting on Cicero's stinking corpse, and found the passageway leading up to the main house.

The door into Reggie's living room was open. We cautiously entered and, using our flashlights, searched for the computer that the security cams would be wired into. I found it in a small, back office. The screen was on, showing the underground church in all its HD vulgarity.

Bobby said, "I wonder if there's a recording of Cicero's torture."

I clicked onto a folder entitled, Retribution. It contained about 20 clips. I clicked on one and it opened, showing Cicero, still very much alive, begging and screaming. It was hard to watch. In the background, I could just make out Reggie and behind him, in shadow, I knew it had to be Clipper. I felt sick, disgusted and wanted nothing more than to rain justice down on that sick son-of-a-bitch.

"We'll take the mainframe."

He looked around and found the alarm system control panel by the back door. "It's on, but if we're quick, we can make it to the van before the rent-a-cops get here."

I unplugged the computer, leaving the monitor on the desk. "Ready."

"I'll bolt and get the van. Hustle down as fast as you can. Just be careful and don't trip."

I nodded and Bobby reached for the handle. That's when the headlights blasted across the front door, as a car pulled up in front of the house.

"Shit." I hustled back into the office, replacing the computer on the desk.

Bobby, standing behind me, pulled out his gun. "Kill 'em?"

"Not unless we have to. Hide."

Before he could respond, the front door opened and the lights flipped on. Arnold Clipper, in all his malevolent glory, accompanied by two guys wearing Los Muertos patches, ambled in. They hadn't seen us, so I motioned Bobby to melt back into the shadows, which he did. I did the same and tried as best I could to slow my breathing.

"Reggie?" No response. I could hear Clipper move closer to the office. "Reggie!"

"Must be out," said a second voice.

"No, he'll be in his office, writing," declared Clipper. "Thinks he's Dostoevski."

Before I could move, he leaned in, the light from the hallway framing him, creating a grey silhouette. I held my breath, sweat running down my face, trigger finger twitching against the cold steel in my hand. Clipper turned around and went back into the hallway.

"He has to be downstairs," he said.

"Loco tio," said one of the bikers.

I could hear the three of them push through the door, then the creaking of the stairs as they descended into the labyrinth.

Bobby moved closer, his face, too, dripping with sweat. "Now," he said hoarsely.

I grabbed the computer and we hotfooted it out the back door. Outside, the air was crisp and cool, it felt like heaven as our sweat dried quickly. In the distance, halfway down the hill, I could see Bobby's blue van; a comforting bulk. I carefully placed the computer inside one of the cabinets. Quickly, we changed back into our civilian clothes, as if that would somehow erase the memory of what had transpired.

Nobody followed us. I tried to imagine the look on Arnold's face when he discovered his uncle lying there on the cold stone floor, his skull cracked open. We drove back to Beachwood and descended back toward Franklin. I was reassured by the sound of Bobby's engine, the gears changing, the throttle first loud then soft.

"Make the left on Franklin and keep straight for a couple'a miles."

Bobby nodded and we cruised on in silence. Somehow the nighttime foot traffic seemed completely fascinating. It was so good to be off that infernal hillside. After a while, Bobby spoke, "I'm starving."

"Yeah, me too."

"We gotta get a big breakfast. I want the blueberry pancakes."

"Make the left on Melrose."

I guided Bobby through the same residential neighborhood I'd driven with Brad the night Ron told me his story; it was a bitter, hollow feeling. I looked at the charming bungalows, small yards with glowing porch lights, the unattached garages and palm trees that floated upward like sentinels.

Finally, Bobby rumbled onto the 101 and headed south, turning off on 4th Street. We drove past my office and continued on through the warehouses and the new condos until we came to Traction Street. We parked and went into Abel's Market Diner. It was just past 3:00 a.m. As always, Bobby was true to his word and ordered a complete heart attack breakfast. So did I. He plied the jukebox with an endless stream of quarters; each song sounded better than the one before: Lynyrd Skynyrd, Creedence, the Chi-Lites and Stevie Wonder.

Bobby nodded slowly. "I don't remember cracking his skull."

I didn't say anything. It was necessary.

CHAPTER III
Never Ask Anything Stupid

We DROVE BACK TO MY office, parked around the corner and went in the front door. The building was deserted but, just in case, we avoided the elevator and took the stairs. The janitors never leave the air on and it was stuffy, smelling of cleaning products. We all but stumbled into my office, extreme fatigue now wrapping its arms around us as our adrenaline took a temporary holiday. In my line of work, it was always temporary. I flipped on the lights and checked my email -- spam advertising narcotic pain pills and penile enhancers. Neither of which I needed.

Bobby made some more coffee and I washed my face with cold water. Sleep was calling and I was having trouble ignoring it. I sat down on the sofa and Bobby handed me a cup of tar.

He grinned. "If that don't keep you awake, nothing will." I nodded, looked at it and put it down. That's the last thing I remember until Bobby shook me awake. "Nick. Nick. Wake up, bro."

I opened my eyes and looked at him, dragging a hand across my tired face. "What time is it?"

"7 a.m."

"Shit!" I sat up with a start.

"We both passed out. Sorry, Boss."

"Not your fault. We needed it."

"Heard that."

"Is there any coffee?"

"Yeah. Just made a fresh pot."

He handed me a cup that looked much less like tar. "Thanks, bro."

"So what now?"

"Gimme a few to collect my thoughts."

"Sure."

He sat down at my desk and flipped on the flat screen TV against the back wall. CNN. Trust Bobby. Any time, any place. Dude's gotta have his news.

Maybe it was the stress, maybe it was the fatigue I couldn't shake, but I felt a certain satisfaction with everything that had transpired. Dominique had, in fact, committed suicide and Cicero was dead, although his death was way disturbing. Tom and Ernie had kidnapped James Halladay. I didn't know where he was, but I did know that this game was far from over, especially as Clipper had, by now, discovered Reggie's body and the missing computer. He would be in a rage, I assumed, as we'd transgressed his inner sanctum, were responsible for the death of his beloved uncle, and had proof that he was a psychotic killer. Richie was still missing, although presumably not far from Clipper. I imagined him hiding out in some Skid Row hotel, wired and paranoid, staring out from behind the curtains, waiting for his boyfriend to return. Jade was in danger as were all of us, including my steadfast wife.

"Let's head to your place. Brad can set up the computer and transfer the surveillance footage onto a flash drive."

"Just make sure he doesn't show it to Jade."

"Yeah."

We grabbed our things and headed out the door. I turned to lock it and that's when I saw the corner of a manila envelope, tucked under the mat. I picked it up and looked at my name that was written across the front in beautiful flowing letters. I didn't need to look inside to know that it was from Clipper. My heart raced and instinctively I reached for my gun. Bobby pulled his, and we both listened intently, but we were alone. I put my .45 away and examined the envelope.

"Careful, bro. It could have Anthrax or something in it."

Taking out a small knife, I carefully opened it. There was no powder, just several sheets of paper that I unfolded. The first page bore the following inscription written in Clipper's stylized flowing script:

He That Troubleth his Own House Shall Inherit the Wind

And the Fool Shall Be Servant to the Wise of Heart

Bobby was reading over my shoulder. "It's from the Bible. *Inherit the Wind.*"

"Yeah. He's given to drama, that's for sure."

I unlocked the door and we went back inside. For good measure, I closed and locked it.

The second page bore an acronym, NAAS, written in large block letters, arranged diagonally from the upper left to the lower right hand corner of the second page.

N~ever

A~sk

A~nything

S~tupid

"Sage advice."

Bobby nodded. "Yeah, but creepy, bro."

The third page was an elaborate pen and ink drawing of what appeared to be an abandoned airfield. The four cardinal points of the compass were sketched in. A runway in the form of two triangles, the smaller a mile or so beyond the larger, occupied the top half of the page. Crumbling buildings drawn with Arnold's typical care and attention to realistic detail suggested a once thriving installation. Sand dunes trailed off to the right and mountains loomed in the distance.

The lower half of the page was divided into four sections, depicting facsimiles of World War II single prop fighter planes. Each drawing was captioned with the name of the aircraft. Two American planes, a P-51A Mustang and a Lockheed P-38 Lightning. The British Submarine Spitfire and the notorious German Messerschmitt Bf 109. As an adjunct to the planes themselves, Clipper included cross-sections of the engines, fuselages and cockpits.

"He loves to break things down, huh?" said Bobby.

"At least they're not human body parts this time."

CICERO (106 BC – 43 BC) was written across the top of the fourth page. Below it were three quotations apparently attributed to the Roman statesman:

Art is Born of the Observation and Investigation of Nature

He Only Employs his Passion Who Can Make No Use of his Reason

In Men of the Highest Character and Noblest Genius There Is to Be

Found an Insatiable Desire for Honor, Command, Power, and Glory

"What's this for?" asked Bobby.

"My guess is that Clipper's referring to himself. A kind of self-portrait."

"Fucking narcissist."

The fifth page was best viewed by turning it on its side. There was a wall of boulders in the shape of a soft hyperbola shielding what appeared to be a storage bunker constructed of brick or masonry. The roof, which inclined upward to a V, was crumbling at its peak and the entrance, which was large and open to the elements, rose to an arch. There was nothing visible on the inside.

The sixth page was disturbing. Skillfully drawn, naked, middle-aged James Halladay lay hog-tied on his stomach, hands and feet strained up into the air. The rope was looped around his throat, forcefully arching his head up and back. The realism was striking --

his broad hairy back, fleshy buttocks, deltoids straining. Halladay's only visible eye, round and birdlike, protruded from the side of his head.

"Torture position," said Bobby. "If you don't keep your head back, you strangle and it doesn't take long."

I fanned through the remaining pages. The seventh page was bizarrely comical. The inscription read, Soul of the Neanderthal. Beneath it, Tom and Ernie, both eyeless, complete with prominent brow ridges and dressed in loin cloths, crouched on their haunches around a small fire. Tom held a stick with which he stirred the embers, and Ernie's large chest and belly were tattooed. Tom had an erection, which angled upward against his loincloth. The drawing, while largely realistic, had an element of caricature and it was hard not to laugh.

"Jesus, bro," chuckled Bobby.

The eighth page read:

Carrot Capital of the World. Sunshine 365 Days a Year.

The ninth page was equally brief:

Great Place to Raise the Kids

"I've heard of this place."

"Use that one and Google it," I gestured.

Bobby sat down at Audrey's computer and typed in, "Carrot Capital of the World." Holtville, California came up immediately and he printed out directions.

Meanwhile, I woke my machine up and typed in, "Abandoned World War II Airfields, California." A few clicks more and I found "Abandoned & Little-Known Airfields; California: El Centro Area."

"Check this out."

He came over and watched as I scrolled through the website that told the story, complete with black-and-white photographs, of a series of abandoned airstrips which had been built in the Imperial Valley during World War II. Scrolling down, I came to a section describing the Holtville Naval Auxiliary Air Station.

"N.A.A.S," said Bobby.

"Never ask anything stupid."

After the war, the Navy had relinquished its interest. Over the years, it had served as a civilian airport, a tuberculosis sanitarium, and a staging area for crop dusting. Now it was completely abandoned except for periodic drag races and occasional war games. Most of the buildings were torn down but the ammunition bunker, depicted by Clipper, was still standing. His drawing was a close replica of the website's photograph. The airfield was approximately eight miles east of Holtville, which was near El Centro, a few miles north of the Mexican border.

It was 8:16 when we climbed back into Bobby's van. "You mind driving, Boss?"

"Sure."

"I wanna get some zees before we get there."

"Okay and I'm gonna stop by your place to check on everyone."

"We're also gonna need some heavy firepower."

"Yeah, I guess we will."

By the time we pulled onto the 10, he was asleep, snoring quietly. Relaxed now, he looked even sadder than when he was awake. I hadn't stopped to think about the psychological toll this could be taking on him, and wondered if his PTSD would be aggravated because of everything that had gone down. He was still snoring when I pulled up in front of his place.

"Bobby." He didn't stir. "Bobby, we're here."

Again, no response so I shook him. He exploded to life, his left arm pinned me to the seat, his Bowie knife in his right. This time he was all the way gone, his 1000 yard stare drilled into me. His breath, hard, jittery. I knew better then to struggle and remained calm.

"Dude, relax, it's me."

The strength is his arm was incredible. I couldn't move. He brought the knife up to my throat and that was when I really started to worry. He face, drenched in sweat. His jaw, clenched tight. His eyes looked at me, but saw nothing. He was back in Nam, facing down the NVA. Suddenly the passenger door was yanked open and Cassady's Beretta pressed hard into the back of his neck.

"Freeze, soldier," she hissed.

It was either her voice or the familiarity of cold gunmetal pressing into him that brought him around, but his eyelids twitched and the 1000 yard stare slowly dissipated.

"Put the knife down, and I mean now."

The venom in her words was clear and unmistakable, assisted by her jacking back the hammer. The sound cut through the tension, and he let me go. She kept the gun pressed into his neck, moving with him as he put the knife on the dash.

"Please, put the gun away," he said as meekly as he could.

Cassady looked at me and I nodded. She removed it, but didn't release the hammer.

I said to him, "You okay?"

He nodded and looked ashen as he clambered out of the van. He glanced at Cassady, but didn't say anything and went inside the house.

I got out and grinned at her. "Thanks, sweetheart."

She nodded, eased the hammer off, clicked on the safety and put the gun into her waistband. "What the hell happened?"

"Can I get a kiss first?"

She smiled and leaned toward me. Tough as things were, she tasted delicious.

"Let's go in."

"I've gotta get something out of the back."

She held the doors open for me as I pulled out Reggie's computer. "Who's is that?"

"Clipper's."

"But why do you have it?"

"I'll tell you when we get inside."

I grabbed it and we went into the house.

Brad and Jade were cooking in the kitchen. I put the computer in his room and came back out to find breakfast for the five of us ready on the kitchen table. Jade looked forlorn, her eyes as downturned as her beautiful mouth. She sighed heavily and sat down, staring at the bacon and scrambled eggs.

"Hey."

She threw a glance at me, then returned to her untouched plate. "Hi."

"What's going on?"

Cassady looked at me and shook her head, 'no.'

I let it go and sat down as Brad brought out the coffee. "Let's eat."

I asked, "Where's Bobby?"

"In the shower."

"We should wait for him."

"He said to go ahead and eat," assured Brad, taking a bite of toast.

Although I'd eaten breakfast earlier, I was hungry again and ate the eggs, but left the bacon.

Cassady smiled at Jade and said, "You need to eat."

"Did you find my brother?" she replied as she looked at me.

"No, but I've got a good idea where he is."

Bobby came back in, dressed in clean shorts and tee-shirt. He sat down, mumbled something and ate his food. The tension in the room rose and all conversation ceased.

I pushed my chair back and stood up. "Brad, I need to talk to you."

"Sure."

He followed me into his room. "Hook that computer up and transfer all the files onto that hard drive please."

"Consider it done."

"I snatched it from Reggie Mount's place. On it are a series of clips from surveillance cams inside his place. It shows Cicero dying. Whatever you do, don't let Jade see it."

"Christ, man."

"Yeah, it was something, bro."

"Don't show me what?" said Jade.

We turned to find her in the doorway.

"Nothing."

"What can't I see, Nick?"

"You hired me to find Richie, which I'm about to do."

"I hired you to help me, including finding out who murdered Cicero."

I was trapped. She knew it. Brad knew it. I knew it. It was going to make CNN anyway, once I closed out the case. The cops, or someone, would sell some of the clips or screenshots to TMZ or whichever tabloid was the highest bidder. Cassady and Bobby appeared behind her. The circle of what could be her emotional demise was now complete.

"Jade, I now know how your father died, but it's nothing you want to see. Believe me."

"Show me."

"Are you sure?"

"Yes." Gone was the forlorn little girl I'd seen just a few minutes earlier. This was the Jade I'd seen several times now -- intense, focused. Her green eyes as hard as marbles.

I nodded. "Brad."

He said, "Bobby, can I wire it into your TV?"

"Yeah, sure."

Brad picked up the computer and took it into the living room. "Can someone please bring the keyboard and mouse?"

I grabbed them and we followed him in. I handed them to him and sat next to Cassady on the sofa. Jade sat on one of the chairs in the corner and Bobby sat on the sofa arm, next to me. He wrapped a big arm around me, his way of trying to make up for my near disaster. We waited quietly as Brad hooked everything up and once again, the tension in the room ramped up.

Bobby leaned over and whispered, "Bro, this ain't a good idea."

"I know, but it's what she wants."

He nodded and glanced at Jade. She was deep in thought. Brad flicked on the computer and TV and waited as it came to life.

"Click on any folder and then on one of the clips."

Brad nodded and maneuvered the mouse. Cassady held my hand and we all stared at the screen. The first clip that came up was of Cicero on his deathbed. He was struggling against the ropes as Reggie taunted him with a piece of cake, holding it close to his mouth, then pulling it away and greedily devouring it. I looked at Jade who was staring transfixed at the screen.

"Is there sound?" asked Jade.

Brad looked at me. I shrugged and he replied, "Yeah, but you don't really wanna hear that, right?"

"Yes, I do."

He sighed and turned it up. We all sat there horrified not only by the sight of a starving Cicero, but by Reggie Mount's taunting laugh.

I stood up and grabbed my guns. "I've seen enough."

Her eyes burning with intense rage, Jade looked at me. "I haven't."

Brad clicked on another clip. It was of Bobby and me as Reggie fired his gun, the bullet slamming into Cicero's, long dead skull. Jade whimpered and Cassady squeezed my hand. Brad closed out the clip and brought up another. It was of Bobby smashing Reggie's head open on the concrete floor and his sickening scream as he died. All eyes turned to Bobby who was holding his breath. He let it out, stood up and left the room.

"Jesus Christ," said Brad quietly.

Tears streamed down Jade's face. She went into the bathroom and began sobbing. Cassady followed her.

"Brad, make sure you copy all the files."

"I will."

I went into Bobby's room. He was loading a double banana clip into an AK-47. A second AK, already with a double mag, lay on the bed. "You should've let me blow that hell hole to kingdom come."

"Evidence. You know that."

"Yeah, of me killing him."

"I already told you, it's self-defense. Nothing's gonna happen to you."

"I lost control."

"You saved our lives."

Jade rushed past me and flung her arms around him. Bobby, completely taken aback, didn't know how to react. I made the motion for him to hug her, which he did.

"Thank you for avenging Daddy," she said, and started crying again as she buried her head into his big chest.

He held her tight and I left them alone, closing the door. Cassady was in the hallway waiting for me. We held each other, but said nothing, the images from the video clips stealing any possible dialogue. The door opened and Bobby stepped out, an AK-47 in each of his bear paws, looking like any action movie star. Except this was real.

"Let's smoke those mothers."

He handed me an AK and we headed for the front door.

CHAPTER IV
Firefight

I PINNED THE SPEEDOMETER AT 70 and kept it there. East of
Riverside we headed up into the rugged San Gorgonio Pass, which
connects the Los Angeles Basin to the Coachella Valley. Bobby went
back to sleep while I drove and thought things over. At the very least,
Tom and Ernie would be waiting for us when we got to the airfield.
They had undoubtedly re-armed but so had we. An AK-47 is a
fearsome weapon; 30 rounds in the banana clip and bullets over 2.5
inches in length that'll go right through a cinder block without any
hesitation, killing anything they hit along the way.

We came down out of the Pass and entered the Coachella Valley.
I could see for miles in every direction, with the San Jacinto and
Santa Rosa mountain ranges to the south and east. Palm Springs
came and went. It's often said that Orange County is the fraud capital
of the world, but Palm Springs can't be far behind. Shifty land
developers jockey for the rights to desert acreage in order to build
lavish golf courses ringed by multi-million dollar retirement homes.
Hapless investors cough up their funds. Sometimes they get a return;
sometimes the funds just vanish. Speculation and outright thievery
contrast with the hard work and dedication of the Mexican date
farmers who populate the southeastern end of the Valley around

Thermal. Here, migrant families have gained their citizenship and built small date palm and citrus empires -- swatches of green in the surrounding desert. Just before Thermal, I turned off the 10 and headed south onto Highway 86, which skirts the southwestern edge of the Valley.

Bobby woke up and stretched, wiping sleep from his eyes. "Where are we?"

"Coming to the Salton Sea."

We passed dilapidated tin-roofed houses, old tire dumps and abandoned vehicles. The flat, almost featureless desert to our right gave off the distinctive odor of creosote. Cottonwoods and willows rose in the salt marshes. The champagne-colored sky, swept by gulls and migrating geese, laid its heavy fingers across the uncertain blue of the lake water, while the smell of rotting fish and algae bloom wafted across the highway.

Bobby rested his chin on his right fist, staring off across the desert at ghost towns that had never really gained a foothold. Farther south we came to the Wildlife Refuge. Here, exotic birds dine on fish and local insect life. An owl passed right in front of us, sailing in a huge arc completely in control of its environment. At the base of the Salton Sea, the desert broadens into the Imperial Valley, which extends clear to the Mexican border. Water diverted from the Colorado River irrigates this agricultural oasis. Alfalfa fields alternate with vegetables; sheep and cattle graze under the broiling sun.

As we neared our destination, Bobby sat up straight, ran his hands across his stubble and took a sip from a water bottle. "We're close, aren't we?"

I nodded.

He looked at me curiously. "How do you wanna handle this?"

"Obviously it's a trap. We know it, and they know we know it."

Bobby nodded. "It sure ain't to save Halladay."

"And Clipper's not gonna be there. It's gonna be Tom and Ernie."

"So why won't he be there?"

"I'm not sure. Maybe he's too preoccupied with Richard."

After that, we drove on in silence. This part of the desert is very isolated. The occasional 18-wheeler. Few cars. No cops. An endless vista of alternating green and brown rows of earth and alfalfa, growing rapidly under the hot California sun, vanishing in the hazy distance. Bobby checked his guns, laying out multiple spare clips, readying himself.

I said, "If we can, we bring 'em in alive."

He looked at me sideways. "You know that's not gonna happen, right?"

"We can try."

"Okay, Boss."

Again we fell silent. As we neared El Centro, the traffic thickened, and we stopped at a Valero Station for gas and water. Then we turned east onto the Evan Hewes Highway, passing carrot fields and groups of cross-country bicyclists laden down with gear.

When we reached Holtville, population just under 6,000, we turned north on Holt Road and then east on Norrish. Then we came to a sign: Holtville Airfield, 6 Miles. A few miles out of town, the fields turned brown and we were back in the desert. Off-road vehicles towing dirt bikes joined us in a steady caravan. It was nearly ten o'clock and I knew we had to hurry.

We crossed a canal and approached the airfield. The paved road ended in a parking lot. In hard economic times, people will find any convenient place to set up a makeshift home, particularly if they have a family. As with other semi-public areas, this was no exception. More than a dozen RVs, some in clusters, most sitting solo, had staked out their claim to a little piece of desert. It was heartbreaking to see the families, complete with barefoot, shabbily-dressed children. It reminded me of old photos of the Great Depression.

The caravan of weekend off-roaders were also pulling into the massive parking lot, unloading their dirt bikes and quads and strapping on their gear. We pulled over and took stock.

"This won't work," said Bobby. "We're too exposed."

"Yeah, so are all these families and off-roaders."

"I'll recon. Maybe we made a mistake."

"Okay."

Bobby got out and went over to a grizzled looking guy, sitting out in front of his RV, sipping on a beer. Again, I looked over Clipper's drawings, trying to get a handle on his deranged mind and what exactly might be waiting for us. Bobby clambered back in and closed the door.

"At the back of the airfield, due east from here, there's a dirt road that leads to the old runway and the barracks, mostly fallen down now, and a bunker that's apparently pretty much intact. That has to be the one in Clipper's picture.

"Is that where the off-roaders go?"

"No. They've staked out an area north of here, about half a click."

"You ready?"

"Let's get to it."

I cranked the motor to life and we took the perimeter road around the massive triangle that formed the airport. At its farthest point, the road made a hard right, running east in a straight line for at least a mile, dwindling into dirt. From the ruts, it was obvious that a fair amount of traffic had recently passed through.

"Hang on," said Bobby. "Pull over. I gotta check something."

As soon as he got out of the van, I knew where he was going. When he got back in, the whisper of wry smile played on his lips. "Harley tracks."

"Los Muertos."

"Yep."

223

"Route 8 is only about 3 miles south and it runs parallel to the Mexican border."

"Maybe that's why Clipper chose this area."

"Because of its proximity, you mean?"

"I dunno, bro, but it kind'a makes sense that maybe they've got plans to jump the border once it's done."

I nodded. "Yeah. They're outta East LA, but when I ran a check on them, the origins of the club is in Mexicali."

"Anyway, we're not just gonna be dealing with those fake cops. The tire tracks prove it."

He was right and there was nothing we could do about it but man up or turn around and drive back with our tails between our legs. And that was out of the question. Nevertheless, I felt the cold flush of fear. What most everyday citizens don't understand is that a bar fight is nothing compared to premeditated violence. The first happens in the heat of the moment, mostly without time to think it through. The latter, though, that's a whole different story. You get ready to do battle knowing there's a very good chance of getting seriously hurt, or seriously dead. Up ahead several old, crumbling buildings, similar to the ones Clipper had drawn, leaned crazily, being slowly subsumed by the ancient desert floor. I didn't see any other vehicles or people, so I pulled over and killed the motor. We slipped on our Kevlar vests, pulling the multi-pocketed jackets over them. We grabbed our sidearms, making sure they were locked and loaded, and the AK-47s.

In silent meditation, Bobby and I climbed out of the van and walked toward the airstrip, which appeared to be deserted. The sun was already blazing and beads of sweat formed on my forehead. The old runway was now a wasteland of cracked, buckled asphalt. The whole installation was no more than 65 years old, but the merciless sun and man's restlessness had turned it into a ghost town. We walked slowly toward what had once been Navy training barracks. Not much remained other than the concrete flooring slabs. Here and there squatters had built campfires; charcoal and ash were still visible in the dirt. The carcasses of small animals, etched white by the sun, lay in heaps as if swept together by some unseen janitor.

As we moved toward the back of the installation, we came to a crumbling retaining wall built of mortared rocks. A flock of ravens, perched on the wall, croaked a warning but held their ground, their ancient eyes expressionless. We skirted the wall and stopped at a jumble of boulders, perhaps 50 yards long and 20 feet tall that formed a natural barricade in front of us. It formed a soft "U" and I figured it surrounded the bunker, at least partly, on three sides. Bobby clambered to the top while I covered him. For a long time he crouched among the rocks studying the scene. Then he came back down.

"It's there, all right. Looks just like the picture. No door. Concrete walls and roof, but no signs of life."

"Let's pincer them and try to get the drop on 'em. If a firefight starts, we'll catch 'em in our crossfire."

We both drank some water and as we waited, gathering ourselves, we heard voices coming from the other side of the boulders. Although we couldn't make out what they were saying, it didn't take a genius to figure out it was most likely about us. They were expecting us and must have emerged from the bunker. I put my index finger up to my mouth and Bobby nodded. From here on in, it was silent running; we turned our cellphones to vibrate. Bobby motioned that he was going left and that I should go right. I made my way slowly along the base of the boulders, trying not to crunch gravel. It was hot and getting hotter. I heard the rattle and froze. About 10 feet in front of me and just above my head, was a large Southwestern Speckled Rattlesnake, clearly irritated that I'd disturbed its morning sun time. Eyeing me with great suspicion, its perfect stone camouflage had blended it in with the rocks, rendering it all but invisible. Stepping away from the warning sound, I had to avoid the rattler by making a wide semi circle. I knew this could expose me, but had no choice.

Safely past the rattlesnake, I moved back toward the wall just far enough away that if it decided to attack, at least I'd have a chance to escape.

As I neared to the end of the boulders, the voices grew louder. I peered around the corner and froze. Standing on top of the bunker was a lookout; a massive biker wearing his club cut, Los Muertos. Sitting in the shade not far from the bunker entrance were Ernie and 3 other Los Muertos, all armed to the teeth with automatic weapons. I didn't want to stick my head out any further, so I pulled out my phone and clicked on the camera icon, carefully edging it around the wall. This way I could press my face up against the boulders, and see where Bobby was. My phone buzzed as his text came in.

'2 many. Surprise lost. We go it hot.'

I texted back, 'I'll clip the lookout. Draw their attention. U cover me.'

'K.'

I flipped up the sight on the AK and very quietly eased the barrel around the side of the wall. Although I knew they would kill us given the chance, I didn't want to do the same, so I took careful aim at the biker's leg.

That's when I heard it -- a man's scream, wretched, tortured, sub-human. I froze and watched as Ernie got to his feet, pulled out his gun and went inside the bunker. En masse, the bikers flexed toward the door when several gunshots rang out. They got to their feet, clearly agitated as Ernie came back out, a gun in his hand. No one said anything, but this was a bad turn of events. All I could think of was that he'd killed Halladay. Either him or Tom, I didn't know which. Maybe that wasn't the plan. Maybe their orders were to take me alive so I could end up hogtied next to Halladay. I didn't like the idea and I felt cold emotion come over me. It felt good in a weird way and I knew I was ready. One of the bikers, a hard looking dude covered in black, jailhouse tats, got in Ernie's face. Now distracted, they'd given us back the element of surprise. I stood up and moved quickly around the wall. The argument was heated and no one realized I was there, that was until I let go with burst of AK rounds over their heads: BRAAAPPPPPPPPPP! The disagreement came to an abrupt halt as they froze and looked at me, the nasty business end of my AK aimed right at them.

"Anyone of you motherfuckas makes a move and I'll fucking kill all of you!"

Ernie looked at me, his expression more admiring curiosity than dread fear. The other bikers didn't look scared either so much as insulted that a single gringo had got the drop on them. They probably thought they were worth an entire SWAT team. Of course they had no idea I had Bobby in reserve, a one-man wrecking crew, his AK equally trained on their nasty asses.

The biker who had been arguing with Ernie stepped toward me, his Tech 9 still in his hand. "You got some fucking balls, cabron."

I aimed my AK at him. "Drop your weapons and I mean now, bro!"

I hadn't seen the biker at the back slowly bringing up his gun, but Bobby had. BANG! A single round from his AK hit the biker in the side, exited his back and slammed into the bunker wall before the blood spray had time to hit the dirt, and dry instantly in the blazing desert sun.

Something strange happens to humans when they make the decision to engage in a deadly firefight, and I have seen it before in some of the other gun battles I've been in. The eyes stop blinking. The jaw sets hard. The face loses all expression. It's the complete opposite of what is portrayed in the movies. As one mind, they brought up their guns. As one, Bobby and I cut loose. As one, they opened fire. In a gun battle, you don't have time to think. You react. As Sheriff "Little Bill" Daggett said in The Unforgiven: "Look son, being a good shot, being quick with a pistol, that don't do no harm, but it don't mean much next to being cool-headed. A man who will keep his head and not get rattled under fire, like as not, he'll kill ya. It ain't so easy to shoot a man anyhow, especially if the son-of-a-bitch is shootin' back at you." This was no exception. AK-47 rounds make a terrible mess of a person, tearing flesh, snapping bones, exploding blood and gore with equal enthusiasm. Our bullets obliterated them in a hail of angry lead.

The shooting stopped and the fading death sounds echoed across the desert. Weirdly, Ernie was still left standing. The others were broken, bloody and dead. The redhead had been hit multiple times yet didn't yet fully comprehend that he too was about to join his compadres. He looked at me, his eyes bulging, face contorted in pain. His trigger finger twitched and his gun discharged harmlessly into the rocks. Then he toppled forward, hitting the ground hard.

The loud ringing in my ears compounded the pain in my chest. I couldn't catch my breath. I looked at the heap of crumpled, bloody bodies and took a couple of steps forward. Although my Kevlar vest had stopped the brace of bullets that had hit me, the blunt force trauma still hurt like a mother. I grimaced and looked over at Bobby. Ashen faced, he was slumped against the wall, clutching his left shoulder. I took a painful breath and made my way over. It was maybe 150 feet but it seemed a lot longer. When I got there I could see his left arm hanging limply, blood dripping steadily out onto the ground. A bullet, Ernie's, maybe, had hit him in the front of his bicep, coming out the back. Blood was oozing out around the bone that protruded like a shark's tooth from the wound.

I knelt down. "It's through and through, Bobby."

He grimaced, his face grey. "At least they won't have to dig it out."

"Can you get up?"

"Yeah."

But he couldn't and I had to pull him to his feet. I slung his AK over my shoulder and we staggered over to Ernie. Pink saliva bubbles were pushing their way out of his mouth, as he tried to suck air into lungs that leaked too much. His eyes alternately protruded and spun back in his head, as blood ran out of the several holes in his torso; soaking into the greedy, dry desert. I wanted to feel something for him, but all I felt was contempt. He kind of cocked his head and stared at me with his dying eyes.

"Where's Clipper?" I asked.

"Fuck you, bitch," he spat his reply and began his death cough.

Bobby looked at me. "This piece'a shit's not gonna tell us."

"I'm gonna check on Halladay."

Bobby looked at his arm and said through clenched teeth. "Make it quick."

Here in this land of merciless sun and bone-chilling nights, as I crossed to the bunker, the apprehension returned, pounding in my bruised chest. I stepped into the black maw of the bunker and took the six crumbled stone steps that led down into a cavernous basement. There in the back I could see two motionless figures and as I got closer, I could feel and smell their death. The horror of it caught in my throat. Tom lay on his back, shot through the face and head. For some reason I was reminded of a cat in rictus, the moment after it's struck by a car. His jaw was elongated, his open mouth displaying pieces of brown tobacco-stained teeth, now covered in red ooze. A few feet away, Halladay, completely naked, lay hogtied on his stomach, just like in Clipper's picture. His hands were wrenched behind his back, the rope looped around his neck, with his head slung forward, strangled by his own weakness. His tongue, now thick and blue, bulged from his mouth. Even in death, they'd stripped away his dignity; a carrot protruded out of his ass. My head started to spin. I caught myself, turned and walked out.

"Let's go."

Bobby nodded and as we retraced our steps toward the boulders, Ernie called out, half-rasp, half child's shriek, "Help me...please!"

We turned the corner and found ourselves staring down the barrel of a Los Muertos biker. Either he'd played possum during the gun battle, or had escaped right at the beginning and somehow had gotten past me. The look in his eyes told me that he wasn't interested in dialogue, only death. Ours. For what seemed like an eternity, we just looked at each other, hatred and fear coursing its way between us. The gun in his hand was a revolver, a Colt .45. It could have been mine. He thumbed back the hammer. Savored the moment. He hadn't seen the large Southwestern Speckled Rattlesnake just above his head, but it had seen him and was clearly unimpressed. The unmistakable sound of imminent death cut through the desert stillness like a chainsaw through a twig. The biker, justifiably horrified, spun around at the sound of the rattle. Not a great idea. The rattlesnake struck with lightning speed, fangs stabbing directly into his jugular. He staggered back, screaming with fear-laced pain. Getting bitten is bad enough, but getting bitten so close to the brain and heart, is a death sentence. The biker sank to his knees, a desperate hand holding the snakebite as if that might help. It didn't. His eyes rolled up and he collapsed onto his back, writhing in agony, perverse poetic justice.

"Finish him off," said Bobby.

I shook my head. "He's already finished."

Like the song says, we walked on, or rather we staggered on, but we got to the van and rumbled back toward the Airfield entrance, past the gathering RVs and the squatters who looked as lost and forlorn as any group of Skid Row denizens.

Most of the traffic was flowing into the Airfield, and the road heading west was clear. There was no obvious clinic in Holtville so instead of wasting time, I gunned it down Evan Hewes Highway to El Centro. Bobby was in too much pain to talk. Once there, I found the hospital and pulled to the curb.

"Bobby, listen, bro, if I take you in there, they'll probably detain me and that can't happen."

"I'll get out and walk myself into Emergency."

"Call me after they've seen you."

"Will do, bro." Bobby's lips were a weird mix of blue and grey and I had to swallow hard to beat back my emotion.

A police car cruised past us and pulled into the emergency entrance. We waited 'til the cops entered the hospital. He looked at me, kind'a smiled, which was more of a grimace and choked me up, then saluted me. I held in the emotion, set my jaw hard, nodded shortly and drove away.

I was heading toward the freeway when my phone buzzed.

"Brad, what's--"

"--Jade's gone."

"What?"

"I went to the store with Cassady and when we got back, she'd split."

"Shit."

"She left a note. Says Lake Forest Exxon Mobil Station, Lake Forest Drive."

"Did she write it?"

"I dunno her handwriting, bro."

"Get on Bobby's computer."

I waited as he ran into Bobby's room and fired it up.

"I'm in."

"Okay, now log onto Merlin and search out Arnold Clipper."

"There's only one, on Beachwood Canyon."

"That's his old residence, so look for his parents, his dad, same name, around 60."

"Not there. No other Arnold Clippers in California."

"Shit. Son-of-a-bitch must have figured out a way to have it deleted."

Brad was silent.

"Bobby keeps an extra set of keys to my office on the wallboard next to the refrigerator."

"Hold on."

I waited. "Got 'em."

"Go to my office and dial 8350 to get in the building."

"On my way."

I could hear him exiting the house at top speed and getting into his car. "Remember when I was writing stuff on the whiteboard?"

"Yeah."

"I wrote old man Clipper's address down on a sheet of typing paper and attached it."

"I'll call you soon as I get there."

I headed west toward San Diego. It was at least a three-hour drive to Lake Forest, which meant I wouldn't get there until mid-afternoon. I still had an almost full tank and held the tachometer at a steady 3500 RPM. Interstate 8 rises out of the valley up a long grade into the mountains. The temperature drops and you pass through the southern California badlands, a jumble of lunar rocks, sunken mesas and mud hills. The landscape matched my mood and I tried to empty my mind of everything except for the highway. But it was eating at me. We'd seen and done too much and for all my bravado, I knew there would surely be a terrible price to pay.

My phone buzzed. "Yeah?"

"21347 Sterling Silver Drive. Lake Forest."

"Okay. Text it to me, please."

"Sure."

"My guess is that Jade's there."

"How you gonna spring her?"

"Not sure."

"I can meet you there."

"No. Stay where you are."

"But…wha…if…"

The mountains cut off reception. Alone with my thoughts, I knew that if I brought in the cops, Clipper would go down fighting, but he'd take Jade and Richie with him. If I went in alone they still might die and I might go with them. Clipper had outsmarted all of us. The death images of Cicero and Halladay, the dark paintings in

Clipper's subterranean labyrinth, and Bobby, his expressive face blanched grey staggering toward ER, seared my mind. I rolled down the window and screamed into the on-rushing air, but the wind swallowed my voice like a toad trapping a fly. I shut the window and shut my mouth. I drove on.

It seemed like the longest three hours of my life but I finally came down out of the mountains, and headed into the chaparral country east of San Diego. Here, the road cuts through the wooded canyons in great sweeping curves. Just north of San Diego, I turned north onto I-805 which merges with I-5. The traffic moved steadily, passing beautiful seaside towns west of the Interstate. From there it was a straight shot past the Camp Pendleton Marine Base, and on to San Juan Capistrano.

In Mission Viejo I gassed up and got cleaned up. There was hot water in the restroom and I washed up, carefully combing my hair, refusing to stare at my bruised and swollen face. I bought some liquid makeup in the station convenience store along with a large hot dog and some coffee. I chewed slowly and sipped the mud. When I was done, I got into the van and, using the rearview mirror, applied some of the makeup to try and cover the disaster area that dominated my face. It worked pretty well. Then I pulled out of the parking lot. 10 minutes later, I turned onto Lake Forest Drive.

CHAPTER V
Last Dance

LAKE FOREST IS ONE OF the newer, post-modern, Orange County cities. There's no traditional downtown area and no discernible city center. The Exxon Mobil Station in Jade's note was the first thing I came to after turning off the Interstate. I parked, suddenly aware that Jade could not have known about the station had Arnold not informed her. Which meant that Arnold wanted me to track him down. I suppressed a shudder and went inside.

A middle-aged Hispanic woman eyed me from behind the counter. I grabbed a water bottle from the cooler, smiled and handed her five bucks.

As she retrieved my change, I asked, "Senora, I'm looking for a muy bonita dark-haired young woman, early twenties, coffee-colored skin, well dressed. She may have been here earlier this morning."

She looked at me, smiled and replied in perfect English, "Is she your girlfriend?"

Good thing I was wearing makeup so she couldn't see my reddening face. "No, just a friend, but she's missing."

"Lemme see your badge."

"Not a cop. I'm a PI." I flipped her my license.

She looked at it and sadness came over. "We hear about so many missing persons all the time."

"It's the interstate, I guess. Easy access."

She nodded. "And most are never found or end up dead. It's awful."

"I know what you mean. Nobody's safe."

"Sometimes they end up in trunks. It's gotten so bad I'm almost scared to go outside."

"So you haven't seen her?"

"I wish I had but, sorry, no."

"Thanks anyway."

"Good luck. Hope you find her."

"I will. Thank you."

Back in the van, I punched in the address on my phone's Google map; it was two miles east and a few blocks off the main drag. Lake Forest is long and narrow. I passed a small shopping center, a gated lake community and a number of residential sections. The houses were attractive tile-roofed, two story numbers with small, manicured yards. They had all been built in the last 20 years and the streets were virtually empty. I passed a mother pushing a baby carriage, and some older couples taking walks. Nearly everyone was Caucasian, middle class and no one seemed happy. I was struck by the odd thought that this community could use someone like Halladay dressed in his jogging clothes -- sweaty, hairy, armed with a stop-watch and an insatiable desire to better his last time.

I turned right onto Rimgate Park Drive, which skirted a canyon and fed onto Sterling Silver Drive. Welcome to Clipperville. Their residence was halfway down the block on the right, a blue, two-story home set back from the street on a gentle slope. It boasted a three-car garage and a circular driveway. There were no cars parked in front, and if Clipper was there, he would probably park in the garage. Plantation shutters and window boxes gave the house a welcoming feel. I drove around the block and parked.

Obviously, I needed to legitimize the events of the last few days, particularly today's shootout, so I called Tony. Over the last 20 years, although he and I had spent a lot of time together, we'd never worked directly on a case jointly. He'd always been very generous when it came to dispensing information, and I reciprocated whenever I could, but that was as far as it went.

By now Clipper would have tried to contact Tom and Ernie, and would know something had gone wrong. He'd set me up like a bowling pin knowing that no matter what happened at the airfield, I would be MIA for most of the day and he'd have a clear playing field to get to Jade. I was here with little choice but to walk into the lion's den. Normally, staking out the joint would have been the way to go, but here, with each passing moment, Jade was in ever-increasing danger of being tortured or killed. The one thing I knew for sure was that I needed back up.

Tony picked up on the second ring. "You okay?"

"Yeah, Tony. Thanks."

"Cassady called me. What the fuck's going on?"

I gave him a thumbnail sketch of what had happened.

"Bobby got shot?"

"Yeah, it was a through and through in his arm. He'll be alright."

"How many dead?"

"Including Cicero and Reggie Mount, 9. Of those, Bobby and I are personally responsible for seven. Four Los Muertos bikers, the two fake cops and some psycho called Reggie Mount. All self-defense. Mount and Clipper, along with persons unknown, murdered Cicero Lamont and the lawyer, Halladay."

"Jesus Christ, dude. This is bad."

"What was I supposed to do? Let 'em shoot Bobby and me? As it is we're lucky to be alive."

"Nick, I can't cover that many bodies."

"I'm not asking you to. Anyway, let's not worry about that now. Where are you?"

"In my cruiser on I-5. Should be there in 45 minutes."

"I'll text you the address when we hang up."

"Don't John Wayne it. Wait for me."

"Just get here as fast as you can. I've parked Bobby's blue van right down the street from the Clipper house. If it's still there when you arrive, that means I'm inside the house and you need to do what you do best."

"Okay. I'll be there a.s.a.p."

I grabbed an extra clip for my Walther, which I placed in the concealed inside pocket of my cargo pants, locked up the van and strolled down the block to the Clipper house. Stepping onto the porch, I rang the doorbell and waited. 30 seconds passed so I rang it again. Finally, a woman I assumed was Mrs. Clipper swung open the door. She was about 60, tall and well-preserved but with a pinched, bird-like face. Her tired grey eyes peered at me from under her carefully coiffed hair.

"Yes? What can I do for you?"

"My name is Peter Gustafson. I've been commissioned by the art firm of Black, Fleur & Olive to locate your son, Arnold. Mr. Olive would like to represent him." I handed her my card, which she examined carefully.

"Don't you think you could have phoned?"

"My apologies. Perhaps that would have been more appropriate."

"Yes, it would."

"The problem is I didn't have your number. I spoke to Mr. Mount a few days ago and he gave me your address and told me to just come on over. Told me you were good people." I smiled pleasantly.

"How is Reggie?"

I shrugged. "You know Reggie. Everyday is a brand new challenge."

"What type of artists do you represent?"

"Not me, the agency."

"Where did they see his paintings?"

"Arnold's drawings are well-known among select Los Angeles art circles. Mr. Olive places great faith in your son."

"That's nice to hear. I've long thought that Arnold's work is under-appreciated. He's never tried to sell it, though. What does Mr. Olive propose?"

"If I could come inside, we could go over everything?"

"What happened to your face? It looks swollen."

"It is. I had an accident up by Mammoth Lake. It's beautiful this time of year, but I slipped on some rocks."

"Looks like you took a nasty fall."

I nodded ruefully. "I did, but I'll live."

Mrs. Clipper considered. "I guess you can come in, but only for a few minutes. My husband, Arnold Sr., doesn't like visitors."

"Thank you."

She motioned for me to enter and I stepped inside. Mrs. Clipper stopped me and whispered, "My husband's in a wheel chair, you know. He's very sensitive. I don't know if Reggie told you that."

"Yes, ma'am," I lied. "He said something about an accident. I'm very sorry."

Mrs. Clipper turned and I followed her down the hallway. We passed by a formal parlor and came to the dining room.

"Let's sit here. Perhaps you would like some lemonade?"

"If it's anything like Reggie's, I would love some."

"Actually, I gave him that recipe," she beamed. "The trick is the water must be fresh and the lemons ripe, but not too ripe."

"Wouldn't you know it? He learned it from you."

Mrs. Clipper headed for the kitchen while I surveyed my surroundings. The dining room had a formal feeling. Twin bronze candelabra stood atop a mahogany sideboard. The shutters were drawn and the light dim. A dog began barking ferociously in the backyard. I heard a muffled shout and the dog stopped. Mrs. Clipper returned carrying two lemonades on a crystal serving tray. She placed it on the table, sat down across from me and handed me a glass of lemonade.

"You're really too kind. Thank you." I took a sip and smacked my lips. "This is great. You can't imagine how parched I was. You have a beautiful home, Mrs. Clipper. I love the window boxes -- nice touch. Takes me back to when I was a kid and my mother grew geraniums, back in Delaware."

"We were fortunate to do well in business."

"Such a blessing," I said. "What was your business?"

"Seatbelts. Arnold Sr. was in seatbelts." Her grey eyes were clear and seemed to have no depth.

"I'm not sure if you realize this but according to Mr. Olive, your son has something of Picasso about him. The gift of de-centering the real which, ironically, makes it all the realer."

She nodded and I knew she wasn't really listening. "I'm a little worried that your proposition might put too much pressure on Arnold."

"Mr. Olive would only take ten per cent of the proceeds and arranges all of the showings. Arnold's work would be showcased in the finest galleries and he wouldn't even have to appear if he didn't want to. He could remain artist incognito."

"That might work if he wouldn't have to appear in public. I know," she threw me a bright, false smile, "let's see what Arnold Sr. thinks."

The ferocious barking started up again. Again, I heard a shout that seemed to come from the backyard.

"I'll call him," said Mrs. Clipper. She got up and spoke into the intercom.

"Arnold, dear, we have a visitor, a friend of Reggie's."

"What does he want?" responded an irritated older man's voice.

"He wants to represent Arnold's paintings."

"No visitors. You know the rules."

"This is different, dear, so please come in and meet with him."

"Fine."

The intercom clicked off and she glanced at me. "Just be patient with him. He won't be able to resist. He's so proud of Arnold's work."

I nodded respectfully and sipped my lemonade. Mrs. Clipper fell silent and I felt her scrutinizing me. Then she spoke. "You'll like Arnold Sr. Everybody does."

"I'm sure I will."

A long taut silence was finally broken by the hum of Arnold Sr.'s electric wheelchair as he came rolling in. Immense suffering was etched into the craggy face of this tall, thin old man. Deep hollows had formed in his cheeks; his forehead was prominent and protruded slightly. Sightless eyes now blank, but still holding something that unnerved me. What had perhaps once been a strong mouth was now a pinched line of displeasure. He wore a blue dress shirt and khakis that exposed his ankles. He wheeled past me and parked, just far enough back so that I could only make him out peripherally, and although he couldn't see me, I could feel his malevolent scrutiny. Mrs. Clipper stared past me, her manner suddenly guarded. It was unsettling and I felt trapped.

"Just exactly why are you here?" Arnold Sr.'s voice was hoarse and the words came slowly.

I craned my head around. "As I explained to Mrs. Clipper, I've been commissioned by Black, Fleur & Olive to find your son. Mr. Olive wants to represent Arnold's paintings. It's a great opportunity."

"Frankly," said Arnold Sr., "that's impossible. No one knows anything about our son's artwork. It's our family secret."

"Word gets around. His talent speaks for itself."

"Everyone has secrets," said Mrs. Clipper in an accusing voice. "Don't *you*, Mr. Crane?"

I turned toward her feeling extremely naked. Her face was hard, accusatory and she wagged her finger at me like a schoolmarm. I had the weird desire to laugh, but the stun gun that Arnold Sr. pressed into my side nixed that plan. The pain was excruciating, yet I couldn't cry out. Paralyzed, my lips wouldn't move. I was dimly aware of a look of intense pleasure in Mrs. Clipper's eyes. She sucked in her breath. The pain, confusion and muscle spasms seemed to last an eternity, until I fell out of my chair and rolled to the floor.

I was only dimly aware of voices, movement, something being dragged across the floor. When I hit my head on a doorway, I realized that something was me. My mind was a sea of black ripples that parted soundlessly as I sank into deep, black water. I was dimly aware of resting on an ocean floor, with a large white stone near my head. I watched a crab scuttle out from under it and then retreat as if I were an unwelcome intruder.

Slowly, I came out of it. My head was throbbing and my muscles still trembled. We were in the family room, with Arnold Sr. across from me perched in a canvas-backed director's chair. I was lying on my side on a white leather settee, trying my damnedest to focus on an electric globe that was on a sideboard, rotating slowly. North America was blue. Europe, orange. My guns were arranged next to the globe and the clips had been removed. I felt something dripping down my right cheek. I reached up slowly and tried to touch whatever it was, but my arms still tingled. I shifted my position and this time managed to touch the gash above my right temple. I looked at the blood as I rubbed it between index and thumb. I forced myself to stop and sat up.

"Not on the sofa!" screeched Mrs. Clipper. "Don't wipe your blood on there."

"Get a cloth," ordered Arnold Sr.

"Now you've gone and got mother mad. Not good. No one should ever make mother mad."

I swept my eyes toward the new voice and met the gaze of an extremely handsome and much younger version of Clipper Sr. Arnold was smiling, studying me intently. His complexion bore a hint of olive. His high, smooth forehead and bright blue eyes exuded a curious good will. He wore a chambray work shirt with the cuffs rolled up, and railroad-striped overalls. The straps were unbuttoned and dangled to his waist. He wore his trademark ancient tennis shoes. He was holding a pistol in one hand; the other was folded calmly across his stomach.

"Nick," he said. "It's good to finally meet you. I knew you would eventually catch up with me or," he paused briefly, "die trying."

I swallowed and took a breath. "You know how it goes, curiosity leads a man forward."

"Indeed it does."

"May I?" I pointed toward the Walther.

"You may not."

"That's not very sociable."

"No more so than when you murdered Uncle Reggie."

"He was going to--"

CRACK! Mrs. Clipper slapped me hard across the head, almost knocking me out again.

"Mother!"

"Give me the stun gun!" she screamed.

"There'll be time enough for all that. For now, leave him alone."

The fog cleared and I looked up at Mrs. Clipper. Fear had replaced anger and she nodded, lowered her eyes and backed away. It was uncanny to see she too feared her son.

"It appears mother doesn't like you very much."

I sat up again. "Fuck the bitch."

Arnold smiled, but this time the warmth, no matter how false it had been, was gone -- cold venom in its place. He stood up and stretched, and I was aware of muscles rippling under his work shirt.

"I'm going to enjoy killing you," he said.

"Where's Jade?"

"Safe."

"Richie?"

Clipper pursed his lips and gently sucked in some air. "With his sister."

"Can I talk to her?"

"In due course."

"In due course, I'm gonna kill you."

He almost laughed but caught himself. "I took Jade to see her father. She didn't like it much."

I've met some cruel bastards, particularly in my line of work, but he was an exceptional specimen. I wanted nothing better than to rip him apart with my bare hands. Yeah, I know, not socially acceptable, but there are times when you have to fight evil with evil. And I was feeling about as evil as I ever have in my entire life.

Clipper smirked at my obvious hatred. "I loved my uncle."

"I loved smashing his skull."

"I loved breaking Jade's fingers, one-by-one."

Every muscle in my body was taught, adrenaline overload, screaming for release. Clipper smiled. His lips curled back exposing a large pink tongue and wet mouth that reminded me of a fat snake. It was as if there was a force field surrounding him that made him more than human, not a god, but some fallen demonic creature sent here to wreak havoc and vengeance. I hated to resort to the homophobic drivel I was raised with in northern Minnesota but knew I had to goad him. Get him so enraged that he would do something out of character. I needed him to attack me. I looked at him with utter disgust and said a silent prayer hoping my gay friends would forgive me.

"I hate pussy-assed faggots like you," I sneered quietly.

Clipper's face and neck turned red. His lips curled back, white at the corners, exposing his perfect teeth. He looked like any rabid dog about to attack.

"What did you say?"

"You heard me, faggot."

He balled his left hand into a fist while his right hand knuckled the gun.

"Arnold, don't!" hissed Clipper Sr.

It was too late. His body stiffened and he stood up, pointing the gun toward me. I lunged, hitting him low, slamming my head and shoulders into his midsection. He fired, but the bullet seared past me, exploding into the flat screen TV in a bright flash and shower of glass. Someone screamed as we skidded backward. He dropped his gun and we crashed to the floor pummeling each other.

"Stop it! Stop it!" yelled Mrs. Clipper.

Arnold, wild-eyed, grabbed my cheek and tried to rip my face. In a brawl, your adrenaline raises your body temperature, masking your pain. I grabbed his wrist, yanking it away from my face and dug my thumb into his eye. He screamed and let go. I punched him, rolled us both over, got him in a chokehold and started squeezing. It was nasty, I heard him choking, gasping for breath and he started to go limp.

Mrs. Clipper stuck her pistol into my face. "Let him go!"

I let him go. He rolled off me, choking and spluttering air back into his lungs. She pulled back the hammer on her nasty looking .32 and glared undying hatred at me. I didn't move, or try to avoid the impending bullet, or hold my hands up defensively. Instead, I smirked at her, hocked up a blood filled loogie and spat it right in her face. It smacked on the corner of her mouth. Instead of shooting me, disgust creased her face and she stepped back, wiping it away with her sleeve. Arnold kicked me in the ribs so hard, that I felt at least two of them crack. The pain was intense, and I screamed, barely able to breath.

"Fucking piece of shit!"

"Fuck your mother."

He bent down and grabbed my throat, squeezing harder and harder. I felt myself passing out as the darkness rolled in. I woke when someone threw water over my face and waited for my vision to come back into focus. Arnold and his mother were looking down at me with the same expressionless, dead-eye glare. They were both armed and it appeared that I wasn't long for this world.

"Get up!" It was half-command, half jubilant exhortation.

"I can't."

He looked toward the door. "Richard, get in here."

I gave Richie the once over as he sashayed in, moving sideways, for all the world like a ferret. Black jeans, expensive black leather jacket, silver chain around his neck. A movie star persona complete with demented director.

"Help him up," commanded Arnold.

Richie bent down and grabbed me, pulling me to my feet. I was still unsteady, so he leaned me against the sideboard.

"Thanks." He backed away. "Good to finally meet you."

Arnold stuck his gun into my chest. "You don't get to speak to him."

"What's the matter? Afraid he'll find out what you did to his dad?"

Arnold squinted hatred, so pure, so vile, that despite myself, a chill fingered its way down my spine. Everyone turned to look as a black-and-tan Rottweiler snarled up to the French doors, pressing its massive head against the glass, dripping saliva, giving me the evil eye. This dog wanted nothing more than to sink his teeth into me.

"Richard, be a love and go calm him down."

"Sure."

He opened the French door and bent down, whispering something to the dog. It calmed and assumed the sit position, its gaze wandering from him to me. I took advantage of the distraction and quickly picked up my Walther, which was on the sideboard, slipping it into my inside pocket. Richie came back in and closed the door. I locked eyes with the dog and snarled, showing him my teeth. The dog exploded, barking furiously, butting the door.

Arnold tapped the glass to get its attention. "Quiet, Brutus."

The dog stopped barking but continued to growl, his beady eyes locked on yours truly.

I let out a sarcastic chuckle. "Brutus?"

"Yes, why?" glared Arnold.

"How appropriate."

He pointed his gun at me and trying hard to control himself, hissed, "Outside."

I didn't move. "Not with that fucking thing out there."

Arnold couldn't hide his amusement. He shook his head in dismay and turned to Richard. "Sweetheart, if you would, please?"

Richard stepped outside, grabbing the dog by the collar and led it away.

Arnold waved me out with his gun and then followed, along with his mother. I had the feeling she would shoot me through the head at the slightest provocation. Richard chained the dog up and I stopped in front of a white gazebo, complete with sweet peas growing up and through the latticework. It was built on a knoll at the back of the yard with towering bamboo hedges on either side; in fact, the entire backyard was ringed with them. I thought I saw movement in the bamboo, but it could have been my imagination.

I looked at Richie. "Where's Jade?"

Arnold pushed me back. "I told you not to speak to him."

"What're you gonna do, kill me?" I snorted with contempt.

Richie came over and that's when I noticed that his pupils were dilated. He was, as Ron Cera would say, wired as a power station. He blurted, "Why did you murder Ron?"

"You've got it all wrong. I never touched him."

"That's enough," interrupted Arnold.

I pointed at Clipper. "He killed him, or at least he had it done."

"Shut up," said Arnold.

"I was questioned by the cops and they told me that eye witnesses saw Ernie, Tom and Arnold drop off Ron's corpse."

Arnold took a menacing step toward me, jacking back the hammer on his gun. "One more word."

I locked eyes with him and smirked. Richard, trying to make sense of it all, came up to me and pulled out a knife which he pointed at me, punctuating each word with an air stab.

"You...are...a...liar."

"No, I'm not."

"I don't believe--"

"--Go ahead, ask lover boy."

Arnold smiled. "This is quite ridiculous, and I've heard--"

"--Go on, ask him," I said, challenge edging my words.

Richard tried to form the words, but his mouth didn't want to cooperate.

Arnold didn't have that problem. "You wanna see Jade?"

"Is that rhetorical?"

He jerked the gun as if he was going to shoot me and changed his mind. "Richard, go get your sister."

Richard didn't move. Instead he squinted and asked, "Who killed Ron?"

Arnold could no longer control himself and shouted maniacally, "He did! He did! HE DIIIIIIIIIIIIIIID!"

"Calm down, dear," said Mrs. Clipper, strangely calm.

But Richard wasn't going to be deterred so easily. "Don't lie to me, dude. I hate liars." His mobile features congealed into a look of anguish.

"Have I ever lied to you?" snapped Arnold.

"You hurt Jade."

"She deserved it."

"Did you have Ron's head cut off?"

"What does it matter? Huh? What difference does it make? Who do you love? Me or that dumb actor?"

"Richard," said Mrs. Clipper sharply, "don't let this vile liar confuse you."

Richard ignored her and although high, managed to keep somewhat focused on Arnold. "I don't understand." The words came out broken, like a child mourning a misplaced toy.

"It's okay," said Arnold. "We're going to make everything okay."

"But--"

"--Please go and let Jade out."

Richard shrugged and moved over to a shed set off from the gazebo. He unlocked it and Jade seemed to catapult into view. Her left arm hung uselessly, her broken fingers dark and discolored. Her eyes were wild, her pupils huge. It was obvious that she had been drugged. She stared at us, her once radiant eyes now pools of vacancy. It was hard to watch.

I stepped forward, smiled and said softly, "Jade, it's me, Nick."

She looked straight at me and there was a glimmer of recognition. "Nick," she repeated slowly as if the word might bring her back to reality.

"We're going to be going home soon."

Drool was leaking out the side of her mouth, slowly making its way down her chin. I wanted to wipe it for her, and then wipe Arnold and his vile parents off the face of the Earth. We stood there, the six of us, in this beautiful back garden with flowers and bees and birds and sunshine and the intoxicating scent of jasmine. It was the most surreal experience.

She turned her gaze on Richard. Her face contorted with grief, then congealed into a delicate pleading smile. She pitched toward him and he opened his arms, a boyish smile breaking across his handsome face. As they met, she raked the nails of her right hand across his cheek, driving him to the ground, falling on top of him. He screamed in pain and she dug her nails into his face.

I grabbed Jade, trying to pull her off Richard. "Stop, Jade! Let him go!"

She made not a sound, but Richard was screaming loud enough for both of them.

"Jade!" I yelled with one final violent tug, pulling her up off him.

I steadied her on her feet and she pulled away from me. Mrs. Clipper stepped forward, unsure what to do. Arnold helped up Richard, who was crying, and handed him back his knife.

"It's okay, it's just a scratch," he reassured him, gently wiping the blood away with his sleeve.

Richard turned to Jade, pain, fear, love, confusion rippling across his face. He stepped toward her and she smiled, but it was a weird contortion, without warmth, without soul.

"I'm sorry," he said.

Jade nodded and came forward. Richard's blade flashed and dug deep in her chest.

"No!" I shouted and ran over, catching her as she collapsed into my arms.

Arnold looked surprised and turned to Richard, who was obviously having trouble comprehending what had just happened. He rubbed his eyes and stared at his sister, the handle of the knife still in her chest. I could just make out the butterfly tattoos above her breasts, purple and gold. Her right breast was pooling with bright red blood. I laid Jade gently on the grass, stood up and glared at Arnold. He shrugged, smirked and aimed his gun at me. I dodged to one side and knocked Mrs. Clipper over as I leapt behind the gazebo.

Arnold, his gun leading the way, laughed as he came toward me. "That's not going to help."

Half-hidden behind the latticework, I popped the clip into my Walther.

Richard intercepted Arnold and started screaming at him. "You bastard. Look what you made me do."

He replied, "Calm down. It was an accide--"

CRACK! Richard slapped him hard across the face. I think we were all a little amazed and Arnold stood there, his expression a mixture of pain and embarrassment.

"Richard, stop!" screamed Mrs. Clipper.

Arnold held out his hands to Richard in a pleading manner. He side-stepped Arnold's proffered embrace and swung a glancing blow that caught him square on the jaw, spinning him halfway around. Mrs. Clipper had seen enough. She aimed her pistol directly at Richard and fired three rounds. The first hit Richard in the throat, the other two sailed past his face. His hands flew up to the gaping hole squirting blood like an open tap. He gurgled something indiscernible and sank to the grass. Again Mrs. Clipper took aim at Richard, who was lying on the ground, his life ebbing fast.

"No, Mother!"

Arnold, his face contorted with desperate rage, charged, slamming her to the ground. Instantly he was on top of her, slapping her face and head with both hands. To my amazement, a lean elderly figure emerged from the back door, Mr. Clipper. He was no longer in the wheelchair. Instead, he was walking with reasonable balance, aiming a gun more or less at Arnold.

"Stop! Now!"

Arnold just kept hitting his mother; the steady slap slap slap cutting through the air. Mr. Clipper's bullet slammed into the dirt near Arnold, who looked up at his father, bewildered. He got to his feet, reached into the pocket of his overalls and extracted his pistol.

Mr. Clipper aimed at me, but I fired first, hitting him in the face. His head jerked back as blood and gore exploded out the back of his head. His body hesitated and collapsed to the ground.

"Father!" Arnold screamed.

Tears flooded down his face and slowly, deliberately, he aimed his gun at me. Although I wanted nothing better than to snap the son-of-a-bitch, I shot him in the shoulder. He dropped the gun, but didn't call out or say a word. I didn't see Mrs. Clipper get to her knees, picking up her pistol, but I heard the CRACK as she fired. Only it wasn't hers. It was Tony's and his bullet hit her center mass. She must've been made out of rock because like her son, she didn't make a sound, or drop the gun, or fall to the ground. Instead, she aimed at

Tony as he came across the lawn in the law enforcement attack position.

"Police! Drop the gun!"

Mrs. Clipper smiled a mouthful of blood and took careful aim. Tony fired three more rounds. The police issue bullets punched though her, spraying blood out of her back. She was dead before she hit the ground.

Arnold screamed his rage and charged me. I could have shot him but I wanted something much more close and personal. I tossed my gun away, stepped forward and dropped down, sweeping his feet out from under him. He crashed to the grass and I was all over him, punching as fast and as hard as I could. I beat him for all of the pain, blood, death and misery he had caused. Maybe he felt he deserved it; he stopped resisting and smiled up at me as I beat him bloody.

"That's enough, Nick! Stop!" yelled Tony, pulling me off.

I sat on the grass, blood and teeth around me, one of which, an eyetooth, was stuck in my hand. I pulled it out and threw it at Arnold's face.

Tony snapped the cuffs on him, although it was pointless as he was all but comatose. I went over to Jade, who was unconscious, but still alive.

"I'll call it in," said Tony, getting on his cell.

I held her and looked over at Richie, but he was stone dead. During the melee, I had forgotten about the dog. Someone's stray bullet had apparently found it and it too now lay on the grass. I tried to breathe slowly, but my cracked ribs hurt like hell and I could barely take in air. In a stand of tall trees in a neighbor's garden, a lone, enormous crow settled onto a branch, warily eyeing the carnage. It jerked its head sideways, looked directly at me and shook its head in mock disapproval. "Shit," I thought. "Shit, shit, shit." Then I shut my eyes, wishing I'd never have to open them.

Jade was kind enough to send me a bonus check for another hundred grand. I split it 50-50 with Bobby and put my half into our daughter's college fund. The dead bikers had been wanted felons and since I have a bounty hunter's license, Tony, with the able help of Bill Boxer, was able to eventually negotiate a deal for me with the District Attorney's office. Some kind of bogus misdemeanor conviction. No time and a year of probation, and just to rub it in, 50 hours of community service picking up the trash alongside the freeway with the orange jacket crew. The cops still hated my guts and every now and then would haul me in on some phony charge, just because they could. I understood and kept my big mouth shut and later rather than sooner, they ended up with a sort of grudging respect for me.

Brad moved up to San Francisco and Bobby went back to his goats. I go over there same as always, and every time I see his goats, I can't help thinking about the hog farm. Cassady used some of the hundred grand from Halladay to buy new French doors, which made her very happy for a while. Bur neither she nor I could forget and we finally sold our house and moved across the hill to Avocado Heights.

They say that time heals all wounds and that sleep knits up the raveled sleeve of care and I hope they're right. But sometimes I can't feel anything at all. And other times I feel things no man should ever feel. But most of the time I feel all right, as if some things just are and other things have to be. Once in a while, Cassady insists we look in on Jade. She's about as bad off as you might expect. Maybe worse.

Richie and Cicero are buried side-by-side in Forest Lawn. One day driving by on 134, I stopped in and paid my respects. I don't really care about Cicero but for some reason I wish I'd gotten to know Richie a little better. Maybe because deep down I think he could have been a good man.

In my darkest moments, I curse the day I met James Halladay. He was not a good man. Arnold Clipper was even worse.

When I think about it, I know that I really tried to do the right thing. We all did -- Bobby, me, good old Brad, who from what I hear is still on the wagon, and of course the actor, Ron Cera. I keep telling myself that I owe his mother a visit. I even went so far as to locate her on Merlin one night when I couldn't sleep. But I haven't been out to see her yet. Maybe it's because every time I think I'm ready to go my mind drifts back to the sight of Ron's severed head, lying there on Towne Street, staring out blindly at nothing.